THE OLD WEST SERIES

TWICE BOUGHT

BY

R.M. BALLANTYNE

Illustrated

ORIGINALLY PUBLISHED 1885
REPUBLISHED 1999
PROTECTED

PUBLISHED BY
MANTLE MINISTRIES
228 STILL RIDGE
BULVERDE, TEXAS 78163

TWICE BOUGHT
ISBN 1-889128-56-2

ABOUT THE BOOK

Twice Bought is a tale of the Oregon goldfields in the 1870's. It is not only educational in nature, taking the reader into a bit of America's past, but is a wonderful story of human drama. The Hero Tom Brixon is impeccable in character, and tries, with the help of God and his fine up-bringing, to steer his goldfield friend Fred Westly towards the right path he should follow. The trials that come with gold camp living are innumerable and these two young gold seekers learn to overcome them all.

In *Twice Bought* Fred is hooked on gold, Tom is hooked on God. The difference is obvious and will give the reader the sense to see the shallowness of vain living. The story is full of adventure with Indians, desperados, and friend and foe alike fighting to exist in those turbulent Old West days.

OLD WEST SERIES

It is truly amazing how boys and some girls are still interested in the Old West. I grew up with movie personalities that personified the rugged Old West such as Gary Cooper, Jimmy Stewart, Henry Fonda, Spencer Tracy, and John Wayne and movies like *Guns along the Mohawk, High Noon, Northwest Passage, The Alamo,* and a whole slew of others, and a steady diet of television westerns like *The Rifleman, Have Gun Will Travel, Wyatt Earp, Johnny Yuma, Maverick, Bonanza, Zorro, Daniel Boone, Davy Crockett, Roy Rogers and, Dale Evans, Hop-Along-Cassidy,* and *Little House on the Prairie,* to name a few.

The actors who played key roles are all gone now, but the interest in the Old West continues to survive with a younger generation. The key to all this is the positives examples these Old West stories bore upon our impressionable minds. It was a clear message that the good guys wore white hats, the bad guys wore black hats with no gray shades in between. Evil was always punished, either at the end of a noose or with a six shooter. The character of the hero was always upright, noble, honest, kind, and truthful.

In contrast, today's modern Westerns glorify killing for no purpose other than to "blow someone away," or to exalt improper relationships. The heroes may conveniently lie and deceive. The youth culture today is desperately in need of an alternative. This is the purpose of *The Old West Series*. These stories are full of adventure and do not compromise on historical facts, making them educational as well as enjoyable. The contrast between good and evil is loud and clear. Over a period of time, *The Old West Series* is going to include the great forgotten writers of America's past such as R. M. Ballantyne, Edward Ellis, Harry Castlemon, G.A.

Henty, and a variety of other choice authors who wrote from a moral, and God-fearing perspective.

The stories that will be selected in this series will span the historical time period from the 1820's-1880's, and will traverse the continent from the Canadian Rockies to old Mexico, from old California to the Mississippi River. They will be stories of the American mountain-men of old who blazed trails while hunting and trapping. Indians will surface during encounters with white settlers moving out west, lending educational value on various tribes. Cowboys, gunfighters, soldiers and pioneers will be woven throughout the stories, each with moral values that have been so long neglected. We encourage you to stoke up the fires from *The Old West Series* and enjoy the legacy of our forgotten past.

ABOUT THE AUTHOR

ROBERT MICHAEL BALLANTYNE was born April 24, 1824, in Edinburgh, Scotland. He attended Edinburgh Academy until his father could no longer pay the school fee. Caught in this dilemma, the mother and older sisters completed his study through home education. Robert was nephew of James Ballantyne, the editor and printer of Sir Walter Scott's works. This contact gave him the love of writing, and he adopted Scott's romantic and chivalric ideals of manhood. Their adventures are pictured as glorious and fulfilling daring deeds. In 1841, at the age of sixteen, Ballantyne signed an agreement to work for the Hudson Bay Company in Canada. He worked in the Canadian wilds as a trapper for six years. During this time he met many rugged trappers and began to write boys' novels of the great outdoors.

Ballantyne enjoyed great literary success along with his contemporary, G.A. Henty. Through his diligent labor in writing eighty novels, he became one of the best known and best loved adventure writers of his time, surpassing G.A. Henty in sales. Using his skill, he faithfully supported his mother and sisters. He was a regular attender at the Chalmers Memorial Church in Edinburgh when not traveling throughout the world seeking plots for his numerous books.

His older brother, John, described him in a short family history: "In the late 'fifties I remember Bob as being a brisk and energetic figure, slim of build like the rest of us Ballantynes, active in his movements, and with a fine baritone voice which he used with great effect at our musical evenings. He had the lowland accent of an Edinburgh Scot like myself. Before his marriage he wore his hair long, much in the style of the hunters of the forests of the Frozen North that he knew so well; his face gave one the impression of being bronzed, no matter what the season, and was considered extremely handsome by the ladies. His eyes were keen, and much of his face was hidden by his full-flowing moustache and thick, brown beard. His entrance into a drawing-room would cause every female head to turn and the conversation to give pause; a fact which embarrassed him immensely as he professed to be not in the least vain about his appearance."

In January 1859, in a letter written to his sister-in-law, Ballantyne wrote: "Do you know I have had some serious thoughts this forenoon, while traveling, that young people are my mission! They not only like what I write, but there is no doubt now that I can keep their earnest attention for a long time while speaking. May God direct me in this thought if it is a correct one. You know I have all along kicked at writing for boys. Yet God has given me great success in this very thing."

Due to an error about coconuts in his book, *The Coral Island,* Ballantyne decided not to write on a subject before studying the particulars as much as possible firsthand of the regions he wrote, while often traveling to them for research. He once walked from London to Edinburgh, a trip of 426 miles in order to identify with the common people of the land along the way for the purpose of becoming a better writer. His books became excellent historical fiction and educational in nature without compromising adventure. Ballantyne was a committed Christian which is reflected in his writings, and is one of the few juvenile book authors who can communicate the Gospel whereby boys and girls can receive enough knowledge of Christ, through reading the story, to receive Christ as their Savior and Lord.

Robert Ballantyne married Jane Dickson Grant, July 31, 1866, and they had four children. For health reasons he traveled to Italy suffering from vertigo and never returned home. He died February 8, 1894 in Rome, at the age of 69.

DEAR READERS

You will note as you read the books from *The Old West Series*, that some of the characters in these stories chose to smoke, drink liquor, gamble, and in some cases lead dissipated lives. However, we have selected godly authors who have wisely chosen that the "heroes" in their stories refrain from these bad habits, and inspire to a higher call.

Remember, these books are historical fiction and are based on real, true-to-life situations. The omission of the fact that some characters participate in bad vises would make these educational stories far-fetched. Although, perhaps politically correct, they would be historically inaccurate. These 1800's authors wrote of the times in which they lived, times that were harsh, with rough men. The West was not settled by city slickers who were dainty and civilized, but by men who lived by the gun and were in constant danger of being killed by wild beasts and desperados. These stories are full of historical characters such as trappers, Indians, Mexicans, bandits, cowboys, pioneers, and gold miners.

At Mantle Ministries, we do not approve of smoking, chewing tobacco, drinking liquor, and the vices that many of the characters within this series chose to practice. These are dangerous and harmful habits.

Be a "true hero", and don't smoke, drink, gamble or chew, and don't run with those who do.

Mantle Ministries Press
Richard "Little Bear" Wheeler

CONTENTS.

CHAPTER XIX

CHAPTER XX

CHAPTER XXI

TWICE BOUGHT:

A TALE OF THE OREGON GOLDFIELDS.

———◦◦◦———

CHAPTER I.

" ' HONESTY is the best policy,' Tom, you may depend
on it," said a youth to his companion, one afternoon, as they walked along the margin of one of those
brawling rivulets which, born amid the snows of the
Rocky Mountain peaks, run a wild and plunging course of
many miles before finding comparative rest in the cele-
brated goldfields of Oregon.

"I don't agree with you, Fred," said Tom, sternly ;
" and I don't believe in the proverb you have quoted.
The world's maxims are not all gospel."

"You are right, Tom ; many of them are false ; nevertheless, some are founded on gospel truth."

"It matters not," returned Tom, angrily. "I have
made up my mind to get back from that big thief Gashford what he has stolen from me, for it is certain that he
cheated at play, though I could not prove it at the time.
It is impossible to get it back by fair means, and I hold
it quite allowable to steal from a thief, especially when
that which you take is your own."

Fred Westly shook his head, but did not reply. Many
a time had he reasoned with his friend, Tom Brixton,

about the sin of gambling, and urged him to be content
with the result of each day's digging for gold, but his
words had no effect. Young Brixton had resolved to
make a fortune rapidly. He laboured each day with pick
and shovel with the energy of a hero and the dogged
perseverance of a navvy, and each night he went to
Lantry's store to increase his gains by gambling. As a
matter of course his "luck," as he called it, varied. Sometimes he returned to the tent which he shared with his
friend Westly depressed, out of humour, and empty-
handed. At other times he made his appearance flushed
with success—occasionally, also, with drink,—and flung
down a heavy bag of golden nuggets as the result of his
evening's play. Ultimately, when under the influence of
drink, he staked all that he had in the world, except his
clothes and tools, to a man named Gashford, who was
noted for his size, strength of body, and utter disregard
of God and man. As Brixton said, Gashford had cheated
him at play, and this had rendered the ruined man unusually savage.

The sun was down when the two friends entered their
tent and began to pull off their muddy boots, while a
little man in a blue flannel shirt and a brown wide-awake
busied himself in the preparation of supper.

"What have you got for us to-night, Paddy?" asked
Westly.

"Salt pork it is," said the little man, looking up with a
most expressive grin; "the best o' victuals when there's
nothin' better. Bein' in a luxurious frame o' mind when
I was up at the store, I bought a few split-pays for
seasonin'; but it comes hard on a man to spind his goold
on sitch things when his luck's down. You've not done
much to-day, I see, by the looks of ye."

"Right, Paddy," said Tom Brixton, with a harsh laugh

"we've done nothing—absolutely nothing. See, there is my day's work."

He pulled three small grains of gold, each about the size of a pea, from his trousers pocket, and flung them contemptuously into a washing-pan at his elbow.

"Sure, we won't make our fortins fast at that rate," said Paddy, or Patrick Flinders.

"This won't help it much," said Westly, with a mingled smile and sigh, as he added a small nugget and a little gold-dust to the pile.

"Ah! then, haven't I forgot the shuggar for the tay; but I've not got far to go for to get it. Just kape stirrin' the pot, Mister Westly, I'll be back in a minit."

"Tom," said Westly, when their comrade had gone out, "don't give way to angry feelings. Do try, like a good fellow, to look at things in a philosophical light, since you object to a religious one. Rightly or wrongly, Gashford has won your gold. Well, take heart and dig away. You know I have saved a considerable sum, the half of which is at your service to—"

"Do you suppose," interrupted the other sharply, "that I will consent to become a beggar?"

"No," replied Westly, "but there is no reason why you should not consent to accept an offer when it is made to you by an old chum. Besides, I offer the money on loan, the only condition being that you won't gamble it away."

"Fred," returned Brixton, impressively, "I *must* gamble with it if I take it. I can no more give up gambling than I can give up drinking. I'm a doomed man, my boy; doomed to be either a millionaire or a madman!"

The glittering eyes and wild expression of the youth while he spoke induced his friend to fear that he was already the latter.

"Oh! Tom, my dear fellow," he said, "God did not

doom you. If your doom is fixed, you have yourself fixed it."

"Now, Fred," returned the other impatiently, "don't bore me with your religious notions. Religion is all very well in the old country, but it won't work at all here at the diggin's."

"My experience has proved the contrary," returned Westly, "for religion—or, rather, God—has saved *me* from drink and gaming."

"If it *be* God who has saved you, why has He not saved me?" demanded Brixton.

"Because that mysterious and incomprehensible power of Free Will stands in your way. In the exercise of your free will you have rejected God, therefore the responsibility rests with yourself. If you will now call upon Him, He will, by His Holy Spirit, enable you to accept salvation through Jesus Christ."

"No use, Fred, no use," said Tom, shaking his head. "When you and I left England, three years ago, I might have believed and trusted as you do, but it's too late now —too late I say, so don't worry me with your solemn looks and sermons. My mind's made up, I tell you. With these three paltry little lumps of gold I'll gamble at the store to-night with Gashford. I'll double the stake every game. If I win, well—if not, I'll—"

He stopped abruptly, because at that moment Paddy Flinders re-entered with the sugar; possibly, also, because he did not wish to reveal all his intentions.

That night there was more noise, drinking, and gambling than usual at Lantry's store, several of the miners having returned from a prospecting trip into the mountains with a considerable quantity of gold.

Loudest among the swearers, deepest among the drinkers, and most reckless among the gamblers was Gashford "the

bully," as he was styled.   He had just challenged any
one present to play when Brixton entered the room.

"We will each stake all that we own on a single
chance," he said, looking round.   "Come, that's fair, ain't
it? for you know I've got lots of dust."

There was a general laugh, but no one would accept
the challenge—which Brixton had not heard—though he
heard the laugh that followed.   Many of the diggers,
especially the poorer ones, would have gladly taken him
up if they had not been afraid of the consequences if
successful.

"Well, boys, I couldn't make a fairer offer—all I
possess against all that any other man owns, though it
should only be half an ounce of gold," said the bully,
tossing off a glass of spirits.

"Done! I accept your challenge," cried Tom Brixton,
stepping forward.

"You!" exclaimed Gashford, with a look of contempt;
"why, you've got nothing to stake.   I cleaned you out
yesterday."

"I have this to stake," said Tom, holding out the three
little nuggets of gold which he had found that day.   "It
is all that I possess, and it is more than half an ounce,
which you mentioned as the lowest you'd play for."

"Well, I'll stick to what I said," growled Gashford,
"if it *be* half an ounce.   Come, Lantry, get out your
scales."

The storekeeper promptly produced the little balance
which he used for weighing gold-dust, and the diggers
crowded round with much interest to watch, while Lantry,
with a show of unwonted care, dusted the scales, and put
the three nuggets therein.

"Three-quarters of an ounce," said the storekeeper,
when the balance ceased to vibrate.

"Come along, then, an' let's have another glass of grog
for luck," cried Gashford, striking his huge fist on the
counter.

A throw of the dice was to decide the matter. While
Lantry, who was appointed to make the throw, rattled
the dice in the box, the diggers crowded round in eager
curiosity, for, besides the unusual disparity between the
stakes, there was much probability of a scene of violence
as the result, Brixton having displayed a good deal of
temper when he lost to the bully on the previous day.

"Lost !" exclaimed several voices in disappointed tones,
when the dice fell on the table.

"Who's lost ?" cried those in the rear of the crowd.

"Tom Brixton, to be sure," answered Gashford, with a
laugh. "He always loses ; but it's no great loss this time,
and I am not much the richer."

There was no response to this sally. Every one looked
at Brixton, expecting an outburst of rage, but the youth
stood calmly contemplating the dice with an absent look,
and a pleasant smile on his lips.

"Yes," he said, recovering himself, "luck is indeed
against me. But never mind. Let's have a drink,
Lantry ; you'll have to give it me on credit this time !"

Lantry professed himself to be quite willing to oblige
an old customer to that extent. He could well afford it,
he said ; and it was unquestionable truth that he uttered,
for his charges were exorbitant.

That night, when the camp was silent in repose, and
the revellers were either steeped in oblivion or wandering
in golden dreams, Tom Brixton sauntered slowly down to
the river at a point where it spread out into a lakelet, in
which the moon was brightly reflected. The overhanging
cliffs, fringed with underwood and crowned with trees, shot
reflections of ebony blackness here and there down into

the water, while beyond, through several openings, could be seen a varied and beautiful landscape, backed and capped by the snowpeaks of the great backbone of America.

It was a scene fitted to solemnise and soften, but it had no such influence on Tom Brixton, who did not give it even a passing thought, though he stood with folded arms and contracted brows, gazing at it long and earnestly. After a time he began to mutter to himself in broken sentences.

"Fred is mistaken—*must* be mistaken. There is no law here. Law must be taken into one's own hands. It cannot be wrong to rob a robber. It is not robbery to take back one's own. Foul means are admissible when fair—yet it *is* a sneaking thing to do! Ha! who said it was sneaking?" (He started and thrust his hands through his hair.) "Bah! Lantry, your grog is too fiery. It was the grog that spoke, not conscience. Pooh! I don't believe in conscience. Come, Tom, don't be a fool, but go and— Mother! What has *she* got to do with it? Lantry's fire-water didn't bring *her* to my mind. No, it *is* Fred, confound him! He's always suggesting what she would say in circumstances which she has never been in and could not possibly understand. And he worries me on the plea that he promised her to stick by me through evil report and good report. I suppose that means through thick and thin. Well, he's a good fellow is Fred, but weak. Yes, I've made up my mind to do it, and I *will* do it."

He turned hastily as he spoke, and was soon lost in the little belt of woodland that lay between the lake and the miner's camp.

It pleased Gashford to keep his gold in a huge leathern bag, which he hid in a hole in the ground within his tent during the day, and placed under his pillow during the night. It pleased him also to dwell and work alone, partly because he was of an unsociable disposition, and partly to prevent men becoming acquainted with his secrets.

There did not seem to be much fear of the big miner's secrets being discovered, for Lynch law prevailed in the camp at that time, and it was well known that death was the usual punishment for theft.   It was also well known that Gashford was a splendid shot with the revolver, as well as a fierce, unscrupulous man.   But strong drink revealed that which might have otherwise been safe. When in his cups Gashford sometimes became boastful, and gave hints now and then which were easily understood.   Still his gold was safe, for, apart from the danger of the attempt to rob the bully, it would have been impossible to discover the particular part of his tent-floor in which the hole was dug, and, as to venturing to touch his pillow while his shaggy head rested on it, no one was daring enough to contemplate such an act, although there were men there capable of doing almost anything.

Here again, however, strong drink proved to be the big miner's foe.   Occasionally, though not often, Gashford drank so deeply as to become almost helpless, and, after lying down in his bed, sank into a sleep so profound that it seemed as if he could not have been roused even with violence.

He was in this condition on the night in which his victim made up his mind to rob him.   Despair and brandy had united to render Brixton utterly reckless; so much so, that, instead of creeping stealthily towards his enemy's tent, an act which would probably have aroused the suspicion of a light sleeper, he walked boldly up, entered it, raised Gashford's unconscious head with one hand, pulled out the bag of gold with the other, put it on his shoulder, and coolly marched out of the camp.   The audacity of the deed contributed largely to its success.

Great was the rage and consternation of Gashford when he awoke the following morning and found that his treasure had disappeared. Jumping at once to the conclusion that it had been stolen by Brixton, he ran to that youth's tent and demanded to know where the thief had gone to.

"What do you mean by the thief?" asked Fred Westly, with misgiving at his heart.

"I mean your chum, Tom Brixton," shouted the enraged miner.

"How do you know he's a thief?" asked Westly.

"I didn't come here to be asked questions by you," said Gashford. "Where has he gone to, I say?"

"I don't know."

"That's a lie!" roared the miner, clenching his fist in a threatening manner.

"Poor Tom! I wish I did know where you have gone!" said Fred, shaking his head sadly as he gazed on the floor, and taking no notice whatever of the threatening action of his visitor.

"Look here now, Westly," said Gashford, in a low suppressed voice, shutting the curtain of the tent and drawing a revolver from his pocket, "you know something about this matter, and you know *me*. If you don't tell me all you know and where your chum has bolted to, I'll blow your brains out as sure as there's a God in heaven."

"I thought," said Westly, quietly, and without the slightest symptom of alarm, "you held the opinion that there is no God and no heaven."

"Come, young fellow, none o' your religious chaff, but answer my question."

"Nothing is farther from my thoughts than chaffing you," returned Westly, gently, "and if the mere mention of God's name is religion, then you may claim to be one of the most religious men at the diggings, for you are constantly praying Him to curse people. I have already answered your question, and can only repeat that I *don't know* where my friend Brixton has gone to. But let me ask, in turn, what has happened to *you ?*"

There was no resisting the earnest sincerity of Fred's look and tone, to say nothing of his cool courage. Gashford felt somewhat abashed in spite of himself.

"What has happened to me ?" he repeated, bitterly. "The worst that could happen has happened. My gold has been stolen, and your chum is the man who has cribbed it. I know that as well as if I had seen him do it. But I'll hunt him down and have it out of him with interest; with interest, mark you—if I should have to go to the ends o' the 'arth to find him."

Without another word Gashford thrust the revolver into his pocket, flung aside the tent curtain, and strode away.

Meanwhile Tom Brixton, with the gold in a game-bag slung across his shoulder, was speeding down the valley, or mountain gorge, at the head of which the Pine Tree Diggings lay, with all the vigour and activity of youthful strength, but with none of the exultation that might be supposed to characterise a successful thief. On the contrary, a weight like lead seemed to lie on his heart, and the faces of his mother and his friend, Fred Westly, seemed to flit before him continually, gazing at him with sorrowful expression. As the fumes of the liquor which he had drunk began to dissipate, the shame and depression of spirit increased, and his strength, great though it was, began to give way.

By that time, however, he had placed many a mile between him and the camp where he had committed the robbery. The valley opened into a wide, almost bound-less stretch of comparatively level land, covered here and there with forests so dense, that, once concealed in their recesses, it would be exceedingly difficult, if not impos-sible, for white men to trace him, especially men who were so little acquainted with woodcraft as the diggers. Besides this, the region was undulating in form, here and there, so that, from the tops of many of the eminences, he could see over the whole land, and observe the approach of enemies without being himself seen.

Feeling, therefore, comparatively safe, he paused in his mad flight, and went down on hands and knees to take a long drink at a bubbling spring. Rising, refreshed, with a deep sigh, he slowly mounted to the top of a knoll which was bathed at the time in the first beams of the rising sun.

From the spot he obtained a view of intermingled forest, prairie, lake, and river, so resplendent that even *his* mind was for a moment diverted from its gloomy introspections, and a glance of admiration shot from his eyes and chased the wrinkles from his brow ; but the frown quickly returned, and the glorious landscape was forgotten as the thought of his dreadful condition returned with overwhelming power.

Up to that day Tom Brixton, with all his faults, had kept within the circle of the world's laws. He had been well trained in boyhood, and, with the approval of his mother, had left England for the Oregon goldfields in company with a steady, well-principled friend, who had been a playmate in early childhood and at school. The two friends had experienced during three years the vary-ing fortune of a digger's life ; sometimes working for long periods successfully, and gradually increasing their "pile ;" at other times toiling day after day for nothing and living on their capital, but, on the whole, making what men called a good thing of it, until Tom took to gambling, which, almost as a matter of course, led to drinking. The process of demoralisation had continued until, as we have seen, the boundary line was at last overstepped, and he had become a thief and an outlaw.

At that period and in those diggings Judge Lynch— in other words, off-hand and speedy "justice" by the community of miners—was the order of the day, and, as stealing had become exasperatingly common, the penalty appointed was death, the judges being, in most cases, the prompt executioners.

Tom Brixton knew well what his fate would be if captured, and this unquestionably filled him with anxiety, but it was not this thought that caused him, as he reclined on the sunny knoll, to spurn the bag of gold with his foot.

"Trash!" he exclaimed, bitterly, repeating the kick.

But the love of gold had taken deep root in the fallen youth's heart. After a brief rest he arose, slung the "trash" over his shoulder, and, descending the knoll, quickly disappeared in the glades of the forest.

CHAPTER II.

WHILE Brixton was hurrying with a guilty conscience deeper and deeper into the dark woods which covered the spur of the mountains in the neighbourhood of Pine Tree Diggings, glancing back nervously from time to time as if he expected the pursuers to be close at his heels, an enemy was advancing to meet him in front, of whom he little dreamed.

A brown bear, either enjoying his morning walk or on the look-out for breakfast, suddenly met him face to face, and stood up on its hind legs as if to have a good look at him.

Tom was no coward ; indeed he was gifted with more than an average amount of animal courage. He at once levelled his rifle at the creature's breast and fired. The bear rushed at him, nevertheless, as if uninjured. Drawing his revolver, Tom discharged two shots before the monster reached him. All three shots had taken effect, but bears are noted for tenacity of life, and are frequently able to fight a furious battle after being mortally wounded. The rifle ball had touched its heart, and the revolver bullets had gone deep into its chest, yet it showed little sign of having been hurt.

Knowing full well the fate that awaited him if he stood to wrestle with a bear, the youth turned to run, but the bear was too quick for him. It struck him on the back and felled him to the earth.

Strange to say, at that moment Tom Brixton's ill-
gotten gains stood him in good stead. There can be no
question that the bear's tremendous claws would have
sunk deep into the youth's back, and probably broken
his spine, if they had not been arrested by the bag of
gold which was slung at his back. Although knocked
down and slightly stunned, Brixton was still unwounded,
and, even in the act of falling, had presence of mind to
draw his long knife and plunge it up to the haft in the
creature's side, at the same time twisting himself violently
round so as to fall on his back and thus face the
foe.

In this position, partly owing to the form of the ground,
the bear found it difficult to grasp its opponent in its
awful embrace, but it held him with its claws and seized
his left shoulder with its teeth. This rendered the use of
the revolver impossible, but fortunately Brixton's right
arm was still free, and he drove the keen knife a second
time deep into the animal's sides. Whether mortal or
not, the wound did not immediately kill. Tom felt that
his hour was come, and a deadly fear came over him as
the thought of death, his recent life, and judgment,
flashed through his brain. He drew out the knife, however, to make another desperate thrust. The bear's great
throat was close over his face. He thought of its jugular
vein, and made a deadly thrust at the spot where he
imagined that to run.

Instantly a flood of warm blood deluged his face and
breast; at the same time he felt as if some dreadful
weight were pressing him to death. Then consciousness
forsook him.

While this desperate fight was going on, the miners of
Pine Tree camp were scouring the woods in all directions
in search of the fugitive. As we have said, great indigna-

THE FIGHT WITH THE BEAR.

tion was felt at that time against thieves, because some
of them had become very daring, and cases of theft were
multiplying. Severe penalties had been imposed on the
culprits by the rest of the community without curing the
evil. At last death was decided on as the penalty for
any act of theft, however trifling it might be. That these
men were in earnest was proved by the summary execu-
tion of the next two offenders who were caught. Immediately after that thieving came to an abrupt end, insomuch
that if you had left a bag of gold on an exposed place,
men would have gone out of their way to avoid it!

One can understand, therefore, the indignation that was
roused in the camp when Tom Brixton revived the practice
in such a cool and impudent manner. It was felt that,
despite his being a favourite with many of the diggers, he
must be made an example. Pursuit was, therefore, organised on an extensive scale and in a methodical manner.
Among others, his friend Fred Westly took part in it.

It cost those diggers something thus to give up the
exciting work of gold-finding for a chase that promised to
occupy time and tax perseverance. Some of them even
refused to join in it, but on the whole the desire for
vengeance seemed general.

Bully Gashford, as he did not object to be called, was,
in virtue of his size, energy, and desperate character,
tacitly appointed leader. Indeed he would have assumed
that position if it had not been accorded to him, for he
was made of that stuff which produces either heroes of
the highest type or scoundrels of the deepest dye. He
arranged that the pursuers should proceed in a body to
the mouth of the valley, and there, dividing into several
parties, scatter themselves abroad until they should find
the thief's trail and then follow it up. As the miners
were not much accustomed to following trails, they

engaged the services of several Indians who chanced to be at the camp at that time.

" What direction d'ye think it 's likely your precious chum has taken ?" asked Gashford, turning abruptly to Fred Westly when the different parties were about to start.

" It is impossible for me to tell."

"I know that," retorted Gashford, with a scowl and something of a sneer, " but it ain't impossible for you to guess.   However, it will do as well if you tell me which party you intend to join."

"I shall join that which goes to the south-west," replied Westly.

" Well, then, *I* will join that which goes to the south-east," returned the bully, shouldering his rifle. " Go ahead, you red reptile," he added, giving a sign to the Indian at the head of the party he had selected to lead.

"The Indian at once went off at a swinging walk, amounting almost to a trot.   The others followed suit, and the forest soon swallowed them all in its dark embrace.

In making this selection Gashford had fallen into a mistake not uncommon among scoundrels—that of judging other men by themselves.   He knew that Westly was fond of his guilty friend, and concluded that he would tell any falsehood or put the pursuers on any false scent that might favour his escape.   He also guessed—and he was fond of guessing—that Fred would answer his question by indicating the direction which he thought it most probable his friend had *not* taken.   In these guesses he was only to a small extent right.   Westly did indeed earnestly hope that his friend would escape ; for he deemed the intended punishment of death most unjustly severe, and, knowing intimately the character and tendencies of Tom Brixton's mind and tastes, he had a pretty shrewd guess as to the direction he had taken, but, so far from desiring to throw the pursuers off the scent, his main anxiety was to join the party which he thought most likely to find the fugitive—if they should find him at all—in order that he might be present to defend him from sudden or unnecessary violence.

Of course Paddy Flinders went with the same party, and we need scarcely add that the little Irishman sympathised with Fred.

"D'ee think it's likely we'll cotch 'im?" he asked, in a whisper, on the evening of that day, as they went rapidly through the woods together, a little in rear of their party.

"It is difficult to say," answered Westly. "I earnestly hope not; indeed I think not, for Tom has had a good start; but the search is well organised, and there are bloodthirsty, indignant, and persevering men among the various parties, who won't be easily baffled. Still Tom is a splendid runner. We may depend on having a long chase before we come up with him."

"Ah, then, it's glad I am that ye think so, sor," returned Paddy, "for I've been afear'd Mister Tom hadn't got quite so much go in him, since he tuk to gambling and drinkin'."

"Look here, Paddy," exclaimed his companion, stopping abruptly, and pointing to the ground, "are not these the footprints of one of your friends?"

"Sure it's a bar," said the little man, going down on his knees to examine the footprints in question with deep interest.

Flinders was a remarkably plucky little man, and one of his great ambitions was to meet with a bear, when alone, and slay it single-handed. His ambition had not, up to that time, been gratified, fortunately for himself,

for he was a bad shot and exceedingly reckless, two
qualities which would probably have insured his own
destruction if he had had his wish.

"Let's go after it, Mister Westly," he said, springing to
his feet with an excited look.

"Nonsense, it is probably miles off by this time;
besides, we should lose our party."

"Niver a taste, sor; we could soon overhaul them agin.
An' won't they have to camp at sundown anyhow?   Moreover, if we don't come up wi' the bar in a mile or so we
can give it up."

"No, no, Paddy, we must not fall behind.   At least, I
must not; but you may go after it alone if you choose."

"Well, I will, sor.   Sure it's not ivery day I git the
chance; an'• there's no fear o' ye overhaulin' Mister
Tom this night.   We'll have to slape over it, I'll be
bound.   Just tell the boys I'll be after them in no time."

So saying Paddy shouldered his rifle, felt knife and axe
to make sure of their being safe in his belt, and strode
away in the track of the bear.

He had not gone above a quarter of a mile when he
came to the spot where the mortal combat had taken
place, and found Tom Brixton and the bear dead—as he
imagined—on the blood-stained turf.

He uttered a mighty cry, partly to relieve his feelings
and partly to recall his friend.   The imprudence of this
flashed upon him when too late, for others, besides Fred,
might have heard him.

But Tom Brixton was not dead.   Soon after the dying
bear had fallen on him, he recovered consciousness, and
shaking himself clear of the carcass with difficulty had
arisen; but, giddiness returning, he lay down, and while
in this position, overcome with fatigue, had fallen asleep.
Paddy's shout aroused him.   With a sense of deadly peril

hanging over him he leaped up and sprang on the Irishman.

"Hallo, Paddy!" he cried, checking himself, and endeavouring to wipe from his face some of the clotted blood with which he had been deluged. "*You* here? Are you alone?"

"It's wishin' that I was," replied the little man, looking round anxiously. "Mister Fred 'll be here d'rectly, sor—an'—an' I hope that 'll be all. But it's alive ye are, is it? An' didn't I take ye for dead. Oh! Mister Brixton, there's more blood on an' about ye, I do belave, than yer whole body could howld."

Before an answer could be returned, Fred Westly, having heard Paddy's shout, came running up.

"Oh! Tom, Tom," he cried, eagerly, "are you hurt? Can you walk? Can you run? The whole camp is out after you."

"Indeed?" replied the fugitive, with a frown. "It would seem that even my *friends* have joined in the chase."

"We have," said the other, hurriedly, "but not to capture—to save, if possible. Come, Tom, can you make an effort? Are you hurt much? You are so horribly covered with blood—"

He stopped short, for at that moment a shout was heard in the distance. It was replied to in another direction nearer at hand.

There happened to be a man in the party which Westly had joined, named Crossby. He had suffered much from thieves, and had a particular spite against Brixton because he had lost to him at play. He had heard Paddy Flinders's unfortunate shout, and immediately ran in the direction whence it came; while others of the party, having discovered the fugitive's track, had followed it up.

"Too late," groaned Fred on hearing Crossby's voice.

"Not too late for *this*," growled Brixton, bitterly, as he quickly loaded his rifle.

"For God's sake don't do that, Tom," cried his friend earnestly, as he laid his hand on his arm ; but Tom shook him off and completed the operation just as Crossby burst from the bushes and ran towards them. Seeing the fugitive standing ready with rifle in hand, he stopped at once, took rapid aim, and fired. The ball whistled close past the head of Tom, who then raised his own rifle, took deliberate aim, and fired, but Westly threw up the muzzle and the bullet went high among the tree-tops.

With an exclamation of fury Brixton drew his knife, while Crossby rushed at him with his rifle clubbed.

The digger was a strong and fierce man, and there would doubtless have been a terrible and fatal encounter if Fred had not again interfered. He seized his friend from behind, and, whirling him sharply round, received on his own shoulder the blow which was meant for Tom's head. Fred fell, dragging his friend down with him.

Flinders, who witnessed the unaccountable action of his companion with much surprise, now sprang to the rescue, but at the moment several of the other pursuers rushed upon the scene, and the luckless fugitive was instantly overpowered and secured.

"Now, my young buck," said Crossby, "stand up ! Hold him, four of you, till I fix his hands wi' this rope. There, it 's the rope that you 'll swing by, so you 'll find it hard to break."

While Tom was being bound he cast a look of fierce anger on Westly, who still lay prostrate and insensible on the ground, despite Paddy's efforts to rouse him.

"I hope he is killed," muttered Tom between his teeth.

"Och! no fear of him, he's not so aisy kilt," said Flinders, looking up. "Bad luck to ye for wishin' it."

As if to corroborate Paddy's opinion, Westly showed signs of returning consciousness, and soon after sat up.

"Did ye kill that bar all by yerself?" asked one of the men who held the fugitive.

But Tom would not condescend to reply, and in a few minutes Crossby gave the word to march back towards Pine Tree Diggings.

They set off—two men marching on either side of the prisoner with loaded rifles and revolvers, the rest in front and in rear. A party was left behind to skin the bear and bring away the tit-bits of the carcass for supper. Being too late to return to Pine Tree Camp that night, they arranged to bivouac for the night in a hollow where there was a little pond fed by a clear spring which was known as the Red Man's Teacup.

Here they kindled a large fire, the bright sparks from which, rising above the tree-tops, soon attracted the attention of the other parties, so that, ere long, the whole band of pursuers was gathered to the spot.

Gashford was the last to come up. On hearing that the thief had been captured by his former chum Westly, assisted by Flinders and Crossby, he expressed considerable surprise, and cast a long and searching gaze on Fred, who, however, being busy with the fire at the time, was unconscious of it. Whatever the bully thought, he kept his opinions to himself.

"Have you tied him up well?" he said, turning to Crossby.

"A wild horse couldn't break his fastenings," answered the digger.

"Perhaps not," returned Gashford, with a sneer, "but you are always too sure by half o' yer work. Come, stand up," he added, going to where Tom lay, and stirring his prostrate form with his toe.

Brixton having now had time to consider his case coolly, had made up his mind to submit with a good grace to his fate, and, if it were so decreed—to die "like a man." "I deserve punishment," he reasoned with himself, "though death is too severe for the offence. However, a guilty man can't expect to be the chooser of his reward. I suppose it is fate, as the Turks say, so I'll submit—like them."

He stood up at once, therefore, on being ordered to do so, and quietly underwent inspection.

"Ha! I thought so!" exclaimed Gashford, contemptuously. "Any man could free himself from that in half an hour. But what better could be expected from a land-lubber?"

Crossby made some sharp allusions to a "sea-lubber," but he wisely restrained his voice so that only those nearest overheard him.

Meanwhile Gashford undid the rope that bound Tom Brixton's arms behind him, and, holding him in his iron grip, ordered a smaller cord to be fetched.

Paddy Flinders, who had a schoolboy tendency to stuff his various pockets full of all sorts of miscellaneous articles, at once stepped forward and handed the leader a piece of strong cod-line.

"There ye are, sor," said he.

"Just the thing, Paddy. Here, catch hold o' this end of it an' haul."

"Yis, gineral," said the Irishman, in a tone and with

a degree of alacrity that caused a laugh from most of
those who were looking on. Even the "gineral" observed
it, and remarked with a sardonic smile—

"You seem to be pleased to see your old chum in this
fix, I think."

"Well now, gineral," returned Flinders, in an argu-
mentative tone of voice, "I can't exactly say that, sor, for
I'm troubled with what ye may call amiable weaknesses.
Anyhow, I might see 'im in a worse fix."

"Well, you're like to see him in a worse fix if you
live long enough," returned the leader. "Haul now on
this knot. It'll puzzle him to undo that. Lend me your
knife."

Flinders drew his glittering bowie-knife from its sheath
and handed it to his leader, who cut off the superfluous
cordage with it, after having bound the prisoner's wrists
behind his back in a sailor-like manner.

In returning the knife to its owner, Gashford, who was
fond of a practical joke, tossed it high in the air towards
him with a "Here, catch."

The keen glittering thing came twirling down, but to
the surprise of all, the Irishman caught it by the handle
as deftly as though he had been a trained juggler.

"Thank your gineralship," exclaimed Paddy, amid a
shout of laughter and applause, bowing low in mock
reverence. As he rose he made a wild flourish with the
knife, uttered an Indian war-whoop, and cut a caper.

In that flourish he managed to strike the cord that
bound the prisoner, and severed one turn of it. The
barefaced audacity of the act (like that of a juggler) caused
it to pass unobserved. Even Tom, although he felt
the touch of the knife, was not aware of what had
happened, for, of course, a number of uncut turns of the
cord still held his wrists painfully tight.

"Now, lie down on your back," said Gashford, sternly, when the laugh that Paddy had raised subsided.

Either the tone of this command, or the pain caused by his bonds, roused Tom's anger, for he refused to obey.

"Lie down, ye spalpeen, whin the gineral bids ye," cried Flinders, suddenly seizing his old friend by the collar and flinging him flat on his back, in which act he managed to trip and fall on the top of him.

The opportunity was not a good one, nevertheless the energetic fellow managed to whisper, "The rope's cut! Lie still!" in the very act of falling.

"Well done, Paddy," exclaimed several of the laughing men, as Flinders rose with a pretended look of discomfiture, and went towards the fire, exclaiming—

"Niver mind, boys, I'll have me supper now. Hi! who's bin an' stole it whin I was out on dooty? Oh! here it is all right. Now then, go to work, an' whin the pipes is lighted I'll maybe sing ye a song, or tell ye a story about ould Ireland."

CHAPTER III.

OBEDIENT to orders, Tom Brixton lay perfectly still on his back, just where he had fallen, wondering much whether the cord was really cut, for he did not feel much relaxation of it or abatement of the pain. He resolved, at any rate, to give no further cause for rough treatment, but to await the issue of events as patiently as he could.

True to his promise, the Irishman after supper sang several songs, which, if not characterised by sweetness of tone, were delivered with a degree of vigour that seemed to make full amends in the estimation of his hearers. After that he told a thrilling ghost story, which drew the entire band of men round him. Paddy had a natural gift in the way of relating ghost stories, for, besides the power of rapid and sustained discourse, without hesitation or redundancy of words, he possessed a vivid imagination, a rich fancy, a deep bass voice, an expressive countenance, and a pair of large coal-black eyes, which, as one of the Yankee diggers said, "would sartinly bore two holes in a blanket if he only looked at it long enough."

We do not intend to inflict that ghost story on the reader. It is sufficient to say that Paddy began it by exclaiming in a loud voice—

"'Now or niver, boys—now or niver.' That's what the ghost said."

"What's that you say, Paddy?" asked Gashford, leaving his own separate and private fire, which he enjoyed with one or two chosen comrades, and approaching that round which the great body of the diggers were already assembled.

"I was just goin' to tell the boys, sor, a bit of a ghost story."

"Well, go on, lad, I'd like to hear it too."

"'Now or niver!'" repeated the Irishman, with such startling emphasis that even Tom Brixton, lying bound as he was under the shelter of a spreading tree at some distance from the fire, had his curiosity aroused. "That's what the ghost said, under somewhat pecooliar circumstances; an' he said it twice so that there might be no mistake at all about it. 'Now or niver! now or niver!' says he, an' he said it earnestly—"

"I didn't know that ghosts could speak," interrupted Crossby, who, when not in a bad humour, was rather fond of thrusting bad jokes and blunt witticisms on his comrades.

"Sure, I'm not surprised at that, for there's many things ye don't know, Crossby; besides, no ghost with the smallest taste of propriety about it would condescind to spake wid *you*. Well, boys, that's what the ghost said in a muffled vice—their vices are muffled, you know, an their virtues too, for all I know to the contrairy. It's a good sentiment is that 'Now or niver' for every wan of ye—so ye may putt it in yer pipes an' smoke it, an' those of ye who haven't got pipes can make a quid of it an' chaw it, or subject it to meditation. 'Now or niver!' Think o' that! You see I'm partikler about it, for the whole story turns on that pint, as the ghost's life depended on it, but ye'll see an' onderstan' better whin I come to the ind o' the story."

A FOOLISH THROW OF THE DICE

Paddy said this so earnestly that it had the double effect of chaining the attention of his hearers and sending a flash of light into Tom Brixton's brain.

"Now or never!" he muttered to himself, and turned gently on his side so as to be able to feel the cord that bound his wrists. It was still tight, but, by moving his fingers, he could feel that one of its coils had really been cut, and that with a little patience and exertion he might possibly free his hands.

Slight as the motion was, however, Gashford observed it, for the fire-light shone brightly on Tom's recumbent figure.

"Lie still, there!" he cried, sternly.

Tom lay perfectly still, and the Irishman continued his story. It grew in mystery and in horror as he proceeded, and his audience became entranced, while some of the more superstitious among them cast occasional glances over their shoulders into the forest behind, which ere long was steeped in the blackness of an unusually dark night. A few of those outside the circle rose and drew nearer to the story-teller.

At that moment a gleam of light which had already entered Brixton's brain flashed into that of Fred Westly, who arose, and, under pretext of being too far off from the speaker, went round to the opposite side of the fire so as to face him. By so doing he placed himself between the fire and his friend Tom. Two or three of the others followed his example, though not from the same motive, and thus, when the fire burnt low, the prisoner found himself lying in deep shadow. By that time he had freed his benumbed hands, chafed them into a condition of vitality, and was considering whether he should endeavour to creep quietly away or spring up and make a dash for life,

" 'Now or niver,' said the ghost, in a solemn mufflled vice," continued Paddy—

" Who did he say that to ?" asked Gashford, who was by that time as much fascinated as the rest of the party.

" To the thief, sor, av coorse, who was standin' tremblin' fornint him, while the sexton was diggin' the grave to putt him in alive—in the dark shadow of a big tombstone."

The Irishman had now almost reached the climax of his story, and was intensely graphic in his descriptions— especially at the horrible parts. He was obviously spinning it out, and the profound silence around told how completely he had enchained his hearers. It also warned Tom Brixton that his time was short, and that in his case it was indeed " now or never."

He crept quietly towards the bushes near him. In passing a tree against which several rifles had been placed he could not resist the temptation to take one. Laying hold of that which stood nearest, and which seemed to be similar in make to the rifle they had taken from himself when he was captured, he drew it towards him. Unfortunately it formed a prop to several other rifles, which fell with a crash, and one of them exploded in the fall.

The effect on Paddy's highly-strung audience was tremendous. Many of them yelled as if they had received an electric shock. All of them sprang up and turned round just in time to see their captive vanish, not unlike a ghost, into the thick darkness !

That glance, however, was sufficient to enlighten them. With shouts of rage many of them darted after the fugitive, and followed him up like bloodhounds. Others, who had never been very anxious for his capture or death, and had been turned somewhat in his favour by the bold stand he had made against the bear, returned to the fire after a short run.

If there had been even a glimmering of light Tom would certainly have been retaken at once, for not a few of his pursuers were quite as active and hardy as himself, but the intense darkness favoured him. Fortunately the forest immediately behind him was not so dense as else-where, else in his first desperate rush, regardless of consequences, he would probably have dashed himself against a tree. As it was he went right through a thicket and plunged headlong into a deep hole. He scrambled out of this with the agility of a panther, just in time to escape Gashford, who chanced to plunge into the same hole, but not so lightly. Heavy though he was, however, his strength was equal to the shock, and he would have scrambled out quickly enough if Crossby had not run on the same course and tumbled on the top of him.

Amid the growling half-fight, half-scramble that ensued, Tom crept swiftly away to the left, but the pursuers had so scattered themselves that he heard them panting and stumbling about in every direction—before, on either hand, and behind. Hurrying blindly on for a few paces, he almost ran into the arms of a man whom he could hear, though he could not see him, and stopped.

"Hallo! is that you, Bill Smith?" demanded the man.

"Ay, that's me," replied Tom, promptly, mimicking Bill Smith's voice and gasping violently. "I thought you were Brixton. He's just passed this way. I saw him."

"Did you?—where?"

"Away there—to the left!"

Off went the pursuer as fast as he dared, and Tom continued his flight with more caution.

"Hallo! hi! hooroo!" came at that moment from a long distance to the right, in unmistakable tones. "Here he is, down this way. Stop, you big thief! Howld him, Dick! Have ye got him?"

There was a general rush and scramble towards the
owner of the bass voice, and Tom, who at once perceived
the ruse, went quietly off in the opposite direction.

Of course, the hunt came to an end in a very few
minutes. Every one, having more or less damaged his
head, knees, elbows, and shins, came to the natural conclusion that a chase in the dark was absurd as well as
hopeless, and in a short time all were reassembled round
the fire, where Fred Westly still stood, for he had not
joined in the pursuit. Gashford was the last to come up,
with the exception of Paddy Flinders.

The bully came forward, fuming with rage, and strode
up to Fred Westly with a threatening look.

"You were at the bottom of this!" he cried, doubling
his huge fist. "It was you who cut the rope, for no
mortal man could have untied it!"

"Indeed I did not!" replied Fred, with a steady but
not defiant look.

"Then it must have bin your little chum Flinders.
Where is he?"

"How could Flinders ha' done it when he was tellin' a
ghost story?" said Crossby.

Gashford turned with a furious look to the speaker,
and seemed on the point of venting his ill-humour upon
him, when he was arrested by the sound of the Irishman's
voice shouting in the distance.

As he drew nearer the words became intelligible.
"Howld him tight, now! d'ye hear? Och! whereiver
have ye gone an' lost yersilf? Howld him tight till I
come an' help ye! What! is it let him go ye have? Ah!
then it's wishin' I had the eyes of a cat this night, for I
can't rightly see the length of my nose. Sure ye've niver
gone an' let him go? Don't say so, now!" wound up

Paddy as, issuing from the wood, he advanced into the circle of light.

"Who's got hold of him, Flin?" asked one of the men as he came up.

"Sorrow wan o' me knows," returned the Irishman, wiping the perspiration from his brow; "d'ye suppose I can see in the dark like the moles? All I know is that half a dozen of ye have bin shoutin' 'Here he is!' an' another half-dozen, 'No, he's here—this way!' an' sure I ran this way an' then I ran that way—havin' a nat'ral disposition to obey orders, acquired in the Louth Militia —an' then I ran my nose flat on a tree—bad luck to it!— that putt more stars in me hid than you'll see in the sky this night. Ah! ye may laugh, but it's truth I'm tellin'. See, there's a blob on the ind of it as big as a chirry!"

"That blob's always there, Paddy," cried one of the men; "it's a grog-blossom."

"There now, Peter, don't become personal. But tell me—ye've got him, av coorse?"

"No, we haven't got him," growled Crossby.

"Well, now, you're a purty lot o' hunters. Sure if—"

"Come, shut up, Flinders," interrupted Gashford, swallowing his wrath. (Paddy brought his teeth together with a snap in prompt obedience.) "You know well enough that we haven't got him, and you know you're not sorry for it; but mark my words, I'll hunt him down yet. Who'll go with me?"

"I'll go," said Crossby, stepping forward at once. "I've a grudge agin the puppy, and I'll help to make him swing if I can."

Half a dozen other men, who were noted for leading idle and dissipated lives, and who would rather have hunted men than nothing, also offered to go, but the

C

most of the party had had enough of it, and resolved to
return home in the morning.

" We can't go just now, however," said Crossby, " we 'd
only break our legs or necks."

" The moon will rise in an hour," returned Gashford ;
" we can start then."

He flung himself down sulkily on the ground beside
the fire and began to fill his pipe.   Most of the others
followed his example, and sat chatting about the recent
escape, while a few, rolling themselves in their blankets,
resigned themselves to sleep.

About an hour later, as had been predicted, the moon
rose, and Gashford with his men set forth.   But by that
time the fugitive, groping his way painfully with many a
stumble and fall, had managed to put a considerable
distance between him and his enemies, so that when the
first silvery moonbeans tipped the tree-tops and shed a
faint glimmer on the ground, which served to make
darkness barely visible, he had secured a good start, and
was able to keep well ahead.   The pursuers were not
long in finding his track, however, for they had taken a
Red Indian with them to act as guide, but the necessity
for frequent halts to examine the footprints carefully
delayed them much, while Tom Brixton ran straight on
without halt or stay.   Still he felt that his chance of
escape was by no means a good one, for as he guessed
rightly, they would not start without a native guide, and
he knew the power and patience of these red men in
following an enemy's trail.   What made his case more
desperate was the sudden diminution of his strength.
For it must be borne in mind that he had taken but
little rest and no food since his flight from Pine Tree
Diggings, and the wounds he had received from the bear,
although not dangerous, were painful and exhausting.

A feeling of despair crept over the stalwart youth when the old familiar sensation of bodily strength began to forsake him. Near daybreak he was on the point of casting himself on the ground to take rest at all hazards, when the sound of falling water broke upon his ear. His spirit revived at once, for he now knew that in his blind wandering he had come near to a well-known river or stream, where he could slake his burning thirst, and, by wading down its course for some distance, throw additional difficulty in the pursuers' way. Not that he expected by that course to throw them entirely off the scent, he only hoped to delay them.

On reaching the river's brink he fell down on his breast, and, applying his lips to the bubbling water, took a deep refreshing draught.

"God help me!" he exclaimed, on rising, and then feeling the burden of gold (which, all through his flight, had been concealed beneath his shirt, packed flat so as to lie close), he took it off and flung it down.

"There," he said bitterly, "for *you* I have sold myself body and soul, and now I fling you away!"

Instead of resting as he had intended, he now, feeling strengthened, looked about for a suitable place to enter the stream and wade down so as to leave no footprints behind. To his surprise and joy he observed the bow of a small Indian canoe half hidden among the bushes. It had apparently been dragged there by its owner, and left to await his return, for the paddles were lying under it.

Launching this frail bark without a moment's delay, he found that it was tight; pushed off and went rapidly down with the current. Either he had forgotten the gold in his haste, or the disgust he had expressed was genuine, for he left it lying on the bank.

He now no longer fled without a purpose. Many

miles down that same stream there dwelt a gold-digger in a lonely hut. His name was Paul Bevan. He was an eccentric being, and a widower with an only child, a daughter, named Elizabeth—better known as Betty.

One phase of Paul Bevan's eccentricity was exhibited in his selection of a spot in which to search for the precious metal. It was a savage, gloomy gorge, such as a misanthrope might choose in which to end an unlovely career. But Bevan was no misanthrope. On the contrary, he was one of those men who are gifted with amiable dispositions, high spirits, strong frames, and unfailing health. He was a favourite with all who knew him, and, although considerably past middle life, possessed much of the fire, energy, and light-heartedness of youth. There is no accounting for the acts of eccentric men, and we make no attempt to explain why it was that Paul Bevan selected a home which was not only far removed from the abodes of other men, but which did not produce much gold. Many prospecting parties had visited the region from time to time, under the impression that Bevan had discovered a rich mine, which he was desirous of keeping all to himself; but, after searching and digging all round the neighbourhood, and discovering that gold was to be found in barely paying quantities, they had left in search of more prolific fields, and spread the report that Paul Bevan was an eccentric fellow. Some said he was a queer chap; others, more outspoken, styled him an ass, but all agreed in the opinion that his daughter Betty was the finest girl in Oregon.

Perhaps this opinion may account for the fact that many of the miners—especially the younger among them —returned again and again to Bevan's Gully to search for gold although the search was not remunerative. Among those persevering though unsuccessful diggers had been, for a considerable time past, our hero Tom Brixton. Perhaps the decision with which Elizabeth Bevan repelled him had had something to do with his late reckless life.

But we must guard the reader here from supposing that Betty Bevan was a beauty. She was not. On the other hand, she was by no means plain, for her complexion was good, her nut-brown hair was soft and wavy, and her eyes were tender and true. It was the blending of the graces of body and of soul that rendered Betty so attractive. As poor Tom Brixton once said in a moment of confidence to his friend Westly, while excusing himself for so frequently going on prospecting expeditions to Bevan's Gully, "There's no question about it, Fred; she's the sweetest girl in Oregon—pshaw! in the world, I should have said. Loving-kindness beams in her eyes, sympathy ripples on her brow, grace dwells in her every motion, and honest, straightforward simplicity sits enthroned upon her countenance!"

Even Crossby, the surly digger, entertained similar sentiments regarding her, though he expressed them in less refined language. "She's a bu'ster," he said once to a comrade, "that's what *she* is, an' no mistake about it. What with her great eyes glarin' affection, an' her little mouth smilin' good-natur', an' her figure goin' about as graceful as a small cat at play—why, I tell ee what it is, mate, with such a gal for a wife a feller might snap his fingers at hunger an' thirst, heat an' cold, bad luck an' all the rest of it. But she's got one fault that don't suit me. She's overly religious—an' that don't pay at the diggin's."

This so-called fault did indeed appear to interfere with Betty Bevan's matrimonial prospects, for it kept a large number of dissipated diggers at arm's-length from her, and it made even the more respectable men feel shy in her presence.

Tom Brixton, however, had not been one of her timid admirers. He had a drop or two of Irish blood in his veins which rendered that impossible! Before falling into dissipated habits he had paid his addresses to her boldly. Moreover, his suit was approved by Betty's father, who had taken a great fancy to Tom. But, as we have said, this Rose of Oregon repelled Tom. She did it gently and kindly, it is true, but decidedly.

It was, then, towards the residence of Paul Bevan that the fugitive now urged his canoe, with a strange turmoil of conflicting emotions however; for, the last time he had visited the Gully he had been at least free from the stain of having broken the laws of man. Now, he was a fugitive and an outlaw, with hopes and aspirations blighted and the last shred of self-respect gone.

CHAPTER IV.

WHEN Tom Brixton had descended the river some eight or ten miles he deemed himself pretty safe from his pursuers, at least for the time being, as his rate of progress with the current far exceeded the pace at which men could travel on foot; and besides, there was the strong probability that, on reaching the spot where the canoe had been entered and the bag of gold left on the bank, the pursuers would be partially satisfied as well as baffled, and would return home.

On reaching a waterfall, therefore, where the navigable part of the river ended and its broken course through Bevan's Gully began, he landed without any show of haste, drew the canoe up on the bank, where he left it concealed among bushes, and began quietly to descend by a narrow footpath with which he had been long familiar.

Up to that point the unhappy youth had entertained no definite idea as to why he was hurrying towards the hut of Paul Bevan, or what he meant to say for himself on reaching it. But towards noon, as he drew near to it, the thought of Betty in her innocence and purity oppressed him. She rose before his mind's eye like a reproving angel.

How could he ever face her with the dark stain of a mean theft upon his soul? How could he find courage to confess his guilt to her? or, supposing that he did not confess it, how could he forge the tissue of lies that would be necessary to account for his sudden appearance, and in such guise—bloodstained, wounded, haggard, and worn out with fatigue and hunger? Such thoughts now drove him to the verge of despair. Even if Betty were to refrain from putting awkward questions, there was no chance whatever of Paul Bevan being so considerate. Was he then to attempt to deceive them, or was he to reveal all? He shrank from answering the question, for he believed that Bevan was an honest man, and feared that he would have nothing further to do with him when he learned that he had become a common thief. A thief! How the idea burned into his heart now that the influence of strong drink no longer warped his judgment!

"Has it *really* come to this?" he muttered, gloomily. Then, as he came suddenly in sight of Bevan's hut, he exclaimed more cheerfully, "Come, I'll make a clean breast of it."

Paul Bevan had pitched his hut on the top of a steep rocky mound, the front of which almost overhung a precipice that descended into a deep gully where the tormented river fell into a black and gurgling pool. Behind the hut flowed a streamlet, which being divided by the mound into a fork, ran on either side of it in two deep channels, so that the hut could only be reached by a plank bridge thrown across the lower or western fork. The forked streamlet tumbled over the precipice and descended into the dark pool below in the form of two tiny silver threads. At least it would have done so if its two threads had not been dissipated in misty spray long before reaching the bottom of the cliff. Thus it will be seen that the gold-digger occupied an almost impregnable fortress, though why he had perched himself in such a position no one could guess and he declined to tell. It was there fore set down, like all his other doings, to eccentricity.

Of course there was so far a pretext for his caution in the fact that there were scoundrels in those regions who sometimes banded together and attacked people who were supposed to have gold-dust about them in large quantities, but as such assaults were not common, and as every one was equally liable to them, there seemed no sufficient ground for Bevan's excessive care in the selection of his fortress.

On reaching it Tom found its owner cutting up some firewood near his plank-bridge.

"Hallo, Brixton!" he cried, looking up in some surprise as the young man advanced; "you seem to have bin in the wars. What have 'e been fightin' wi', lad?"

"With a bear, Paul Bevan," replied Tom, sitting down on a log, with a long-drawn sigh.

"You're used up, lad, an' want rest; mayhap you want grub also. Anyhow you look awful bad. No wounds, I hope, or bones broken, eh?"

"No, nothing but a broken heart," replied Tom with a faint attempt to smile.

"Why, that's a queer bit o' you for a b'ar to break. If you had said it was a girl that broke it, now, I could have—"

"Where is Betty?" interrupted the youth, quickly, with an anxious expression.

"In the hut, lookin' arter the grub. You'll come in an' have some, of course. But I'm coorious to hear about that b'ar. Was it far from here you met him?"

"Ay, just a short way this side o' Pine Tree Diggings."

"Pine Tree Diggin's!" repeated Paul in surprise. "Why, then, didn't you go back to Pine Tree Diggin's to wash yourself, an' rest, instead o' comin' all the way here?"

"Because—because, Paul Bevan," said Tom with sudden earnestness, as he gazed on the other's face, "because I 'm a thief!"

"You might be worse," replied Bevan, while a peculiarly significant smile played for a moment on his rugged features.

"What do you mean?" exclaimed Tom, in amazement.

"Why, you might have bin a murderer, you know," replied Bevan, with a nod.

The youth was so utterly disgusted with this cool, indifferent way of regarding the matter that he almost regretted having spoken. He had been condemning himself so severely during the latter part of his journey, and the meanness of his conduct as well as its wickedness had been growing so dark in colour, that Bevan's unexpected levity took him aback, and for a few seconds he could not speak.

"Listen," he said at last, seizing his friend by the arm and looking earnestly into his eyes. "Listen, and I will tell you all about it."

The man became grave as Tom went on with his narrative.

"Yes, it 's a bad business," he said, at its conclusion, "an uncommon bad business. Got a very ugly look about it."

"You are right, Paul," said Tom, bowing his head, while a flush of shame covered his face. "No one, I think, can be more fully convinced of the meanness—the sin—of my conduct than I am now—"

"Oh! as to that," returned Bevan, with another of his peculiar smiles, "I didn't exactly mean that. You were tempted, you know, pretty bad. Besides, Bully Gashford is a big rascal, an' richly deserves what he got. No, it wasn't that I meant—but it's a bad look-out for you, lad, if they nab you. I knows the temper o' them Pine Tree men, an' they're in such a wax just now that they'll string you up, as sure as fate, if they catch you."

Again Tom was silent, for the lightness with which Bevan regarded his act of theft only had the effect of making him condemn himself the more.

"But, I say, Brixton," resumed Bevan, with an altered expression, "not a word of all this to Betty. You haven't much chance with her as it is, although I do my best to back you up; but if she came to know of this affair, you'd not have the ghost of a chance at all—for you know the gal is religious, more's the pity; though I will say it, she's a good obedient gal, in spite of her religion, an' a 'fectionate darter to me. But she'd never marry a thief, you know. You couldn't well expect her to."

The dislike with which Tom Brixton regarded his companion deepened into loathing as he spoke, and he felt it difficult to curb his desire to fell the man to the ground, but the thought that he was Betty's father soon swallowed up all other thoughts and feelings. He resolved in his own mind that, come of it what might, he would certainly tell all the facts to the girl and then formally give her up, for he agreed with Bevan at least on one point, namely, that he could not expect a good religious girl to marry a thief!

"But you forget, Paul," he said, after a few moments' thought, "that Betty is sure to hear about this affair the first time you have a visitor from Pine Tree Diggings."

"That's true, lad, I did forget that. But you know you can stoutly deny that it was you who did it. Say

there was some mistake, and git up some cock-an'-
a-bull story to confuse her. Anyhow, say nothing about
it just now."

Tom was still meditating what he should say in reply
to this, when Betty herself appeared, calling her father to
dinner.

"Now, mind, not a word about the robbery," he whispered as he rose, "and we'll make as much as we can of
the b'ar."

"Yes, not a word about it," thought Tom, "till Betty
and I are alone, and then—a clean breast and good-bye
to her, for ever!"

During dinner the girl manifested more than usual
sympathy with Tom Brixton. She saw that he was
almost worn out with fatigue, and listened with intense
interest to her father's embellished narrative of the encounter with the "b'ar," which narrative Tom was forced
to interrupt and correct several times in the course of its
delivery. But this sympathy did not throw her off her
guard. Remembering past visits, she took special care
that Tom should have no opportunity of being alone with
her.

"Now, you must be off to rest," said Paul Bevan, the
moment his visitor laid down his knife and fork, "for, let
me tell you, I may want your help before night. I've
got an enemy, Tom, an enemy who has sworn to be the
death o' me, and who *will* be the death o' me, I feel sure
o' that, in the long-run. However, I'll keep him off as
long as I can. He'd have been under the sod long afore
now, lad—if—if it hadn't bin for my Betty. She's a
queer girl is Betty, and she's made a queer man of her
old father."

"But who is this enemy, and when—what—? explain
yourself."

"Well, I 've no time to explain either 'when' or 'what' just now, and you have no time to waste. Only I have had a hint from a friend, early this morning, that my enemy has discovered my whereabouts, and is following me up. But I 'm ready for him and right glad to have your stout arm to help—-though you couldn't fight a babby just now. Lie down, I say, an' I 'll call you when you 're wanted."

Ceasing to press the matter, Tom entered a small room, in one corner of which a narrow bed, or bunk, was fixed. Flinging himself on this, he was fast asleep in less than two minutes. "Kind nature's sweet restorer" held him so fast that for three hours he lay precisely as he fell, without the slightest motion, save the slow and regular heaving of his broad chest.

At the end of that time he was rudely shaken by a strong hand. The guilty are always easily startled. Springing from his couch he had seized Bevan by the throat before he was quite awake.

"Hist! man, not quite so fast," gasped his host, shaking him off. "Come, they 've turned up sooner than I expected."

"What—who?" said Brixton, looking round.

"My enemy, of coorse, an' a gang of redskins to help him. They expect to catch us asleep, but they 'll find out their mistake soon enough. That lad there brought me the news, and, you see, he an' Betty are getting things ready."

Tom glanced through the slightly opened doorway, as he tightened his belt, and saw Betty and a boy of about fourteen years of age standing at a table busily engaged loading several old-fashioned horse-pistols with buckshot.

"Who 's the boy?" asked Tom.

"They call him Tolly. I saved the little chap once

from a grizzly b'ar, an' he's a grateful feller, you see—
has run a long way to give me warnin' in time. Come,
here's a shot-gun for you charged wi' slugs. I'm not
allowed to use ball, you must know, 'cause Betty thinks
that balls kill an' slugs only wound! I humour the
little gal, you see, for she's a good darter to me. We've
both on us bin lookin' forward to this day, for we knowed
it must come sooner or later, an' I made her a promise
that when it did come I'd only defend the hut wi' slugs.
But slugs ain't bad shots at a close range, when aimed
low."

The man gave a sly chuckle and a huge wink as he
said this, and entered the large room of the hut.

Betty was very pale and silent. She did not even
look up from the pistol she was loading when Tom
entered. The boy Tolly, however, looked at his tall,
strong figure with evident satisfaction.

" Ha!" he exclaimed, ramming down a charge of slugs
with great energy ; " we'll be able to make a good fight
without your services, Betty. Won't we, old man?"

The pertly-put question was addressed to Paul Bevan,
between whom and the boy there was evidently strong
affection.

" Yes, Tolly," replied Bevan, with a pleasant nod, " three
men are quite enough for the defence of this here castle."

" But, I say, old man," continued the boy, shaking a
powder-horn before his face, " the powder's all done.
Where'll I git more?"

A look of anxiety flitted across Bevan's face.

" It's in the magazine.   I got a fresh keg last week,
an' thought it safest to put it there till required—an'
haven't I gone an' forgot to fetch it in!"

"Well, that don't need to trouble you," returned the boy,
"just show me the magazine, an' I'll go an' fetch it in!"

"The magazine's over the bridge," said Bevan. "I dug it there for safety. Come, Tom, the keg's too heavy for the boy. I must fetch it myself, and you must guard the bridge while I do it."

He went out quickly as he spoke, followed by Tom and Tolly.

It was a bright moonlight night, and the forks of the little stream glittered like two lines of silver at the bottom of their rugged bed on either side of the hut. The plank-bridge had been drawn up on the bank. With the aid of his two allies Bevan quickly thrust it over the gulf, and, without a moment's hesitation, sprang across. While Tom stood at the inner end, ready with a double-barrelled gun to cover his friend's retreat if necessary, he saw Bevan lift a trap-door not thirty yards distant and disappear. A few seconds, and he re-appeared with a keg on his shoulder.

All remained perfectly quiet in the dark woods around. The babbling rivulet alone broke the silence of the night. Bevan semed to glide over the ground, he trod so softly.

"There's another," he whispered, placing the keg at Tom's feet, and springing back towards the magazine. Again he disappeared, and, as before, re-issued from the hole with the second keg on his shoulder. Suddenly a phantom seemed to glide from the bushes and fell him to the earth. He dropped without even a cry, and so swift was the act that his friends had not time to move a finger to prevent it. Tom, however, discharged both barrels of his gun at the spot where the phantom seemed to disappear, and Tolly Trevor discharged a horse pistol in the same direction. Instantly a rattling volley was fired from the woods, and balls whistled all round the defenders of the hut.

Most men in the circumstances would have sought shelter, but Tom Brixton's spirit was of that utterly reckless character that refuses to count the cost before action. Betty's father lay helpless on the ground in the power of his enemies! That was enough for Tom. He leaped across the bridge, seized the fallen man, threw him on his shoulder, and had almost regained the bridge, when three painted Indians uttered a hideous war-whoop and sprang after him.

Fortunately, having just emptied their guns, they could not prevent the fugitive from crossing the bridge, but they reached it before there was time to draw in the plank, and were about to follow, when Tolly Trevor planted himself in front of them with a double-barrelled horse-pistol in each hand.

"We don't want *you* here, you—red—faced—baboons!" he cried, pausing between each of the last three words to discharge a shot, and emphasising the last word with one of the pistols, which he hurled with such precision that it took full effect on the bridge of the nearest red man's nose. All three fell, but rose again with a united screech and fled back to the bushes.

A few moments more and the bridge was drawn back, and Paul Bevan was borne into the hut amid a scattering fire from the assailants, which, however, did no damage.

To the surprise and consternation of Tolly, who entered first, Betty was found sitting on a chair with blood trickling from her left arm. A ball entering through the window had grazed her, and she sank down, partly from the shock coupled with alarm. She recovered, however, on seeing her father carried in, sprang up, and ran to him.

"Only stunned, Betty," said Tom; "will be all right soon, but we must rouse him, for the scoundrels will be upon us in a minute. What—what's this—wounded?"

"Only a scratch. Don't mind me. Father! dear

father—rouse up! They will be here—oh! rouse up, dear father!"

But Betty shook him in vain.

"Out o' the way, *I* know how to stir him up," said Tolly, coming forward with a pail of water and sending the contents violently into his friend's face—thus drenching him from head to foot.

The result was that Paul Bevan sneezed, and, sitting up, looked astonished.

"Ha! I thought that 'ud fetch you," said the boy, with a grin. "Come, you'd better look alive if you don't want to lose yer scalp."

"Ho! ho!" exclaimed Bevan, rising with a sudden look of intelligence and staggering to the door, "here, give me the old sword, Betty, and the blunderbuss. Now then."

He went out at the door, and Tom Brixton was following, when the girl stopped him.

"Oh! Mr. Brixton," she said, "do not *kill* any one if you can help it."

"I won't if I can help it. But listen, Betty," said the youth, hurriedly seizing the girl's hand. "I have tried hard to speak with you alone to-day to tell you that I am *guilty*, and to say good-bye *for ever.*"

"Guilty! what do you mean?" she exclaimed in bewildered surprise.

"No time to explain. I may be shot, you know, or taken prisoner, though the latter's not likely. In any case remember that I confess myself *guilty!* God bless you, dear, *dear* girl."

Without waiting for a reply, he ran to a hollow on the top of the mound where his friend and Tolly were already ensconced, and whence they could see every part of the clearing around the little fortress.

" I see the reptiles," whispered Bevan, as Tom joined
them. "They are mustering for an attack on the south
side. Just what I wish," he added, with a suppressed
chuckle, "for I 've got a pretty little arrangement of cod-
hooks and man-traps in that direction."

As he spoke several dark figures were seen gliding
among the trees. A moment later, and these made a
quick silent rush over the clearing to gain the slight
shelter of the shrubs that fringed the streamlet.

"Just so," remarked Bevan, in an undertone, when a
crash of branches told that one of his traps had taken
effect, "an' from the row I should guess that two have
gone into the hole at the same time. Ha ! that 's a fish
hooked !" he added, as a short sharp yell of pain, mingled
with surprise, suddenly increased the noise.

"An' there goes another !" whispered Tolly, scarcely
able to contain himself with delight at such an effective
yet comparatively bloodless way of embarrassing their
foes.

"And another," added Bevan; "but look out now;
they 'll retreat presently. Give 'em a dose o' slug as they
go back, but take 'em low, lads—about the feet and ankles.
It 's only a fancy of my dear little gal, but I like to humour
her fancies."

Bevan was right. Finding that they were not only
surrounded by hidden pit-falls, but caught by painfully
sharp little instruments, and entangled among cordage,
the Indians used their scalping-knives to free themselves.
and rushed back again towards the wood, but before gain-
ing its shelter they received the slug-dose above referred
to, and instantly filled the air with shrieks of rage rather
than of pain. At that moment a volley was fired from
the other side of the fortress, and several balls passed
close over the defenders' heads.

"Surrounded and outnumbered!" exclaimed Bevan, with something like a groan.

As he spoke another but more distant volley was heard, accompanied by shouts of anger and confusion among the men who were assaulting the fortress.

"The attackers are attacked," exclaimed Bevan, in surprise; "I wonder who by."

He looked round for a reply, but only saw the crouching figure of Tolly beside him.

"Where's Brixton?" he asked.

"Bolted into the hut," answered the boy.

"Betty," exclaimed Tom, springing into the little parlour or hall, where he found the poor girl on her knees, "you are safe now. I heard the voice of Gashford, and the Indians are flying. But I too must fly. I am guilty, as I have said, but my crime is not worthy of death, yet death is the award, and, God knows, I am not fit to die. Once more—farewell."

He spoke rapidly, and was turning to go without even venturing to look at the girl, when she said—

"Whatever your crime may be, remember that there is a Saviour from sin. Stay! You cannot leap the creek, and even if you did you would be caught, for I hear voices near us. Come with me."

She spoke in a tone of decision that compelled obedience. Lifting a trap-door in the floor she bade her lover descend. He did so, and found himself in a cellar half full of lumber and with several casks ranged round the walls. The girl followed, removed one of the casks, and disclosed a hole behind it.

"It is small," she said, quickly, "but you will be able to force yourself through. Inside it enlarges at once to a low tunnel, along which you will creep for a hundred yards, when you will reach open air in a dark, rocky dell!

close to the edge of the precipice above the river. Descend
to its bed, and, when free, use your freedom to escape
from death—but much more, to escape from sin. Go
quickly !"

Tom Brixton would fain have delayed to seize and kiss
his preserver's hand, but the sound of voices overhead
warned him to make haste. Without a word he dropped
on hands and knees and thrust himself through the
aperture. Betty replaced the cask, returned to the upper
room, and closed the trap-door just a few minutes before
her father ushered Gashford and his party into the hut.

CHAPTER V.

WHEN our hero found himself in a hole, pitch dark and barely large enough to permit of his creeping on hands and knees, he felt a sudden sensation of fear— of undefinable dread—come over him, such as one might be supposed to experience on awaking to the discovery that he had been buried alive. His first impulse was to shout for deliverance, but his manhood returned to him and he restrained himself.

Groping his way cautiously along the passage or tunnel, which descended at first steeply, he came to a part which he could feel was regularly built over with an arch of brickwork or masonry, and the sound of running water overhead told him that this was a tunnel under the rivulet. As he advanced the tunnel widened a little and began to ascend. After creeping what he judged to be a hundred yards or so, he thought he could see a glimmer of light, like a faint star in front of him. It was the opening to which Betty had referred. He soon reached it, and emerged into the fresh air.

As he raised himself, and drew a long breath of relief, the words of his deliverer seemed to start up before him in letters of fire—" Use your freedom to escape from death—but *much more, to escape from sin.*"

"I will, so help me God !" he exclaimed, clasping his hands convulsively and looking upward. In the strength of the new-born resolution thus induced by the Spirit of God, he fell on his knees and tried to pray. Then he rose and sat down to think, strangely forgetful of the urgent need there was for flight.

Meanwhile Gashford and his men proceeded to question Paul Bevan and his daughter. The party included, among others, Fred Westly, Paddy Flinders, and Crossby. Gashford more than suspected the motives of the first two in accompanying him, but did not quite see his way to decline their services, even if he had possessed the power to do so. He consoled himself, however, with the reflection that he could keep a sharp eye on their movements.

"No, no, Bevan," he said, when the man brought out a case-bottle of rum and invited him to drink, "we have other work on hand just now. We have traced that young thief Brixton to this hut, and we want to get hold of him."

"A thief is he?" returned Bevan, with a look of feigned surprise. "Well, now, that *is* strange news. Tom Brixton don't look much like a thief, do he?" (appealing to the by-standers). "There must be some mistake, surely."

"There's no mistake," said Gashford, with an oath. "He stole a bag o' gold from my tent. To be sure he dropped it in his flight, so I've got it back again, but that don't affect his guilt."

"But surely, Mister Gashford," said Bevan slowly, for, having been hurriedly told in a whisper by Betty what she had done for Tom, he was anxious to give his friend as much time as possible to escape, "surely as you've come by no loss, ye can afford to let the poor young feller off this time."

"No, we can't," shouted Gashford, fiercely. "These mean pilferers have become a perfect pest at the diggin's, an' we intend to stop their little game, we do, by stoppin' their windpipes when we catch them. Come, don't shilly-shally any longer, Paul Bevan. He's here and no mistake, so you'd better hand him over. Besides, you owe us something, you know, for coming to your help agin the redskins in the nick of time."

" Well, as to that, I *am* much obliged, though, after all, it wasn't to help me you came."

" No matter," exclaimed the other impatiently, "you know he is here, an' you're bound to give him up."

" But I *don't* know that he's here, an' I *can't* give him up, cause why? he's escaped."

" Escaped! impossible, there is only one bridge to this mound, and he has not crossed that since we arrived, I'll be bound. There's a sentry on it now."

" But an active young feller can jump, you know."

" No, he couldn't jump over the creek unless he was a human flea or a Rocky Mountain goat. Come, since you won't show us where he is, we'll take the liberty of sarchin' your premises. But stay, your daughter's got the name o' bein' a religious gal. If there's any truth in that she'd be above tellin' a lie. Come now, Betty, tell us, like a good gal, is Tom Brixton here?"

" No, he is not here," replied the girl.

" Where is he, then?"

" I do not know."

" That's false, you *do* know. But come, lads, we'll sarch, and here's a cellar to begin with."

He laid hold of the iron ring of the trap-door, opened it, and seizing a light, descended, followed by Bevan, Crossby, Flinders, and one or two others. Tossing the lumber about he finally rolled aside the barrels ranged beside the wall, until the entrance to the subterranean way was discovered,

"Ho ! ho !" he cried, lowering the light and gazing into it. " Here's something, anyhow."

After peering into the dark hole for some time he felt with his hand as far as his arm could reach.

" Mind he don't bite !" suggested Paddy Flinders, in a tone that drew a laugh from the by-standers.

" Hand me that stick, Paddy," said Gashford, " and keep your jokes to a more convenient season."

" Ah ! then 'tis always a convanient season wid me, sor," replied Paddy, with a wink at his companions as he handed the stick.

" Does this hole go far in ?" he asked, after a fruitless poking about with the stick.

" Ay, a long way. More 'n a hundred yards," returned Bevan.

" Well, I 'll have a look at it."

Saying which Gashford pushed the light as far in as he could reach, and then, taking a bowie-knife between his teeth, attempted to follow.

We say attempted, because he was successful only in a partial degree. It must be remembered that Gashford was an unusually large man, and that Tom Brixton had been obliged to use a little force in order to gain an entrance. When, therefore, the huge bully had thrust himself in about as far as his waist he stuck hard and fast, so that he could neither advance nor retreat ! He struggled violently, and a muffled sound of shouting was heard inside the hole, but no one could make out what was said.

" Och ! the poor cratur," exclaimed Paddy Flinders, with a look of overdone commiseration, " what 'll we do for 'im at all at all ?"

" Let's try to pull him out," suggested Crossby.

They tried and failed, although as many as could manage it laid hold of him.

"Sure he minds me of a stiff cork in a bottle," said
Flinders, wiping the perspiration from his forehead, "an'
what a most awful crack he'll make whin he does come
out! Let's give another heave, boys."

They gave another heave, but only caused the muffled
shouting inside to increase. "Och! the poor cratur's
stritchin' out like a injinrubber man; sure he's a fut
longer than he used to be—him that was a sight too long
already," said Flinders.

"Let's try to shove him through," suggested the
baffled Crossby.

Failure again followed their united efforts—except as
regards the muffled shouting within, which increased in
vigour and was accompanied by no small amount of kick-
ing by what of Gashford remained in the cellar.

"I'm afeared his legs'll come off altogether if we try
to pull harder than we've done," said Crossby, contemplating the huge and helpless limbs of the victim with a
perplexed air.

"What a chance, boys," suddenly exclaimed Flinders,
"to pay off old scores with a tree-mendous wallopin'!
We could do it aisy in five or tin minutes, an' then lave
'im to think over it for the rest of his life."

As no one approved of Paddy's proposal, it was finally
resolved to dig the big man out, and a pick and shovel
were procured for the purpose.

Contrary to all expectations, Gashford was calm, almost
subdued, when his friends at last set him free.   Instead
of storming and abusing every one, he said quietly but
quickly, "Let us search the bush now.   He can't be far
off yet, and there's moonlight enough."

Leading the way, he sprang up the cellar stair, out at
the hut-door, and across the bridge, followed closely by
his party.

"Hooroo!" yelled Paddy Flinders, as if in the irrepressible ardour of the chase, but in reality to give Brixton intimation of the pursuit if he should chance to be within earshot.

The well-meant signal did indeed take effect, but it came too late. It found Tom still seated in absorbed meditation. Rudely awakened to the consciousness of his danger and his stupidity, he leaped up and ran along the path that Betty had described to him. At the same moment it chanced that Crossby came upon the same path at its river-side extremity, and in a few moments each ran violently into the other's arms, and both rolled upon the ground.

The embrace that Crossby gave the youth would have been creditable even to a black bear, but Tom was a match for him in his then condition of savage despair. He rolled the rough digger over on his back, half strangled him, and bumped his shaggy head against the conveniently-situated root of a tree. But Crossby held on with the tenacity of sticking-plaster, shouting wildly all the time, and before either could subdue the other Gashford and his men coming up stopped the combat.

It were vain attempting to describe the conflict of Brixton's feelings as they once more bound his arms securely behind him and led him back to Paul Bevan's hut. The thought of death while fighting with man or beast had never given him much concern, but to be done to death by the rope as a petty thief was dreadful to contemplate, while to appear before the girl he loved humiliated and bound was in itself a sort of preliminary death. Afterwards, when confined securely in the cellar and left to himself for the night, with a few pine branches as a bed, the thought of home and mother came to him with overwhelming power, and finally mingled with his

dreams. But those dreams, however pleasant they might
be at first and in some respects, invariably ended with
the branch of a tree and a rope with a noose dangling at
the end thereof, and he awoke again and again with a
choking sensation, under the impression that the noose
was already tightening on his throat.

The agony endured that night while alone in the dark
cellar was terrible, for Tom knew the temper of the
diggers too well to doubt his fate. Still hope, blessed
hope, did not utterly desert him. More than once he
struggled to his knees and cried to God for mercy in the
Saviour's name.

By daybreak next morning he was awakened out of
the first dreamless sleep that he had enjoyed, and bid
get up. A slight breakfast of bread and water was
handed to him, which he ate by the light of a home-
made candle stuck in the neck of a quart bottle. Soon
afterwards Crossby descended, and bade him ascend the
wooden stair or ladder. He did so, and found the
party of miners assembled under arms and ready for the
road.

" I 'm sorry I can't help 'ee," said Paul Bevan, drawing
the unhappy youth aside, and speaking in a low voice.
" I would if I could, for I owe my life to you, but they
won't listen to reason. I sent Betty out o' the way, lad,
a-purpose. Thought it better she shouldn't see you,
but—"

"Come, come, old man, time's up," interrupted Gashford, roughly ; "we must be off. Now, march, my
young slippery-heels. I needn't tell you not to
try to bolt again. You'll find it difficult to do
that."

As they moved off and began their march through the
forest on foot, Tom Brixton felt that escape was indeed

out of the question, for, while three men marched in front of him, four marched on either side, each with rifle on shoulder, and the rest of the band brought up the rear. But even if his chances had not been so hopeless he would not have made any further effort to save himself, for he had given himself thoroughly up to despair. In the midst of this a slight sense of relief mingled with the bitterness of disappointment when he found that Betty had been sent out of the way, and that he would see her no more, for he could not bear the thought of her seeing him thus led away.

"May I speak with the prisoner for a few minutes?" said Fred Westly to Gashford, as they plodded through the woods. "He has been my comrade for several years, and I promised his poor mother never to forsake him. May I, Gashford?"

"No," was the sharp reply, and then, as if relenting, "Well, yes, you may; but be brief, and no underhand dealing, mind, for if you attempt to help him you shall be a dead man the next moment, as sure as I'm a living one. An' you needn't be too soft, Westly," he added, with a cynical smile. "Your chum has— Well, it's no business o' mine. You can go to him."

Poor Tom Brixton started as his old friend went up to him, and then hung his head.

"Dear Tom," said Fred, in a low voice, "don't give way to despair. With God all things are possible, and even if your life is to be forfeited it is not too late to save the soul, for Jesus is able and willing to save to the uttermost. But I want to comfort you with the assurance that I will spare no effort to save you. Many of the diggers are not very anxious that you should bear the extreme punishment of the law, and I think Gashford may be bought over. If so, I need not tell you

that my little private store hidden away under the pine-
tree—"

"There is no such store, Fred," interrupted Tom, with
a haggard look of shame.

"What do you mean, Tom?"

"I mean that I gambled it all away unknown to you.
Oh! Fred, you do not, you cannot know what a fearful
temptation gambling is when given way to, especially
when backed by drink. No, it's of no use your trying
to comfort me. I do believe, now, that I deserve to
die."

"Whatever you deserve, Tom, it is my business to save
you, if I can—both body and soul; and what you now
tell me does not alter my intentions or my hopes. By
the way, does Gashford know about this?"

"Yes, he knows that I have taken your money."

"And that's the reason," said Gashford himself, coming up at the moment, "that I advised you not to
be too soft on your chum, for he's a bad lot altogether."

"Is the man who knows of a crime, and connives at
it, and does not reveal it, a much better 'lot'?" demanded
Fred, with some indignation.

"Perhaps not," replied Gashford, with a short laugh;
"but as I never set up for a good lot, you see, there's no
need to discuss the subject. Now, fall to the rear, my
young blade. Remember that I'm in command of this
party, and you know, or ought to know, that I suffer no
insolence in those under me."

Poor Fred fell back at once, bitterly regretting that he
had spoken out, and thus injured to some extent his
influence with the only man who had the power to aid
his condemned friend.

It was near sunset when they reached Pine Tree Diggings. Tom Brixton was thrust into a strong block-house, used chiefly as a powder magazine, but sometimes as a prison, the key of which was kept on that occasion in Gashford's pocket, while a trusty sentinel paced before the door.

That night Fred Westly sat in his tent the personification of despair. True, he had not failed all along to lay his friend's case before God, and, up to this point, strong hope had sustained him ; but now, the only means by which he had trusted to accomplish his end were gone. The hidden hoard, on which he had counted too much, had been taken and lost by the very man he wished to save, and the weakness of his own faith was revealed by the disappearance of the gold—for he had almost forgotten that the Almighty can provide means at any time and in all circumstances.

Fred would not allow himself for a moment to think that Tom had *stolen* his gold. He only *took* it for a time, with the full intention of refunding it when better times should come. On this point Fred's style of reasoning was in exact accord with that of his unhappy friend. Tom never for a moment regarded the misappropriation of the gold as a theft. Oh no ! it was merely an appropriated loan—a temporary accommodation. It would be interesting, perhaps appalling, to know how many thousands of criminal careers have been begun in this way !

"Now, Mister Westly," said Flinders, entering the tent in haste, "what's to be done ? It's quite clear that Mister Tom's not to be hanged, for there's two or three of us 'll commit murder before that happens ; but I've bin soundin' the boys, an' I'm afeared there's a lot o' the worst wans that 'll be glad to see him scragged, an' there's a lot as won't risk their own necks to save him, an' what

betune the wan an' the other, them that'll fight for
him are a small minority—so again I say, what's to
be done?"

Patrick Flinders's usually jovial face had by that
time become almost as long and lugubrious as that of
Westly.

"I don't know," returned Fred, shaking his head.
"My one plan, on which I had been founding much hope,
is upset. Listen. It was this. I have been saving a
good deal of my gold for a long time past and hiding it
away secretly, so as to have something to fall back upon
when poor Tom had gambled away all his means. This
hoard of mine amounted, I should think, to something
like five hundred pounds. I meant to have offered it to
Gashford for the key of the prison, and for his silence
while we enabled Tom once more to escape. But this
money has, without my knowledge, been taken away
and—"

"Stolen, you mean!" exclaimed Flinders, in surprise.

"No, not stolen—taken! I can't explain just now.
It's enough to know that it is gone, and that my plan
is thus overturned."

"D'ee think Gashford would let him out for that?"
asked the Irishman, anxiously.

"I think so; but, after all, I'm almost glad that the
money's gone, for I can't help feeling that this way of
enticing Gashford to do a thing, as it were slily, is underhand. It is a kind of bribery."

"Faix, then, it's not c'ruption anyhow, for the baste is
as c'rupt as he can be already. An', sure, wouldn't
it just be bribin' a blackguard not to commit
murther?"

"I don't know, Pat. It is a horrible position to be
placed in. Poor, poor Tom!"

" Have ye had supper ?" asked Flinders, quickly.

" No—I cannot eat."

" Cook it then, an' don't be selfish. Other people can ait though ye can't.   It 'll kape yer mind employed —an' I 'll want somethin' to cheer me up whin I come back."

Pat Flinders left the tent abruptly, and poor Fred went about the preparation of supper in a half mechanical way, wondering what his comrade meant by his strange conduct.

Pat's meaning was soon made plain, that night, to a dozen or so of his friends, whom he visited personally and induced to accompany him to a sequestered dell in an out-of-the-way thicket, where the moonbeams struggled through the branches and drew a lovely pale-blue pattern on the green-sward.

" My frinds," he said, in a low, mysterious voice, " I know that ivery mother's son of ye is ready to fight for poor Tom Brixton to-morrow, if the wust comes to the wust.   Now, it has occurred to my chum Westly an' me that it would be better, safer, and surer to buy him up than to fight for him, an' as I know some o' you fellers has dug up more goold than you knows well what to do wid, an' you 've all got liberal hearts—lastewise ye should have, if ye haven't—I propose, an' second the resolootion, that we make up some five hundred pounds betune us an' presint it to Bully Gashford as a mark of our estaim—if he 'll on'y give us up the kay o' the prison put Patrick Flinders, Esq., sintry over it, an' then go to slape till breakfast-time tomorry mornin'."

This plan was at once agreed to, for five hundred pounds was not a large sum to be made up by men who—some of them at least—had nearly made "their pile"—by which they meant their fortune, while the liberality of heart with which they had been credited was not wanting. Having settled a few details, this singular meeting broke up, and Patrick Flinders—acting as the secretary, treasurer, and executive committee—went off, with a bag of golden nuggets and unbounded self-confidence, to transact the business.

CHAPTER VI.

GASHFORD was not quite so ready to accept Flinders's offer as that enthusiast had expected. The bully seemed to be in a strangely unusual mood, too—a mood which at first the Irishman thought favourable to his cause.

"Sit down," said Gashford, with less gruffness than usual, when his visitor entered his hut. "What d'ye want wi' me?"

Flinders addressed himself at once to the subject of his mission, and became quite eloquent as he touched on the grandeur of the sum offered, the liberality of the offerers, and the ease with which the whole thing might be accomplished. A very faint smile rested on Gashford's face as he proceeded, but by no other sign did he betray his thoughts until his petitioner had concluded.

"So you want to buy him off?" said Gashford, the smile expanding to a broad grin.

"If yer honour had bin born a judge an' sot on the bench since iver ye was a small spalpeen ye couldn't have hit it off more nately. That's just what we want—to buy him off. It's a purty little commercial transaction— a man's life for five hundred pound; an', sure it's a good price to give too, consitherin' how poor we all are, an' what a dale o' sweatin' work we've got to do to git the goold."

" But suppose I won't sell," said Gashford, "what then?"

" Faix, then, I'll blow your brains out," thought the Irishman, his fingers tingling with a desire to grasp the loaded revolver that lay in his pocket, but he had the wisdom to restrain himself and to say, "Och! sor, sure ye'll niver refuse such a nat'ral request. An' we don't ask ye to help us. Only to hand me the kay o' the prison, remove the sintry, an' then go quietly to yer bed wid five hundred pound in goold benathe yer hid to drame on."

To add weight to his proposal he drew forth the bag of nuggets from one of his capacious coat pockets and held it up to view.

" It's not enough," said Gashford, with a stern gruffness of tone and look which sank the petitioner's hopes below zero.

" Ah! then, Muster Gashford," said Flinders, with the deepest pathos, " it's yer own mother would plade wid ye for the poor boy's life, av she was here—think o' that. Sure he's young and inexparienced, an' it's the first offince he's iver committed—"

" No, not the first," interrupted Gashford.

" The first that I knows on," returned Flinders.

" Tell me—does Westly know of this proposal of yours?"

" No sor, he doesn't."

" Ah! I thought not. With his religious notions it would be difficult for him to join in an attempt to *bribe* me to stop the course of justice."

" Well, sor, you're not far wrong, for Muster Westly had bin havin' a sort o' tussle wid his conscience on that very pint. You must know, he had made up his mind to do this very thing an' offer you all his savin's—a thousand pound, more or less—to indooce you to help to

save his friud, but he found his goold had bin stolen,
so, you see, sor, he couldn't do it."

" Did he tell you who stole his gold ?"

" No, sor, he didn't—he said that some feller had took
it—on loan, like, though I calls it stailin'—but he didn't
say who."

" And have you had no tussle with *your* conscience,
Flinders, about this business ?"

The Irishman's face wrinkled up into an expression of
intense amusement at this question.

" It 's jokin' ye are, Muster Gashford.   Sure, now, me
conscience—if I 've got wan—doesn't bother me oftin ;
an' if it did, on this occasion, I 'd send it to the right-
about double quick, for it 's not offerin' ye five hundred
pound I am to stop the coorse o' justice, but to save ye
from committin' murther !   Give Muster Brixton what
punishment the coort likes—for stailin'—only don't hang
him.   That 's all we ask."

" You 'll have to pay more for it, then," returned the
bully.   " That 's not enough."

" Sure we haven't got a rap more to kape our pots
bilin', sor," returned Flinders, in a tone of despair.
" Lastewise I can spake for myself, for I 'm claned out—
all but."

" How much does the ' all but ' represent ?"

" Well, sor, to tell you the raal truth, it 's about tshwo
hundred pound, more or less, and I brought it wid me,
for fear you might want it, an' I haven't got a nugget
more if it was to save me own life.   It 's the truth I 'm
tellin' ye, sor."

There was a tone and look of such intense sincerity
about the poor fellow as he slowly drew a second bag of
gold from his pocket and placed it beside the first, that
Gashford could not help being convinced.

"Two hundred and five hundred," he said, meditatively.

"That makes siven hundred, sor," said Flinders, suggestively.

The bully did not reply for a few seconds. Then, taking up the bags of gold, he threw them into a corner. Thereafter he drew a large key from his pocket and handed it to the Irishman, who grasped it eagerly.

"Go to the prison," said Gashford, "tell the sentry you've come to relieve him, and send him to me. Mind, now, the rest of this business must be managed entirely by yourself, and see to it that the camp knows nothing about our little commercial transaction, for, *if it does*, your own days will be numbered."

With vows of eternal secrecy, and invoking blessings of an elaborate nature on Gashford's head, the Irishman hastened away, and went straight to the prison, which stood considerably apart from the huts and tents of the miners.

"Who goes there?" challenged the sentry as he approached, for the night was very dark.

"Mesilf, av coorse."

"An' who may that be, for yer not the only Patlander in camp, more's the pity!"

"It's Flinders I am." Sure any man wid half an ear might know that. I've come to relave ye."

"But you've got no rifle," returned the man, with some hesitation.

"Aren't revolvers as good as rifles, ay, an' better at close quarters? Shut up your tatie-trap, now, an' be off to Muster Gashford's hut, for he towld me to sind you there widout delay."

This seemed to satisfy the man, who at once went away, leaving Flinders on guard.

Without a moment's loss of time Paddy made use of the key and entered the prison.

"Is it there ye are, avic?" he said, in a hoarse whisper, as he advanced with caution and outstretched hands to prevent coming against obstructions.

"Yes; who are you?" replied Tom Brixton, in a stern voice.

"Whist, now, or ye 'll git me into throuble. Sure, I 'm yer sintry, no less, an' yer chum Pat Flinders."

"Indeed, Paddy! I 'm surprised that they should select you to be my jailer."

"Humph! well, they didn't let me have the place for nothing—och! musha!"

The last exclamations were caused by the poor man tumbling over a chair and hitting his head on a table.

"Not hurt, I hope," said Brixton, his spirit somewhat softened by the incident.

"Not much—only a new bump—but it's wan among many, so it don't matter. Now, listen. Time is precious. I 've come for to set you free—not exactly at this momint, howiver, for the boys o' the camp haven't all gone to bed yet; but whin they 're quiet I 'll come again an' help you to escape. I 've only come now to let you know."

The Irishman then proceeded to give Tom Brixton a minute account of all that had been done in his behalf. He could not see how the news affected him, the prison being as dark as Erebus, but great was his surprise and consternation when the condemned man said, in a calm but firm voice, "Thank you, Flinders, for your kind intentions, but I don't mean to make a second attempt to escape."

"Ye don't intind to escape!" exclaimed his friend, with a look of blank amazement at the spot where the voice of the other came from.

"No; I don't deserve to live, Paddy, so I shall remain and be hanged."

"I 'll be hanged if ye do," said Paddy, with much decision. "Come, now, don't be talkin' nonsense. It 's jokin' ye are, av coorse."

"I 'm very far from joking, my friend," returned Tom, in a tone of deep despondency, "as you shall find when daylight returns. I am guilty—more guilty than you fancy—so I shall plead guilty, whether tried or not, and take the consequences. Besides, life is not worth having. I 'm tired of it!"

"Och! but we 've bought you, an' paid for you, an' you 've no manner o' right to do what ye like wi' yourself," returned his exasperated chum. "But it 's of no use talkin' to ye. There 's somethin' wrong wi' your inside, no doubt. When I come back for ye at the right time you 'll have thought better of it. Come, now, give us your hand."

"I wish I could, Flinders, but the rascal that tied me has drawn the cord so tight that I feel as if I had no hands at all."

"I 'll soon putt that right. Where are ye? Ah, that 's it, now, kape stidy."

Flinders severed the cord with his bowie knife, unwound it, and set his friend free.

"Now thin, remain where ye are till I come for ye; an' if any wan should rap at the door an' ax where 's the sintinel an' the kay, just tell him ye don't know, an' don't care; or, if ye prefer it, tell him to go an' ax his grandmother."

With this parting piece of advice Flinders left the prisoner, locked the door, put the key in his pocket, and went straight to Fred Westly, whom he found seated beside the fire with his face buried in his hands.

"If Tom told you he wouldn't attempt to escape," said
Westly, on hearing the details of all that his eccentric
friend had done, "you may be sure that he 'll stick to it."

"D'ye raaly think so, Muster Fred?" said his companion in deep anxiety.

"I do.   I know Tom Brixton well, and when he is in
this mood nothing will move him.   But, come, I must
go to the prison and talk with him."

Fred's talk, however, was not more effective than that
of his friend had been.

"Well, Tom," he said, as he and Flinders were about
to quit the block-house, "we will return at the hour
when the camp seems fairly settled to sleep, probably
about midnight, and I hope you will then be ready to fly.
Remember what Flinders says is so far true—your life
has been bought and the price paid, whether you accept
or refuse it.   Think seriously of that before it be too
late."

Again the prison door closed, and Tom Brixton was
left with this thought turning constantly and persistently
in his brain:

"Bought, and the price paid!" he repeated to himself,
for the fiftieth time that night, as he sat in his dark prison.
"'Tis a strange way to put it to a fellow, but that does
not alter the circumstances.   No, I won't be moved by
mere sentiment.   I 'll try the Turk's plan, and submit to
fate.   I fancy this is something of the state of mind that
men get into when they commit suicide.   And yet I don't
feel as if I would kill myself if I were free.   Bah! what 's
the use of speculating about it?   Anyhow my doom is
fixed, and poor Flinders with his friends will lose their
money.   My only regret is that that unmitigated villain
Gashford will get it.   It would not be a bad thing, now
that my hands are free, to run a-muck amongst 'em.   I

feel strength enough in me to rid the camp of a lot of devils before I should be killed! But, after all, what good would that do me when I couldn't know it—couldn't know it! Perhaps I *could* know it! No, no! Better to die quietly, without the stain of human blood on my soul —if I *have* a soul. Escape! Easy enough, maybe, to escape from Pine Tree Diggings; but how escape from conscience? how escape from facts?—the girl I love holding me in contempt! my old friend and chum regarding me with pity! character gone! a life of crime before me! and death, by rope, or bullet, or knife, sooner or later! Better far to die now and have it over at once; prevent a deal of sin, too, as well as misery. 'Bought, and the price paid!' 'Tis a strange way to put it, and there is something like logic in the argument of Paddy, that I've got no right to do what I like with myself! Perhaps a casuist would say it is my *duty* to escape. Perhaps it is!"

Now, while Tom Brixton was revolving this knotty question in his mind, and Bully Gashford was revolving questions quite as knotty and much more complex, and Fred Westly was discussing with Flinders the best plan to be pursued in the event of Tom refusing to fly, there was a party of men assembled under the trees in a mountain gorge, not far distant, who were discussing a plan of operations which, when carried out, bade fair to sweep away, arrest, and overturn other knotty questions and deep-laid plans altogether.

It was the band of marauders who had made the abortive attack on Bevan's fortress.

When the attack was made, one of the redskins who guided the miners chanced to hear the war-whoop of a personal friend in the ranks of the attacking party. Being troubled with no sense of honour worth mentioning, this faithless guide deserted at once to the enemy, and not

only explained all he knew about the thief that he had
been tracking, but gave, in addition, such information
about the weak points of Pine Tree Diggings' that the
leader of the band resolved to turn aside for a little from
his immediate purposes and make a little hay while the
sun shone in that direction.

The band was a large one—a few on horseback, many
on foot; some being Indians and half-castes, others
disappointed miners and desperadoes. A fierce villain
among the latter was the leader of the band, which was
held together merely by unity of purpose and interest in
regard to robbery, and similarity of condition in regard
to crime.

"Now, lads," said the leader, who was a tall, lanky,
huge-boned, cadaverous fellow with a heavy chin and
hawk-nose, named Stalker, "I'll tell 'e what it is. Seems
to me that the diggers at Pine Tree Camp are a set
of out-an'-out blackguards—like most diggers—except
this poor thief of a fellow Brixton, so I vote for attackin'
the camp, carryin' off all the gold we can lay hands on
in the hurry-skurry, an' set this gentleman—this thief
Brixton—free. He's a bold chap, I'm told by the redskin, an' will no doubt be glad to jine us. An' we want
a few bold men."

The reckless robber-chief looked round with a mingled
expression of humour and contempt as he finished his
speech, whereat some laughed and a few scowled.

"But how shall we find Brixton?" asked a man named
Goff, who appeared to be second in command. "I know
the Pine Tree Camp, but I don't know where's the
prison."

"No matter," returned Stalker. "The redskin helps us
out o' that difficulty. He tells me the prison is a block-
house, that was once used as a powder-magazine, and stands

on a height a little apart from the camp.   I'll go straight
to it, set the young chap free, let him jump up behind
me and ride off, while you and the rest of the boys are
makin' the most of your time among the nuggets.   We
shall all meet again at the Red Man's Teacup."

"And when shall we go to work, captain?" asked the
lieutenant.

"Now.   There's no time like the present.   Strike
when the iron's hot, boys!" he added, looking round at
the men by whom he was encircled.   "You know what
we've got to do.   Advance together, like cats, till we're
within a yard or two of the camp, then a silent rush
when you hear my signal, the owl's hoot.   No shouting, mind, till the first screech comes from the enemy;
then, as concealment will be useless, give tongue all of
you till your throats split if you like, an' pick up the
gold.   Now, don't trouble yourselves much about fighting.
Let the bags be the main look-out—of course you'll have
to defend your own heads, though I don't think there'll
be much occasion for that—an' you know if any of them
are fools enough to fight for their gold, you'll have to
dispose of them somehow."

Having delivered this address with much energy, the
captain of the band put himself at its head and led the
way.

While this thunder-cloud was drifting down on the
camp, Fred Westly and Flinders were preparing for flight.
They did not doubt that their friend would at the last be
persuaded to escape, and had made up their minds to fly
with him and share his fortunes.

"We have nothing to gain, you see, Paddy," said Fred,
"by remaining here, and, having parted with all our gold,
have nothing to lose by going."

"Thrue for ye, sor, an' nothin' to carry except ourselves, worse luck!" said the Irishman, with a deep sigh. "Howiver, we lave no dibts behind us, that's wan comfort, so we may carry off our weapons an' horses wid clear consciences. Are ye all ready now, sor?"

"Almost ready," replied Fred, thrusting a brace of revolvers into his belt and picking up his rifle. Go for the horses, Pat, and wait at the stable for me. Our neighbours might hear the noise if you brought them round here."

Now, the stable referred to was the most outlying building of the camp in the direction in which the marauders were approaching. It was a small log-hut of the rudest description perched on a little knoll which overlooked the camp, and from which Tom Brixton's prison could be clearly seen, perched on a neighbouring knoll.

Paddy Flinders ruminated on the dangers and perplexities that might be in store for him that night as he went swiftly and noiselessly up to the hut. To reach the door he had to pass round from the back to the front. As he did so he became aware of voices sounding softly close at hand. A large log lay on the ground. With speed worthy of a redskin he sank down beside it.

"This way, captain; I've bin here before, an' know that you can see the whole camp from it—if it wasn't so confoundedly dark. There's a log somewhere—ah, here it is; we'll be able to see better if we mount it."

"I wish we had more light," growled the so-called captain; it won't be easy to make off on horseback in such—is this the log? Here, lend a hand."

As he spoke the robber-chief put one of his heavy boots on the little finger of Pat Flinders's left hand, and wellnigh broke it in springing on to the log in question!

A peculiarly Irish howl all but escaped from poor Flinders's lips.

"I see," said Stalker, after a few moments. "There's enough of us to attack a camp twice the size. Now we must look sharp. I'll go round to the prison and set Brixton free. When that's done, I'll hoot three times—so—only a good deal louder. Then you an' the boys will rush in and—you know the rest. Come."

Descending from the log on the other side, the two desperadoes left the spot. Then Paddy rose and ran as if he had been racing, and as if the prize of the race were life!

"Bad luck to you, ye murtherin' thieves," growled the Irishman, as he ran, "but I'll stop yer game, me boys!"

CHAPTER VII.

A S straight, and almost as swiftly, as an arrow,
Flinders ran to his tent, burst into the presence
of his amazed comrade, seized him by both arms, and
exclaimed in a sharp hoarse voice, the import of which
there could be no mistaking—

"Whisht!—howld yer tongue! The camp'll be
attacked in ten minutes! Be obadient, now, an' foller
me."

Flinders turned and ran out again, taking the path to
Gashford's hut with the speed of a hunted hare. Fred
Westly followed. Bursting in upon the bully, who had
not yet retired to rest, the Irishman seized him by both
arms and repeated his alarming words, with this addition :
"Sind some wan to rouse the camp—but *silently!* No
noise—or it's all up wid us!"

There was something in Paddy's manner and look that
commanded respect and constrained obedience—even in
Gashford.

"Bill," he said, turning to a man who acted as his valet
and cook, "rouse the camp. Quietly—as you hear. Let
no man act, however, till my voice is heard. You'll
know it when ye hear it!"

"No mistake about *that!*" muttered Bill, as he ran
out on his errand.

"Now—foller!" cried Flinders, catching up a bit of

rope with one hand and a billet of firewood with the other, as he dashed out of the hut and made straight for the prison, with Gashford and Westly close at his heels.

Gashford meant to ask Flinders for an explanation as he ran, but the latter rendered this impossible by outrunning him. He reached the prison first, and had already entered when the others came up and ran in. He shut the door and locked it on the inside.

" Now, then, listen, all of ye," he said, panting vehemently, "an' take in what I say, for the time's short. The camp 'll be attacked in five minits—more or less. I chanced to overhear the blackguards. Their chief comes here to set Muster Brixton free. Then—och! here he comes ! Do as I bid ye, ivery wan, an' howld yer tongues."

The latter words were said energetically, but in a low whisper, for footsteps were heard outside as if approaching stealthily. Presently a rubbing sound was heard, as of a hand feeling for the door. It touched the handle and then paused a moment, after which there came a soft tap.

" I 'll spake for ye," whispered Flinders in Brixton's ear.

Another pause, and then another tap at the door.

" Arrah ! who goes there ?" cried Paddy, stretching himself, as if just awakened out of a sound slumber and giving vent to a mighty yawn.

" A friend," answered the robber-chief through the keyhole.

" A frind !" echoed Pat. " Sure an' that's a big lie, if iver there was one. Aren't ye goin' to hang me i' the mornin' ?"

" No indeed, I ain't one o' this camp. But surely you can't be the man—the—the thief—named Brixton, for you 're an Irishman."

"An' why not?" demanded Flinders. "Sure the
Brixtons are Irish to the backbone—an' thieves too—
root an' branch, from Adam an' Eve downwards. But go
away wid ye. I don't belave that ye're a frind. You've
only just come to tormint me an' spile my slape the
night before my funeral. Fie for shame! Go away an'
lave me in pace."

"You're wrong, Brixton; I've come to punish the
blackguards that would hang you, an' set you free, as I'll
soon show you. Is the door strong?"

"Well, it's not made o' cast iron, but it's pretty
tough."

"Stand clear, then, an' I'll burst it in wi' my foot,"
said Stalker.

"Och! is it smashin' yer bones you'll be after!
Howld fast. Are ye a big man?"

"Yes, pretty big."

"That's a good job, for a little un would only bust
hisself agin it for no use. You'll have to go at it like a
hoy-draulic ram."

"Never fear. There's not many doors in these diggin's
that can remain shut when I want 'em open," said the
robber, as he retired a few paces to enable him to deliver
his blow with greater momentum.

"Howld on a minit, me frind," said Paddy, who had
quietly turned the key and laid hold of the handle; "let
me git well out o' the way, an' give me warnin' before
you come."

"All right. Now then, look out!" cried Stalker.

Those inside heard the rapid little run that a man
takes before launching himself violently against an object.
Flinders flung the door wide open in the nick of time.
The robber's foot dashed into empty space, and the
robber himself plunged headlong, with a tremendous crash,

on the floor. At the same instant Flinders brought his
billet of wood down with all his might on the spot where
he guessed the man's head to be. The blow was well
aimed, and rendered the robber chief incapable of further
action for the time being.

"Faix, ye'll not 'hoot' to yer frinds this night, anyhow," said Flinders, as they dragged the fallen chief to the
doorway, to make sure, by the faint light, that he was
helpless. "Now, thin," continued Paddy, "we'll away
an' lead the boys to battle. You go an' muster them, sor,
an' I'll take ye to the inimy."

"Have you seen their ambush, and how many there
are?" asked Gashford.

"Niver a wan have I seen, and I've only a gineral
notion o' their whereabouts."

"How then can you lead us?"

"Obey orders, an' you'll see, sor. I'm in command
to-night. If ye don't choose to foller, ye'll have to do
the best ye can widout me."

"Lead on, then," cried Gashford, half amused and half
angered by the man's behaviour.

Flinders led the way straight to Gashford's hut, where,
as he anticipated, the man named Bill had silently
collected most of the able-bodied men of the camp, all
armed to the teeth. He at once desired Gashford to put
them in fighting order and lead them. When they were
ready he went off at a rapid pace towards the stable
before mentioned.

"They should be hereabouts, Muster Gashford," he
said, in a low voice, "so git yer troops ready for action."

"What do ye mean?" growled Gashford.

To this Flinders made no reply, but turning to Westly
and Brixton, who stood close at his side, whispered them
to meet him at the stable before the fight was quite over.

F

He then put his hand to his mouth and uttered three
hoots like an owl.

" I believe you are humbugging us," said Gashford.

" Whisht, sor—listen !"

The breaking of twigs was heard faintly in the distance,
and, a few moments later, the tramp apparently of a
body of men.   Presently dark forms were dimly seen to
be advancing.

" Now's your time, gineral !   Give it 'em hot," whispered
Flinders.

" Ready !   Present !   Fire !" said Gashford, in a deep,
solemn tone, which the profound silence rendered dis-
tinctly audible.

The marauders halted, as if petrified.   Next moment
a sheet of flame burst from the ranks of the miners, and
horrible yells rent the air, high above which, like the roar
of a lion, rose Gashford's voice in the single word :—

" Charge !"

But the panic-stricken robbers did not await the onset.
They turned and fled, hotly pursued by the men of Pine
Tree Diggings.

"That 'll do !" cried Flinders to Brixton ; " they 'll not
need us any more this night.   Come wid me now."

Fred Westly, who had rushed to the attack with the
rest, soon pulled up.   Remembering the appointment, he
returned to the stable, where he found Tom gazing in
silence at Flinders, who was busily employed saddling
their three horses.   He at once understood the situation.

" Of course you 've made up your mind to go, Tom ?"
he said.

" N—no," answered Tom.   " I have not."

" Faix, thin, you 'll have to make it up pretty quick
now, for whin the boys come back the prisoners an'
wounded men 'll be sure to tell that their chief came for

the express purpose of rescuin' that 'thief Brixton '—
an' it 's hangin' that 'll be too good for you then. Roastin'
alive is more likely. It 's my opinion that if they catch
us just now, Muster Fred an' I will swing for it too!
Come, sor, git up!"

Tom hesitated no longer. He vaulted into the saddle.
His comrades also mounted, and in a few minutes more
the three were riding away from Pine Tree Diggings as
fast as the nature of the ground and the darkness of the
hour would permit.

It was not quite midnight when they left the place
where they had toiled so long and had met with so many
disasters, and the morning was not far advanced when
they reached the spring of the Red Man's Teacup. As
this was a natural and convenient halting-place to parties
leaving those diggings, they resolved to rest and refresh
themselves and their steeds for a brief space, although
they knew that the robber-chief had appointed that spot
as a rendezvous after the attack on the camp.

"You see, it 's not likely they 'll be here for an hour or
two," said Tom Brixton, as he dismounted and hobbled
his horse, "for it will take some time to collect their
scattered forces, and they won't have their old leader to
spur them on, as Paddy's rap on the head will keep him
quiet till the men of the camp find him."

"Troth, I 'm not so sure o' that, sor. The rap was a
stiff wan, no doubt, but men like that are not aisy to kill.
Besides, won't the boys o' the camp purshoo them,
which 'll be spur enough, an' if they finds us here, it 'll
matter little whether we fall into the hands o' diggers or
robbers. So ye 'll make haste av ye take my advice."

They made haste accordingly, and soon after left; and
well was it that they did so, for, little more than an
hour later, Stalker—his face covered with blood and his

head bandaged—galloped up at the head of the mounted men of his party.

" We 'll camp here for an hour or two," he said sharply, leaping from his horse, which he proceeded to unsaddle. " Hallo ! somebody 's bin here before us. Their fire ain't cold yet. Well, it don't matter. Get the grub ready, boys, an' boil the kettle. My head is all but split. If ever I have the luck to come across that Irish blackguard Brixton I 'll—"

He finished the sentence with a deep growl and a grind of his teeth.

About daybreak the marauders set out again, and it chanced that the direction they took was the same as that taken by Fred Westly and his comrades. These latter had made up their minds to try their fortune at a recently discovered goldfield, which was well reported of, though the yield had not been sufficient to cause a " rush" to the place. It was about three days' journey on horseback from the Red Man's Teacup, and was named Simpson's Gully, after the man who discovered it.

The robbers' route lay, as we have said, in the same direction, but only for part of the way, for Simpson's Gully was not their ultimate destination. They happened to be better mounted than the fugitives, and travelled faster. Thus it came to pass that, on the second evening, they arrived somewhat late at the camping-place where Fred and his friends were spending the night.

These latter had encamped earlier that evening. Supper was over, pipes were out, and they were sound asleep when the robber band rode up.

Flinders was first to observe their approach. He awoke his comrades roughly.

" Och ! the blackguards have got howld of us. Be aisy, Muster Brixton. No use fightin'. Howld yer tongues, now, an' let *me* spake. Yer not half liars enough for the occasion, aither of ye."

This compliment had barely been paid when they were surrounded and ordered to rise and give an account of themselves.

"What right have *you* to demand an account of us?" asked Tom Brixton, recklessly, in a supercilious tone that was meant to irritate.

"The right of might," replied Stalker, stepping up to Tom, and grasping him by the throat.

Tom resisted, of course, but, being seized at the same moment by two men from behind, was rendered helpless. His comrades were captured at the same moment, and the arms of all bound behind them.

"Now, gentlemen," said the robber chief, "perhaps you will answer with more civility.

"You are wrong, for I won't answer at all," said Tom Brixton, "which I take to be *less* civility."

"Neither will I," said Fred, who had come to the conclusion that total silence would be the easiest way of getting over the difficulties that filled his mind in regard to deception.

Patrick Flinders, however, had no such difficulties. To the amazement of his companions, he addressed a speech to Stalker in language so broken with stuttering and stammering that the marauders around could scarcely avoid laughing, though their chief seemed to be in no mood to tolerate mirth. Tom and Fred did not at first understand, though it soon dawned upon them that by this means he escaped being recognised by the man with whom he had so recently conversed through the keyhole of Tom Brixton's prison door.

"S-s-s-sor," said he, in a somewhat higher key than he was wont to speak, "my c-c-comrades are c-c-cross-

g-grained critters b-both of 'em, th-th-though they're
g-good enough in their way, for all that.   A-a-ax *me*
what ye w-w-want to know."

"Can't you speak without so many k-k-kays an'
g-g-gees?" demanded Stalker, impatiently.

"N-n-no, s-sor, I c-can't, an' the m-more you t-try to
make me the w-w-wus I g-gits."

"Well, then, come to the point, an' don't say more
than's needful."

"Y-y-yis, sor."

"What's this man's name?" asked the chief, settling
the bandages uneasily on his head with one hand, and
pointing to Brixton with the other.

"M-Muster T-T-T-om, sor."

"That's his Christian name, I suppose?"

"W-w-well, I'm not sure about his bein' a c-c-c-Chris-
tian."

"Do you spell it T-o-m or T-h-o-m?"

"Th-that depinds on t-t-taste, sor."

"Bah! you're a fool!"

"Thank yer honour, and I'm also an I-I-Irish m-man
as sure me name's Flinders."

"There's one of your countrymen named Brixton,"
said the chief, with a scowl, "who's a scoundrel of the
first water, and I have a crow to pluck with him some
day when we meet.   Meanwhile I feel half-disposed to
give his countryman a sound thrashing as part payment
of the debt in advance."

"Ah! sure, sor, me counthryman 'll let ye off the dibt,
no doubt," returned Flinders.

"Hallo! you seem to have found your tongue all of a
sudden!"

"F-faix, then, it's b-bekaise of yer not houndin' me on.
I c-c-can't stand bein' hurried, ye s-see.   B-besides, I was

havin' me little j-j-joke, an' I scarcely sp-splutter at all whin I 'm j-j-jokin'."

"Where did you come from?" demanded the chief, sharply.

"From P-Pine Tree D-Diggin's."

"Oh, indeed? When did you leave the camp?"

"On M-Monday mornin', sor."

"Then of course you don't know anything about the fight that took place there on Monday night?"

"D-don't I, sor?"

"Why don't you answer whether you do or not?" said Stalker, beginning to lose temper.

"Sh-shure yer towld me th-that I d-d-don't know, an' I 'm too p-p-purlite to c-contradic' yer honour."

"Bah! you 're a fool."

"Ye t-t-towld me that before, sor."

The robber chief took no notice of the reply, but led his lieutenant aside and held a whispered conversation with him for a few minutes.

Now, among other blessings, Flinders possessed a pair of remarkably acute ears, so that, although he could not make out the purport of the whispered conversation, he heard, somewhat indistinctly, the words "Bevan" and "Betty." Coupling these words with the character of the men around him, he jumped to a conclusion and decided on a course of action in one and the same instant.

Presently Stalker returned, and addressing himself to Tom and Fred, said—

"Now, sirs, I know not your circumstances nor your plans, but I 'll take the liberty of letting you know something of mine. Men give me and my boys bad names. We call ourselves Free-and-easy Boys. We work hard for our living. It is our plan to go round the country collecting taxes—revenue—or whatever you choose to call it, and punishing those who object to pay. Now, we want a few stout fellows to replace the brave men who have fallen at the post of duty. Will you join us?"

"Certainly not," said Fred, with decision.

"Of course not," said Tom, with contempt.

"Well, then, my fine fellows, you may follow your own inclinations, for there's too many willing boys around to make us impress unwilling ones, but I shall take the liberty of relieving you of your possessions. I will tax *you* to the full amount."

He turned and gave orders in a low voice to those near him. In a few minutes the horses, blankets, food, arms, etc., of the three friends were collected, and themselves unbound.

"Now," said the robber chief, "I mean to spend the night here. You may bid us good-night. The world lies before you—go!"

"B-b-but, sor," said Flinders, with a perplexed and pitiful air. "Ye niver axed *me* if I'd j-j-jine ye."

"Because I don't want you," said Stalker.

"Ah! thin, it's little ye know th-the j-j-jewel ye're th-throwin' away."

"What can you do?" asked the robber, while a slight smile played on his disfigured face.

"What c-can I *not* do? ye should ax. W-w-why, I can c-c-c-cook, an' f-f-fight, an' d-dance, an' t-t-tell stories, an' s-s-sing an'—"

"There, that'll do. I accept you," said Stalker, turning away, while his men burst into a laugh, and felt that Flinders would be a decided acquisition to the party.

"Are we to go without provisions or weapons?" asked Fred Westly, before leaving.

"You may have both," answered Stalker, "by joining

us. If you go your own way—you go as you are. Please yourselves."

"You may almost as well kill us as turn us adrift here in the wilderness without food or the means of procuring it," remonstrated Fred. "Is it not so, Tom?"

Tom did not condescend to reply. He had evidently screwed his spirit up—or down—to the Turkish condition of apathy and contempt.

"You're young, both of you, and strong," answered the robber. "The woods are full of game, berries, roots, and fish. If you know anything of woodcraft you can't starve."

"An' s-s-sure Tomlin's Diggin's isn't far—far off—straight f-f-fornint you," said Flinders, going close up to his friends, and whispering, "Kape round by Bevan's Gully. You'll be—"

"Come, none of your whisperin' together!" shouted Stalker. "You're one of *us* now, Flinders, so say good-bye to your old chums an' fall to the rear."

"Yis, sor," replied the biddable Flinders, grasping each of his comrades by the hand and wringing it as he said, " G-g-good-bye, f-f-foolish b-boys (Bevan's Gully—*sharp!*), f-farewell f-for i-i-iver!" and, covering his face with his hands, burst into crocodile's tears while he fell to the rear. He separated two of his fingers, however, in passing a group of his new comrades, in order to bestow on them a wink which produced a burst of subdued laughter.

Surprised, annoyed, and puzzled, Tom Brixton thrust both hands into his trousers pockets, turned round on his heel, and, without uttering a word, sauntered slowly away.

Fred Westly, in a bewildered frame of mind, followed his example, and the two friends were soon lost to view—swallowed up, as it were, by the Oregon wilderness.

CHAPTER VIII.

A FTER walking through the woods a considerable
distance in perfect silence—for the suddenness of
the disaster seemed to have bereft the two friends of
speech—Tom Brixton turned abruptly and said—

"Well, Fred, we're in a nice fix now. What is to be
our next move in this interesting little game?"

Fred Westly shook his head with an air of profound
perplexity, but said nothing.

"I've a good mind," continued Tom, "to return to Pine
Tree Diggings, give myself up, and get hanged right off.
It would be a good riddance to the world at large, and
would relieve me of a vast deal of trouble."

"There is a touch of selfishness in that speech, Tom—
don't you think?—for it would not relieve *me* of trouble ;
to say nothing of your poor mother!"

"You're right, Fred. D'you know, it strikes me that
I'm a far more selfish and despicable brute than I used
to think myself."

He looked at his companion with a sad sort of smile ;
nevertheless, there was a certain indefinable ring of
sincerity in his tone.

"Tom," said the other, earnestly, "will you wait for me
here for a few minutes while I turn aside to pray?"

"Certainly, old boy," answered Tom, seating himself
on a mossy bank. "You know I cannot join you."

"I know you can't, Tom. It would be mockery to pray to One in whom you don't believe; but as *I* believe in God, the Bible, and prayer, you'll excuse my detaining you, just for—"

"Say no more, Fred. Go; I shall wait here for you."

A slight shiver ran through Brixton's frame as he sat down, rested his elbows on his knees, and clasped his hands.

"God help me!" he exclaimed, under a sudden impulse, "I've come down *very* low, God help me!"

Fred soon returned.

"You prayed for guidance, I suppose?" said Tom, as his friend sat down beside him.

"I did."

"Well, what is the result?"

"There is no result as yet—except, of course, the calmer state of my mind, now that I have committed our case into our Father's hands."

"*Your* Father's, you mean."

"No, I mean *our*, for He is your father as well as mine, whether you admit it or not. Jesus has bought you and paid for you, Tom, with His own blood. You are not your own."

"Not my own? bought and paid for!" thought Brixton, recalling the scene in which words of somewhat similar import had been addressed to him. "Bought and paid for—twice bought! Body and soul!" Then, aloud, "And what are you going to do now, Fred?"

"Going to discuss the situation with you."

"And after you have discussed it, and acted according to our united wisdom, you will say that you have been guided."

"Just so! That is exactly what I will say and believe, for ' He is faithful who has promised.'"

" And if you make mistakes and go wrong, you will still hold, I suppose, that you have been guided ?"

" Undoubtedly I will—not guided, indeed, into the mistakes, but guided to what will be best in the long-run, in spite of them."

" But, Fred, how can you call guidance in the wrong direction *right* guidance ?"

" Why, Tom, can you not conceive of a man being guided wrongly as regards some particular end he has in view, and yet that same guidance being right, because leading him to something far better which, perhaps, he has *not* in view ?"

" So that," said Tom, with a sceptical laugh, " whether you go right or go wrong, you are sure to come right in the end !"

" Just so ! '*All* things work together for good to them that love God.'"

" Does not that savour of Jesuitism, Fred, which teaches the detestable doctrine that you may do evil if good is to come of it ?"

" Not so, Tom ; because I did not understand you to use the word *wrong* in the sense of *sinful*, but in the sense of erroneous—mistaken. If I go in a wrong road, knowing it to be wrong, I sin ; but if I go in a wrong road mistakenly, I still count on guidance, though not perhaps to the particular end at which I aimed—nevertheless, guidance to a *good* end. Surely you will admit that no man is perfect ?"

" Admitted."

" Well, then, imperfection implies mistaken views and ill-directed action, more or less, in every one, so that if we cannot claim to be guided by God except when free from error in thought and act, then there is no such thing as Divine guidance at all. Surely you don't hold that !"

"Some have held it."

"Yes; 'the fool hath said in his heart, There is no God,' —some have even gone the length of letting it out of the heart and past the lips. With such we cannot argue; their case admits only of pity and prayer."

"I agree with you there, Fred; but if your views are not Jesuitical, they seem to me to be strongly fatalistic. Commit one's way to God, you say; then, shut one's eyes, drive ahead anyhow, and—the end will be sure to be all right!"

"No, I did not say that. With the exception of the first sentence, Tom, that is your way of stating the case, not God's way. If you ask in any given difficulty, 'What shall I do?' His word replies, 'Commit thy way unto the Lord. Trust also in Him, and He will bring it to pass.' If you ask, 'How am I to know what is best?' the Word again replies, 'Hear, ye deaf; look, ye blind, that you may see.' Surely that is the reverse of shutting the eyes, isn't it? If you say, 'How shall I act?' the Word answers, 'A good man will guide his affairs with discretion.' That's not driving ahead anyhow, is it?"

"You may be right," returned Tom, "I hope you are. But, come, what does your wisdom suggest in the present difficulty?"

"The first thing that occurs to me," replied the other, "is what Flinders said just before we were ordered off by the robbers. 'Keep round by Bevan's Gully,' he said, in the midst of his serio-comic leave-taking; and again he said, 'Bevan's Gully—sharp!' Of course Paddy, with his jokes and stammering, has been acting a part all through this business, and I am convinced that he has heard something about Bevan's Gully; perhaps an attack on Bevan himself, which made him wish to tell us to go there."

"Of course; how stupid of me not to see that before! Let's go at once!" cried Tom, starting up in excitement. "Undoubtedly he meant that. He must have overheard the villains talk of going there, and we may not be in time to aid them unless we push on."

"But in what direction does the gully lie?" asked Fred, with a puzzled look.

Tom returned the look with one of perplexity, for they were now a considerable distance both from Bevan's Gully and Pine Tree Diggings, in the midst of an almost unknown wilderness. From the latter place either of the friends could have travelled to the former almost blindfold; but, having by that time lost their exact bearings, they could only guess at the direction.

"I think," said Fred, after looking round and up at the sky for some time, "considering the time we have been travelling, and the position of the sun, that the gully lies over yonder. Indeed, I feel almost sure it does."

He pointed, as he spoke, towards a ridge of rocky ground that cut across the western sky and hid much of the more distant landscape in that direction.

"Nonsense, man!" returned Tom, sharply, "it lies in precisely the opposite direction. Our adventures have turned your brain, I think. Come, don't let us lose time. Think of Betty; that poor girl may be killed if there is another attack. She was slightly wounded last time. Come!"

Fred looked quickly in his friend's face. It was deeply flushed, and his eye sparkled with unwonted fire.

"Poor fellow! his case is hopeless; she will never wed him," thought Fred, but he only said, "I, too, would not waste time, but it seems to me we shall lose much if we go in that direction. The longer I study the nature of the ground, and calculate our rate of travelling since we left the diggings, the more am I convinced that our way lies westward."

"I feel as certain as you do," replied Tom with some asperity, for he began to chafe under the delay. "But if you are determined to go that way you must go by yourself, old boy, for I can't afford to waste time on a wrong road."

"Nay, if you are so sure, I will give in and follow. Lead on," returned Tom's accommodating friend, with a feeling of mingled surprise and chagrin.

In less than an hour they reached a part of the rocky ridge before mentioned, from which they had a magnificent view of the surrounding country. It was wilderness truly, but such a wilderness of tree and bush, river and lake, cascade and pool, flowering plant and festooned shrub, dense thicket and rolling prairie, backed here and there by cloud-capped hills, as seldom meets the eye or thrills the heart of traveller, except in alpine lands. Deep pervading silence marked the hour, for the air was perfectly still, and though the bear, the deer, the wolf, the fox, and a multitude of wild creatures were revelling there in the rich enjoyment of natural life, the vast region, as it were, absorbed and dissipated their voices almost as completely as their persons, so that it seemed but a grand untenanted solitude, just freshly laid out by the hand of the wonder-working Creator. Every sheet of water, from the pool to the lake, reflected an almost cloudless blue, excepting towards the west, where the sun, by that time beginning to descend, converted all into sheets of liquid gold.

The two friends paused on the top of a knoll, more to recover breath than to gaze on the exquisite scene, for they both felt that they were speeding on a mission that might involve life or death. Fred's enthusiastic admiration, however, would no doubt have found vent in fitting words if he had not at the moment recognised a familiar landmark.

"I knew it!" he cried, eagerly. "Look, Tom, that is Ranger's Hill on the horizon away to the left. It is very faint from distance, but I could not mistake its form."

"Nonsense, Fred! you never saw it from this point of view before, and hills change their shape amazingly from different points of view. Come along."

"No, I am too certain to dispute the matter any longer. If you will have it so, we must indeed part here. But, oh! Tom, don't be obstinate! Why, what has come over you, my dear fellow? Don't you see—"

"I see that evening is drawing on, and that we shall be too late. Good-bye! One friendly helping hand will be better to her than none. I *know* I 'm right."

Tom hurried away, and poor Fred, after gazing in mingled surprise and grief at his comrade until he disappeared, turned with a heavy sigh and went off in the opposite direction.

"Well," he muttered to himself, as he sped along at a pace that might have made even a red man envious, "we are both of us young and strong, so that we are well able to hold out for a considerable time on such light fare as the shrubs of the wilderness produce, and when Tom discovers his mistake he 'll make good use of his long legs to overtake me. I cannot understand his infatuation. But, with God's blessing, all shall yet be well."

Comforting himself with the last reflection, and offering up a heartfelt prayer as he pressed on, Fred Westly was soon separated from his friend by many a mile of wilderness.

Meanwhile Tom Brixton traversed the land with strides not only of tremendous length, but unusual

"WE MUST INDEED PART HERE."—Page 96.

rapidity. His "infatuation" was not without its appropriate cause. The physical exertions and sufferings which the poor fellow had undergone for so long a period, coupled with the grief, amounting almost to despair, which tormented his brain, had at last culminated in fever; and the flushed face and glittering eyes, which his friend had set down to anxiety about Bevan's pretty daughter, were, in reality, indications of the gathering fires within. So also was the obstinacy. For it must be admitted that the youth's natural disposition was tainted with that objectionable quality which, when fever, drink, or any other cause of madness operates in any man, is apt to assert itself powerfully.

At first he strode over the ground with terrific energy, thinking only of Betty and her father in imminent danger; pausing now and then abruptly to draw his hand across his brow and wonder if he was getting near Bevan's Gully. Then, as his mind began to wander, he could not resist a tendency to shout.

"What a fool I am!" he muttered, after having done this once or twice. "I suppose anxiety about that dear girl is almost driving me mad. But she can never—never be mine. I'm a thief! a thief! Ha! ha-a-a-a!"

The laugh that followed might have appalled even a red and painted warrior. It did terrify, almost into fits, all the tree and ground squirrels within a mile of him, for these creatures went skurrying off to holes and topmost boughs in wild confusion when they heard it echoing through the woods.

When this fit passed off Tom took to thinking again. He strode over hillock, swamp, and plain in silence, save when, at long intervals, he muttered the words, "Think, think, thinking. Always thinking! Can't stop think, thinking!"

Innumerable wild fowl, and many of the smaller animals of the woods, met him in his mad career, and fled from his path, but one of these seemed at last inclined to dispute the path with him.

It was a small brown bear, which creature, although insignificant when compared with the gigantic grizzly, is, nevertheless, far more than a match for the most powerful unarmed man that ever lived. This rugged creature chanced to be rolling sluggishly along as if enjoying an evening saunter at the time when Tom approached. The place was dotted with willow bushes, so that when the two met there was not more than a hundred yards between them. The bear saw the man instantly, and rose on its hind legs to do battle. At that moment Tom lifted his eyes. Throwing up his arms, he uttered a wild yell of surprise, which culminated in a fit of demoniacal laughter. But there was no laughter apparent on poor Tom's flushed and fierce visage, though it issued from his dry lips. Without an instant's hesitation he rushed at the bear with clenched fists. The animal did not await the charge. Dropping humbly on its fore-legs, it turned tail and fled, at such a pace that it soon left its pursuer far behind !

Just as it disappeared over a distant ridge Tom came in sight of a small pond or lakelet covered with reeds, and swarming with ducks and geese, besides a host of plover and other aquatic birds—most of them with out-stretched necks, wondering no doubt what all the hubbub could be about. Tom incontinently bore down on these, and dashing in among them was soon up to his neck in water !

He remained quiet for a few minutes and deep silence pervaded the scene. Then the water began to feel chill. The wretched man crept out, and, remembering his errand, resumed his rapid journey. Soon the fever burned again with intensified violence, and the power of connected thought began to depart from its victim altogether.

While in this condition Tom Brixton wandered aimlessly about, sometimes walking smartly for a mile or so, at other times sauntering slowly, as if he had no particular object in view, and occasionally breaking into a run at full speed, which usually ended in his falling exhausted on the ground.

At last, as darkness began to overspread the land, he became so worn-out that he flung himself down under a tree, with a hazy impression on his mind that it was time to encamp for the night. The fever was fierce and rapid in its action. First it bereft him of reason and then left him prostrate, without the power to move a limb except with the greatest difficulty.

It was about the hour of noon when his reasoning powers returned, and, strange to say, the first conscious act of his mind was to recall the words "*twice bought*," showing that the thought had been powerfully impressed on him before delirium set in. What he had said or done during his ravings he knew not, for memory was a blank, and no human friend had been there to behold or listen. At that time, however, Tom did not think very deeply about these words, or, indeed, about anything else. His prostration was so great that he did not care at first to follow out any line of thought, or to move a limb. A sensation of absolute rest and total indifference seemed to enchain all his faculties. He did not even know where he was, and did not care, but lay perfectly still, gazing up through the overhanging branches into the bright blue sky, sometimes dozing off into a sleep that almost resembled death, from which he awoke gently, to wonder, perhaps, in an idle way, what had come over him, and then ceasing to wonder before the thought had become well defined.

The first thing that roused him from this condition was a passing thought of Betty Bevan. He experienced something like a slight shock, and the blood which had begun to stagnate received a new though feeble impulse at its fountain-head, the heart. Under the force of it he tried to rise, but could not, although he strove manfully. At last, however, he managed to raise himself on one elbow, and looked round with dark and awfully large eyes, while he drew his left hand tremblingly across his pale brow. He observed the trembling fingers and gazed at them inquiringly.

" I—I must have been ill. So weak, too ! Where am I ? The forest—everywhere ! What can it all mean ? There was a—a thought—what could it—Ah ! Betty— dear girl—that was it. But what of her ? Danger— yes—in danger. Ha ! *now* I have it !"

There came a slight flush on his pale cheeks, and, struggling again with his weakness, he succeeded in getting on his feet, but staggered and fell with a crash that rendered him insensible for a time.

On recovering, his mind was clearer and more capable of continuous thought; but this power only served to show him that he was lost, and that, even if he had known his way to Bevan's Gully, his strength was utterly gone, so that he could not render aid to the friends who stood in need of it so sorely.

In the midst of these depressing thoughts an intense desire for food took possession of him, and he gazed around with a sort of wolfish glare, but there was no food within his reach—not even a wild berry.

" I believe that I am dying," he said at last, with deep solemnity. " God forgive me ! Twice bought ! Fred said that Jesus had bought my soul before the miners bought my life."

For some time he lay motionless; then, rousing himself, again began to speak in low, disjointed sentences, among which were words of prayer.

"It is terrible to die here—alone!" he murmured, recovering from one of his silent fits. "Oh that mother were here now! dear, dishonoured, but still beloved mother! Would that I had a pen to scratch a few words before—stay, I have a pencil."

He searched his pockets and found the desired implement, but he could not find paper. The lining of his cap occurred to him; it was soft and unfit for his purpose. Looking sadly round, he observed that the tree against which he leaned was a silver-stemmed birch, the inner bark of which, he knew, would serve his purpose. With great difficulty he tore off a small sheet of it and began to write, while a little smile of contentment played on his lips.

From time to time weakness compelled him to pause, and more than once he fell asleep in the midst of his labour. Heavy labour it was, too, for the nerveless hands almost refused to form the irregular scrawl. Still he persevered—till evening. Then a burning thirst assailed him, and he looked eagerly round for water, but there was none in view. His eyes lighted up, however, as he listened, for the soft tinkling of a tiny rill filled his ear.

With a desperate effort he got upon his hands and knees, and crept in the direction whence the sound came. He found the rill in a few moments, and, falling on his breast, drank with feelings of intense gratitude in his heart. When satisfied he rose to his knees again and tried to return to his tree, but even while making the effort he sank slowly on his breast, pillowed his head on the wet green moss, and fell into a profound slumber.

CHAPTER IX.

WE left Fred Westly hastening through the forest to the help of his friends at Bevan's Gully.

At first, after parting from his comrade, he looked back often and anxiously, in the hope that Tom might find out his mistake and return to him ; but, as mile after mile was placed between them, he felt that this hope was vain, and turned all his energies of mind and body to the task that lay before him. This was to outwalk Stalker's party of bandits and give timely warning to the Bevans ; for, although Flinders's hints had been vague enough, he readily guessed that the threatened danger was the descent of the robbers on their little homestead, and it naturally occurred to his mind that this was probably the same party which had made the previous attack, especially as he had observed several Indians among them.

Young, sanguine, strong, and active, Fred, to use a not inapt phrase, devoured the ground with his legs ! Sometimes he ran, at other times he walked, but more frequently he went along at an easy trot, which, although it looked slower than quick walking, was in reality much faster, besides being better suited to the rough ground he had to traverse.

Night came at last, but night could not have arrested him if it had not been intensely dark. This, however, did not trouble him much, for he knew that the same cause would arrest the progress of his foes, and besides, the moon would rise in an hour. He therefore flung himself on the ground for a short rest, and fell asleep, while praying that God would not suffer him to sleep too long.

His prayer was answered, for he awoke with a start an hour afterwards, just as the first pale light of the not quite risen moon began to tinge the clear sky.

Fred felt very hungry, and could not resist the tendency to meditate on beefsteaks and savoury cutlets for some time after resuming his journey; but, after warming to the work, and especially after taking a long refreshing draught at a spring that bubbled like silver in the moonlight, these longings passed away. Hour after hour sped by, and still the sturdy youth held on at the same steady pace, for he knew well that to push beyond his natural strength in prolonged exertion would only deduct from the end of his journey whatever he might gain at the commencement.

Day broke at length. As it advanced the intense longing for food returned, and, to his great anxiety, it was accompanied by a slight feeling of faintness. He therefore glanced about for wild fruits as he went along, without diverging from his course, and was fortunate to fall in with several bushes which afforded him a slight meal of berries. In the strength of these he ran on till noon, when the faint feeling returned, and he was fain to rest for a little beside a brawling brook.

"Oh! Father, help me!" he murmured, as he stooped to drink. On rising, he continued to mutter to himself, "If only a tithe of my ordinary strength were left, or if I had one good meal and a short rest, I could be there in three hours; but—"

Whatever Fred's fears were, he did not express them. He arose and recommenced his swinging trot with something like the pertinacity of a bloodhound on the scent. Perhaps he was thinking of his previous conversation with Tom Brixton about being guided by God in *all* circumstances, for the only remark that escaped him afterwards was, " It is my duty to act, and leave results to Him."

Towards the afternoon of that day Paul Bevan was busy mending a small cart in front of his hut, when he observed a man to stagger out of the wood as if he had been drunk, and approach the place where his plank-bridge usually spanned the brook. It was drawn back, however, at the time, and lay on the fortress side, for Paul had been rendered somewhat cautious by the recent assault on his premises.

" Hallo, Betty !" he cried.

" Yes, father," replied a sweet musical voice, the owner of which issued from the doorway with her pretty arms covered with flour and her face flushed from the exertion of making bread.

" Are the guns loaded, lass ?"

" Yes, father," replied Betty, turning her eyes in the direction towards which Paul gazed. " But I see only one man," she added.

" Ay, an' a drunk man too, who couldn't make much of a fight if he wanted to. But, lass, the drunk man may have any number of men at his back, both drunk and sober, so it's well to be ready. Just fetch the revolvers an' have 'em handy while I go down to meet him."

" Father, it seems to me I should know that figure. Why, it's—no, surely it cannot be young Mister Westly !"

" No doubt of it, girl. Your eyes are better than mine,

but I see him clearer as he comes on.   Young Westly—
drunk—ha! ha!—as a hatter!   I'll go help him over."

Paul chuckled immensely—as sinners are wont to do
when they catch those whom they are pleased to call
"saints" tripping—but when he had pushed the plank
over, and Fred, plunging across, fell at his feet in a state
of insensibility, his mirth vanished and he stooped to
examine him.   His first act was to put his nose to the
youth's mouth and sniff.

"No smell o' drink there," he muttered.   Then he
untied Fred's neckcloth and loosened his belt.   Then, as
nothing resulted from these acts, he set himself to lift
the fallen man in his arms.   Being a sturdy fellow
he succeeded, though with considerable difficulty, and
staggered with his burden towards the hut, where he was
met by his anxious daughter.

"Why, lass, he's no more drunk than you are!" cried
Paul, as he laid Fred on his own bed.   "Fetch me the
brandy-flask—no?   Well, get him a cup of coffee, if ye
prefer it."

"It will be better for him, father; besides, it is fortunately ready and hot."

While the active girl ran to the outer room or "hall"
of the hut for the desired beverage, Paul slily forced a
teaspoonful of diluted brandy into Fred's mouth.   It had,
at all events, the effect of restoring him to consciousness,
for he opened his eyes and glanced from side to side with
a bewildered air.   Then he sat up suddenly, and said—

"Paul, the villains are on your track again.   I've
hastened ahead to tell you.   I'd have been here sooner
—but—but I'm—starving."

"Eat, then—eat before you speak, Mr. Westly," said
Betty, placing food before him.

"But the matter is urgent!" cried Fred.

"Hold on, Mr. Fred," said Paul; "did you an' the enemy—whoever he may be, though I've a pretty fair guess—start to come here together?"

"Within the same hour, I should think."

"An' did you camp for the night?"

"No. At least I rested but one hour."

"Then swallow some grub an' make your mind easy. They won't be here for some hours yet, for you've come on at a rate that no party of men could beat, I see that clear enough—unless they was mounted."

"But a few of the chief men *were* mounted, Paul."

"Pooh! that's nothing. Chief men won't come on without the or'nary men. It needs or'nary men, you know, to make chief 'uns. Ha! ha! Come, now, if you can't hold your tongue, try to speak and eat at the same time."

Thus encouraged, Fred set to work on some bread and cheese and coffee with all the *gusto* of a starving man, and, at broken intervals, blurted out all he knew and thought about the movements of the robber band, as well as his own journey and his parting with Brixton.

"'Tis a pity, an' strange, too, that he was so obstinate," observed Paul.

"But he thought he was right," said Betty, and then she blushed with vexation at having been led by impulse even to appear to justify her lover. But Paul took no notice.

"It matters not," said he, "for it happens that you have found us almost on the wing, Westly. I knew full well that this fellow Buxley—"

"They call him Stalker, if you mean the robber chief," interrupted Fred.

"Pooh! Did you ever hear of a robber chief without half a dozen aliases?" rejoined Paul. "This Buxley,

havin' found out my quarters, will never rest till he kills
me; so as I've no fancy to leave my little Betty in an
unprotected state yet a while, we have packed up our
goods and chattels—they ain't much to speak of—and
intend to leave the old place this very night. Your
friend Stalker won't attack till night—I know the villain
well—but your news inclines me to set off a little sooner
than I intended. So, what you have got to do is to lie
down an' rest while Betty and I get the horse an' cart
ready. We've got a spare horse, which you're welcome
to. We sent little Tolly Trevor off to Briant's Gulch to
buy a pony for my little lass. He should have been
back by this time if he succeeded in gettin' it."

"But where do you mean to go to?" asked Fred.

"To Simpson's Gully."

"Why, that's where Tom and I were bound for when
we fell in with Stalker and his band! We shall probably meet Tom returning. But the road is horrible—
indeed there is no road at all, and I don't think a cart
could—"

"Oh! I know that," interrupted Paul, "and have no
intention of smashing up my cart in the woods. We
shall go round by the plains, lad. It is somewhat longer,
no doubt, but once away, we shall be able to laugh at
men on foot if they are so foolish as to follow us. Come
now, Betty, stir your stumps and finish your packing.
I'll go get the—"

A peculiar yell rent the air outside at that moment,
cutting short the sentence and almost petrifying the
speaker, who sprang up and began frantically to bar the
door and windows of the hut, at the same time growling,
"They've come sooner than I expected. Who'd have
thought it! Bar the small window at the back, Betty,
an' then fetch all the weapons. I was so taken up wi'

you, Fred, that I forgot to haul back the plank ; that's
how they 've got over.   Help wi' this table—so—they'll
have some trouble to batter in the door wi' that agin it,
an' I 've a flankin' battery at the east corner to prevent
them settin' the place on fire."

While the man spoke he acted with violent haste.
Fred sprang up and assisted him, for the shock—coupled,
no doubt, with the hot coffee and bread and cheese—
had restored his energies, at least for the time, almost as
effectually as if he had had a rest.

They were only just in time, for at that moment a
man ran with a wild shout against the door.   Finding it
fast, he kept thundering against it with his heavy boots,
and shouting Paul Bevan's name in unusually fierce
tones.

"Are ye there ?" he demanded at last, and stopped to
listen.

"If you 'll make less noise mayhap ye 'll find out,"
growled Paul.

"Och ! Paul, dear, open av ye love me," entreated the
visitor, in a voice there was no mistaking.

"I do believe it 's my mate Flinders !" said Fred.

Paul said nothing, but proved himself to be of the
same opinion by hastily unbarring and opening the door,
when in burst the irrepressible Flinders, wet from head
to foot, splashed all over with mud and blood, and panting like a race-horse.

"Is that—tay ye 've got there—my dear ?" he asked
in gasps.

"No, it is coffee.   Let me give you some."

"Thank 'ee kindly—fill it up—my dear.   Here 's
wishin'—ye all luck !"

Paddy drained the cup to the dregs, wiped his mouth
on the cuff of his coat, and thus delivered himself—

"Now, don't all spake at wance. Howld yer tongues an' listen. Av coorse, Muster Fred's towld ye when an' where an' how I.jined the blackguards. Ye'll be able now to guess why I did it. Soon after I jined 'em I began to boast o' my shootin' in a way that would ha' shocked me nat'ral mòdesty av I hadn't done it for a raisin o' me own. Well, they boasted back, so I defied 'em to a trial, an' soon showed 'em what I could. do. There wasn't wan could come near me wi' the rifle. So they made me hunter-in-chief to the band then an' there. I wint out at wance an' brought in a good supply o' game. Then, as my time was short, you see, I gave em' the slip nixt day an' comed on here, neck an' crop, through fire an' water, like a turkey-buzzard wi' the cholera. An' so here I am, an' they'll soon find out I've given 'em the slip, an' they'll come after me, swearin', perhaps; an' if I was you, Paul Bevan, I wouldn't stop to say how d'ye do to them."

"No more I will, Paddy—an', by good luck, we're about ready to start, only I've got a fear for that poor boy Tolly. If he comes back arter we're gone an' falls into their hands it'll be a bad look-out for him."

"No fear o' Tolly," said Flinders; "he's a 'cute boy as can look after himself. By the way, where's Muster Tom?"

The reason of Brixton's absence was explained to him by Betty, who bustled about the house packing up the few things that could be carried away, while her father and Fred busied themselves with the cart and horses outside. Meanwhile the Irishman continued to refresh himself with the bread and cheese.

"Ye see it's o' no manner o' use me tryin' to help ye, my dear," he said, apologetically, "for I niver was much of a hand at packin', my exparience up to this time

havin' run pretty much in the way o' havin' little or
nothin' to pack. Moreover, I 'm knocked up as well as
hungry, an' ye seem such a good hand that it would be a
pity to interfere wid ye. Is there any chance o' little
Tolly turnin' up wi' the pony before we start?"

"Every chance," replied the girl, smiling, in spite of
herself, at the man's free-and-easy manner rather than
his words. "He ought to have been here by this time.
We expect him every moment."

But these expectations were disappointed, for, when
they had packed the stout little cart, harnessed and
saddled the horses, and were quite ready to start, the
boy had not appeared.

"We durstn't delay," said Paul, with a look of intense
annoyance, "an' I can't think of how we are to let him
know which way we 've gone, for I didn't think of telling him why we wanted another pony."

"He can read, father. We might leave a note for
him on the table, and if he arrives before the robbers
that would guide him."

"True, Betty; but if the robbers should arrive before
him, that would also guide *them*."

"But we 're so sure of his returning almost immediately," urged Betty.

"Not so sure o' that, lass. No, we durstn't risk it, an'
I can't think of anything else. Poor Tolly! he 'll stand
a bad chance, for he 's sure to come gallopin' up, an'
singin' at the top of his voice in his usual reckless
way."

"Cudn't we stick up a bit paper in the way he 's
bound to pass, wid a big wooden finger to point it out,
and the word 'notice' on it, writ big?"

"Oh! I know what I 'll do," cried Betty Tolly will
oe sure to search all over the place for us, and there 's one

place, a sort of half cave in the cliff, where he and I used to read together. He 'll be quite certain to look there."

"Right, lass, an' we may risk that, for the reptiles won't think o' sarchin' the cliff. Go, Betty; write, 'We're off to Simpson's Gully, by the plains. Follow hard.' That 'll bring him on if they don't catch him— poor Tolly !"

In a few minutes the note was written and stuck on the wall of the cave referred to ; then the party set off at a brisk trot, Paul, Betty, and Flinders in the cart, while Fred rode what its owner styled the spare horse.

They had been gone about two hours, when Stalker, alias Buxley, and his men arrived in an unenviable state of rage, for they had discovered Flinders's flight, had guessed its object, and now, after hastening to Bevan's Gully at top speed, had reached it to find the birds flown.

This they knew at once from the fact that the plank-bridge, quadrupled in width to let the horse and cart pass, had been left undrawn as if to give them a mocking invitation to cross. Stalker at once accepted the invitation. The astute Bevan had, however, anticipated and prepared for this event by the clever use of a saw just before leaving. When the robber-chief gained the middle of the bridge it snapped in two and let him down with a horrible rending of wood into the streamlet, whence he emerged like a half-drowned rat, amid the ill-suppressed laughter of his men. The damage he received was slight. It was only what Flinders would have called "a pleasant little way of showing attintion to his inimy before bidding him farewell."

Of course every nook and corner of the stronghold was examined with the utmost care—also with consider-

able caution, for they knew not how many more traps
and snares might have been laid for them. They did
not, however, find those for whom they sought, and,
what was worse in the estimation of some of the band,
they found nothing worth carrying away. Only one
thing did they discover that was serviceable, namely, a
large cask of gunpowder in the underground magazine
formerly mentioned. Bevan had thought of blowing this
up before leaving, for his cart was already too full to take
it in, but the hope that it might not be discovered, and
that he might afterwards return to fetch it away, induced
him to spare it.

Of course all the flasks and horns of the band were
replenished from this store, but there was still left a full
third of the cask which they could not carry away.
With this the leader determined to blow up the hut, for
he had given up all idea of pursuing the fugitives, he and
his men being too much exhausted for that.

Accordingly the cask was placed in the middle of the
hut and all the unportable remains of Paul Bevan's furniture were piled above it. Then a slow match was made
by rubbing gunpowder on some long strips of calico. This
was applied and lighted, and the robbers retired to a spot
close to a spring about half a mile distant, where they
could watch the result in safety while they cooked some
food.

But these miscreants were bad judges of slow matches!
Their match turned out to be very slow. So slow that
they began to fear it had gone out—so slow that the daylight had time to disappear and the moon to commence
her softly solemn journey across the dark sky—so slow
that Stalker began seriously to think of sending a man
to stir up the spark, though he thought there might be
difficulty in finding a volunteer for the dangerous job—

so slow that a certain reckless little boy came galloping towards the fortress on a tall horse with a led pony plunging by his side—all before the spark of the match reached its destination and did its work.

Then, at last, there came a flash that made the soft moon look suddenly paler, and lighted up the world as if the sun had shot a ray right through it from the antipodes. This was followed by a crash and a roar that caused the solid globe itself to vibrate and sent Paul Bevan's fortress into the sky a mass of blackened ruins. One result was that a fiendish cheer arose from the robbers' camp, filling the night air with discord. Another result was that the happy-go-lucky little boy and his horses came to an almost miraculous halt, and remained so for some time, gazing straight before them in a state of abject amazement!

CHAPTER X.

HOW long Tolly Trevor remained in a state of horrified surprise no one can tell, for he was incapable of observation at the time, besides being alone. On return-ing to consciousness he found himself galloping towards the exploded fortress at full speed, and did not draw rein till he approached the bank of the rivulet. Reflecting that a thoroughbred hunter could not clear the stream, even in daylight, he tried to pull up, but his horse refused. It had run away with him.

Although constitutionally brave, the boy felt an unplea-sant sensation of some sort as he contemplated the inevit-able crash that awaited him ; for, even if the horse should perceive his folly and try to stop on reaching the bank, the tremendous pace attained would render the attempt futile.

"Stop ! won't you ?   Wo-o-o !" cried Tolly, straining at the reins till the veins of his neck and forehead seemed about to burst.

But the horse would neither "stop" nor "wo-o-o !" It was otherwise, however, with the pony.   That amiable creature had been trained well, and had learned obedience. Blessed quality !   Would that the human race—especially its juvenile section—understood better the value of that inestimable virtue !   The pony began to pull back at the sound of "wo !"   Its portion in childhood had probably been woe when it refused to recognise the order.   The result was that poor Tolly's right arm, over which was thrown the pony's rein, had to bear the strain of conflicting opinions.

A bright idea struck his mind at this moment. Bright ideas always do strike the mind of genius at critical moments! He grasped both the reins of his steed in his right hand, and took a sudden turn of them round his wrist. Then he turned about—not an instant too soon—looked the pony straight in the face, and said "WO!" in a voice of command that was irresistible. The pony stopped at once, stuck out its fore legs, and was absolutely dragged a short way over the ground. The strain on Tolly's arm was awful, but the arm was a stout one, though small. It stood the strain, and the obstinate runaway was arrested on the brink of destruction with an almost broken jaw.

The boy slipped to the ground and hastily fastened the steeds to a tree. Even in that hour of supreme anxiety he could not help felicitating himself on the successful application of pony docility to horsey self-will.

But these and all other feelings of humour and satisfaction were speedily put to flight when, after crossing the remains of the plank bridge with some difficulty, he stood before the hideous wreck of his friend's late home, where he had spent so many glad hours listening to marvellous adventures from Paul Bevan, or learning how to read and cipher, as well as drinking in wisdom generally, from the Rose of Oregon.

It was an awful collapse. A yawning gulf had been driven into the earth, and the hut—originally a solid structure—having been hurled bodily skyward, shattered to atoms, and inextricably mixed in its parts, had come down again into the gulf as into a ready-made grave.

It would be vain to search for any sort of letter, sign,

or communication from his friends among the *débris.*
Tolly felt that at once, yet he could not think of leaving
without a search. After one deep and prolonged sigh he
threw off his lethargy, and began a close inspection of the
surroundings.

" You see," he muttered to himself, as he moved quickly
yet stealthily about, " they 'd never have gone off without
leavin' some scrap of information for me, to tell me which
way they 'd gone, even though they 'd gone off in a lightnin'
hurry. But p'raps they didn't. The reptiles may have
comed on 'em unawares, an' left 'em no time to do anything. Of *course* they can't have killed 'em. Nobody
ever could catch Paul Bevan asleep—no, not the sharpest
redskin in the land. That 's quite out o' the question."

Though out of the question, however, the bare thought
of such a catastrophe caused little Trevor's under lip to
tremble, a mist to obscure his vision, and a something-or-
other to fill his throat, which he had to swallow with a
gulp. Moreover, he went back to the ruined hut and
began to pull about the wreck with a fluttering heart, lest
he should come on some evidence that his friends had
been murdered. Then he went to the highest part of the
rock to rest a little, and consider what had best be done
next.

While seated there, gazing on the scene of silent
desolation, which the pale moonlight rendered more
ghastly, the poor boy's spirit failed him a little. He
buried his face in his hands and burst into tears.

Soon this weakness, as he deemed it, passed away.
He dried his eyes, roughly, and rose to resume his search,
and it is more than probable that he would ere long have
bethought him of the cave where Betty had left her note,
if his attention had not been suddenly arrested by a faint
glimmer of ruddy light in a distant part of the forest.

The robbers were stirring up their fires, and sending a tell-tale glow into the sky.

"O-ho!" exclaimed Tolly Trevor.

He said nothing more, but there was a depth of meaning in the tone and look accompanying that "O-ho!" which baffles description.

Tightening his belt, he at once glided down the slope, flitted across the rivulet, skimmed over the open space, and melted into the forest after the most approved method of Red Indian tactics.

The expedition from which he had just returned having been peaceful, little Trevor carried no warlike weapons—for the long bowie-knife at his side, and the little hatchet stuck in his girdle, were, so to speak, merely domestic implements, without which he never moved abroad. But as war was not his object, the want of rifle and revolver mattered little. He soon reached the neighbourhood of the robbers' fire, and, when close enough to render extreme caution necessary, threw himself flat on the ground and advanced à la "snake-in-the-grass."

Presently he came within earshot, and listened attentively, though without much interest, to a deal of boastful small talk with which the marauders beguiled the time, while they fumigated their mouths and noses preparatory to turning in for the night.

At last the name of Paul Bevan smote his ear, causing it, metaphorically, to go on full cock.

"I'm sartin sure," said one of the speakers, "that the old screw has gone right away to Simpson's Gully."

"If I thought that I'd follow him up, and make a dash at the Gully itself," said Stalker, plucking a burning stick from the fire to rekindle his pipe.

"If you did you'd get wopped," remarked Goff, with a touch of sarcasm, for the lieutenant of the band was not

so respectful to his commander as a well-disciplined man
should be.

"What makes you think so?" demanded the chief.

"The fact that the diggers are a sight too many for us,"
returned Goff. "Why, we'd find 'em three to one, if not
four."

"Well, that, coupled with the uncertainty of his having
gone to Simpson's Gully," said the chief, "decides me to
make tracks down south to the big woods on the slopes
of the Sawback Hills. There are plenty of parties travelling thereabouts with lots of gold, boys, and difficulties
enough in the way of hunting us out o' the stronghold.
I'll leave you there for a short time and make a private
excursion to Simpson's Gully, to see if my enemy an' the
beautiful Betty are there."

"An' get yourself shot or stuck for your pains," said
Goff. "Do you suppose that such a hulking, long-legged
fellow as you are can creep into a camp like an or'nary
man without drawin' attention?"

"Perhaps not," returned Stalker; "but are there not
such things as disguises? Have you not seen me with
my shootin'-coat and botanical box an' blue spectacles,
an' my naturally sandy hair—"

"No, no, captain!" cried Goff, with a laugh, "not sandy;
say yellow, or golden."

"Well, golden, then, if you will. You've seen it dyed
black, haven't you?"

"Oh yes! I've seen you in these humblin' circumstances before now," returned the lieutenant, "and I must
say your own mother wouldn't know you. But what's
the use o' runnin' the risk, captain?"

"Because I owe Bevan a grudge!" said the chief,
sternly, "and mean to be revenged on him. Besides, I
want the sweet Betty for a wife, and intend to have her,

whether she will or no. She 'll make a capital bandit's wife—after a little while, when she gets used to the life. So now you know some of my plans, and you shall see whether the hulking botanist won't carry all before him."

" O-ho !" muttered the snake-in-the-grass, very softly ; and there was something so compound and significant in the tone of that second " O-ho !" soft though it was, that it not only baffles description, but—really, you know, it would be an insult to your understanding, good reader, to say more in the way of explanation ! There was also a heaving of the snake's shoulders, which, although un-accompanied by sound, was eminently suggestive.

Feeling that he had by that time heard quite enough, Tolly Trevor effected a masterly retreat, and returned to the place where he had left the horses. On the way he recalled with satisfaction the fact that Paul Bevan had once pointed out to him the exact direction of Simpson's Gully at a time when he meant to send him on an errand thither. " You 've on'y to go over there, lad," Paul had said, pointing towards the forest in rear of his hut, " and hold on for two days straight as the crow flies till you come to it. You can't well miss it."

Tolly knew that there was also an easier though longer route by the plains, but as he was not sure of it he made up his mind to take to the forest.

The boy was sufficiently trained in woodcraft to feel pretty confident of finding his way, for he knew the north side of trees by their bark, and could find out the north star when the sky was clear, besides possessing a sort of natural aptitude for holding on in a straight line. He mounted the obstinate horse, therefore, took the rein of the obedient pony on his right arm, and, casting a last look of profound regret on Bevan's desolated homestead, rode

swiftly away. So eager was he that he took no thought
for the morrow. He knew that the wallet slung at his
saddle-bow contained a small supply of food—as much,
probably, as would last three days with care. That was
enough to render Tolly Trevor the most independent and
careless youth in Oregon.

While these events were occurring in the neighbourhood of Bevan's Gully, three red men, in all the glory of
vermilion, charcoal, and feathers, were stalking through
the forest in the vicinity of the spot where poor Tom
Brixton had laid him down to die. These children of the
wilderness stalked in single file—from habit, we presume,
for there was ample space for them to have walked abreast
if so inclined. They seemed to be unsociable beings, for
they also stalked in solemn silence.

Suddenly the first savage came to an abrupt pause, and
said, "Ho!" the second savage said "He!" and the
third said "Hi!" After which, for full a minute, they
stared at the ground in silent wonder and said nothing.
They had seen a footprint! It did not by any means
resemble that deep, well developed, and very solitary
footprint at which Robinson Crusoe is wont to stare in
nursery picture-books. No; it was a print which was
totally invisible to ordinary eyes, and revealed itself to
these children of the woods in the form of a turned leaf
and a cracked twig. Such as it was, it revealed a track
which the three children followed up until they found
Tom Brixton—or his body—lying on the ground near to
the little spring.

Again these children said "Ho!" "He!" and "Hi!"
respectively, in varying tones according to their varied
character. Then they commenced a jabber, which we
are quite unable to translate, and turned Tom over on his
back. The motion awoke him, for he sat up and stared

THEY STALKED AWAY WITH HIM.—PAGE 125.

Ever that effort proved too much for him in his weak state, for he fell back and fainted.

The Indians proved to be men of promptitude. They lifted the white man up; one got Tom's shoulders on his back, another put his legs over his shoulders, and thus they stalked away with him. When the first child of the wood grew tired, the unburdened one stepped in to his relief; when the second child grew tired, the first one went to his aid; when all the children grew tired, they laid their burden on the ground and sat down beside it. Thus, by easy stages, was Tom Brixton conveyed away from the spot where he had given himself up as hopelessly lost.

Now, it could not have been more than six hours after Tom had thus been borne away that poor Tolly Trevor came upon the same scene. We say "poor" advisedly, for he had not only suffered the loss of much fragmentary clothing in his passage through that tangled wood, but also most of the food with which he had started, and a good deal of skin from his shins, elbows, knuckles, and knees, as well as the greater part of his patience. Truly, he was in a pitiable plight, for the forest had turned out to be almost impassable for horses, and in his journey he had not only fallen oft and been swept out of the saddle by overhanging branches frequently, but had to swim swamps, cross torrents, climb precipitous banks, and had stuck in quagmires innumerable.

As for the horses—their previous owner could not have recognised them. It is true they were what is styled "all there," but there was an inexpressible droop of their heads and tails, a weary languor in their eyes, and an abject waggle about their knees which told of hope deferred and spirit utterly gone. The pony was the better of the two. Its sprightly glance of amiability had changed into a gaze of humble resignation, whereas the

aspect of the oostinate horse was one of impotent ill-
nature. It would have bitten, perhaps, if strength had
permitted, but as to its running away—ha!

Well, Tolly Trevor approached—it could hardly be said
he rode up to—the spring before mentioned, where he
passed the footprints in stupid blindness.

He dismounted, however, to drink and rest a while.

"Come on—you brute!" he cried, almost savagely,
dragging the horse to the water.

The creature lowered its head and gazed as though to
say, "What liquid is that?"

As the pony, however, at once took a long and hearty
draught, it also condescended to drink, while Tolly
followed suit. Afterwards he left the animals to graze,
and sat down under a neighbouring tree to rest and
swallow his last morsel of food.

It was sad to see the way in which the poor boy carefully shook out and gathered up the few crumbs in his
wallet, so that not one of them should be lost; and how
slowly he ate them, as if to prolong the sensation of being
gratified! During the two days which he had spent in
the forest his face had grown perceptibly thinner, and
his strength had certainly diminished. Even the reckless
look of defiant joviality, which was one of the boy's chief
characteristics, had given place to a restless anxiety that
prevented his seeing humour in anything, and induced
a feeling of impatience when a joke chanced irresistibly to
bubble up in his mind. He was once again reduced almost
to the weeping point, but his sensations were somewhat
different, for, when he had stood gazing at the wreck of
Bevan's home, the nether lip had trembled because of the
sorrows of friends, whereas now he was sorrowing because
of an exhausted nature, a weakened heart, and a sinking
spirit. But the spirit had not yet utterly given way!

" Come !" he cried, starting up. "This won't do, Tolly. Be a man ! Why, only think—you have got over two days and two nights. That was the time allowed you by Paul, so your journey 's all but done—*must* be. Of course those brutes—forgive me, pony, *that* brute, I mean—has made me go much slower than if I had come on my own legs, but notwithstanding, it cannot be—hallo ! what 's that ?"

The exclamation had reference to a small dark object which lay a few yards from the spot on which he sat. He ran and picked it up. It was Tom Brixton's cap—with his name rudely written on the lining. Beside it lay a piece of bark on which was pencil-writing.

With eager, anxious haste the boy began to peruse it, but he was unaccustomed to read handwriting, and when poor Tom had pencilled the lines his hand was weak and his brain confused, so that the characters were doubly difficult to decipher. After much and prolonged effort the boy made out the beginning. It ran thus : " This is probably the last letter that I, Tom Brixton, shall ever write. (I put down my name now, in case I never finish it.) O dearest mother !—"

Emotion had no doubt rendered the hand less steady at this point, for here the words were quite illegible—at least to little Trevor—who finally gave up the attempt in despair. The effect of this discovery, however, was to send the young blood coursing wildly through the veins, so that a great measure of strength returned, as if by magic.

The boy's first care was naturally to look for traces of the lost man, and he set about this with a dull fear at his heart, lest at any moment he should come upon the dead body of his friend. In a few minutes he discovered the track made by the Indians, which led him to the spot near to the spring where Tom had fallen. To his now

fully-awakened senses Trevor easily read the story, as far
as signs could tell it.

Brixton had been all but starved to death. He had
lain down under a tree to die—the very tree under which
he himself had so recently given way to despair.   While
lying there he—Brixton—had scrawled his last words on
the bit of birch-bark.   Then he had tried to reach the
spring, but had fainted either before reaching it or after
leaving. This he knew, because the mark of Tom's coat,
part of his waist-belt, and the handle of his bowie-knife
were all impressed on the softish ground with sufficient
distinctness to be discerned by a sharp eye.   The moccasined footprints told of Indians having found Brixton—
still alive, for they would not have taken the trouble to
carry him off if he had been dead.   The various sizes of
the moccasined feet told that the party of Indians
numbered three ; and the trail of the red men, with its
occasional halting-places, pointed out clearly the direction
in which they had gone.   Happily this was also the
direction in which little Trevor was going.

Of course the boy did not read this off as readily as
we have written it all down.   It cost him upwards of an
hour's patient research; but when at last he did arrive at the
result of his studies he wasted no time in idle speculation.
His first duty was to reach Simpson's Gully, discover his
friend Paul Bevan, and deliver to him the piece of birch-
bark he had found, and the information he had gleaned.

By the time Tolly had come to this conclusion his horse
and pony had obtained both rest and nourishment enough
to enable them to raise their drooping heads and tails an
inch or two, so that, when the boy mounted the former
with some of his old dash and energy, it shook its head,
gave a short snort, and went off at a fair trot.

Fortunately the ground improved just beyond this

point, opening out into park-like scenery, which, in
another mile or two, ran into level prairie land. This
Trevor knew from description was close to the mountain
range in which lay the gully he was in quest of. The
hope which had begun to rise increased, and communicat-
ing itself, probably by sympathetic electricity, to the
horse, produced a shuffling gallop, which ere long brought
them to a clump of wood. On rounding this they came
in sight of the longed-for hills.

Before nightfall Simpson's Gully was reached, and little
Trevor was directed to the tent of Paul Bevan, who had
arrived there only the day before.

"It's a strange story, lad," said Paul, after the boy had
run rapidly over the chief points of the news he had to
give, to which Betty, Fred, and Flinders sat listening with
eager interest.

"We must be off to search for him without delay,"
said Fred Westly, rising.

"It's right ye are, sor," cried Flinders, springing up.
"Off to-night, an' not a moment to lose."

"We'll talk it over first, boys," said Paul. "Come
with me. I've a friend in the camp as'll help us."

"Did you not bring the piece of bark?" asked Betty
of the boy, as the men went out.

"Oh! I forgot. Of course I did," cried Trevor, drawing
it from his breast-pocket. "The truth is I'm so knocked
up that I scarce know what I'm about."

"Lie down here on this deer-skin, poor boy, and rest
while I read it."

Tolly Trevor flung himself on the rude but welcome
couch, and almost instantly fell asleep, while Betty Bevan,
spreading the piece of birch-bark on her knee, began to
spell out the words and try to make sense of Tom Brixton's
last epistle.

CHAPTER XL.

WITH considerable difficulty Betty Bevan succeeded in deciphering the tremulous scrawl which Tom Brixton had written on the piece of birch-bark. It ran somewhat as follows :—

"This is probably the last letter that I, Tom Brixton, shall ever write. (I put down my name now, in case I never finish it.) O dearest mother! what would I not now give to unsay all the hard things I have ever said to you, and to undo all the evil I have done. But this cannot be. 'Twice bought!' It is strange how these words run in my mind. I was condemned to death at the gold-fields—my comrades bought me off. Fred— dear Fred—who has been true and faithful to the last, reminded me that I had previously been bought with the blood of Jesus—that I have been *twice bought!* I think he put it in this way to fix my obstinate spirit on the idea, and he has succeeded. The thought has been burned in upon my soul as with fire. I am very, *very* weak—dying, I fear, in the forest, and alone! . . . How my mind seems to wander! I have slept since writing the last sentence, and dreamed of food! Curious mixing of ideas! I also dreamed of Betty Bevan. Ah, sweet girl! if this ever meets your eye, believe that I loved you sincerely. It is well that I should die, perhaps, for I have been a thief, and would not ask your hand now even if I

might. I would not sully it with a touch of mine, and I
could not expect you to believe in me after I tell you that
I not only robbed Gashford, but also Fred—my chum
Fred—and gambled it all away, and drank away my
reason almost at the same time. . . . I have slept again,
and dreamed of water this time—bright, pure, crystal
water—sparkling and gushing in the sunshine. O God!
how I despised it once, and how I long for it now!
I am too weak and wandering, mother, to think about
religion now. But why should I? Your teaching has
not been altogether thrown away; it comes back like a
great flood while I lie here dreaming and trying to write.
The thoughts are confused, but the sense comes home.
All is easily summed up in the words you once taught me,
' I am a poor sinner, and nothing at all, but Jesus Christ
is all in all.' Not sure that I quote rightly. No matter,
the sense is there also. And yet it seems—it is—such a
mean thing to sin away one's life and ask for pardon only
at the end—the very end! But the thief on the cross did
it; why not I? Sleep—*is* it sleep? may it not be slowly-
approaching death?—has overpowered me again. I have
been attempting to read this. I seem to have mixed
things somehow. It is sadly confused—or my mind is.
A burning thirst consumes me—and—I *think* I hear
water running! I will—"

Here the letter ended abruptly.

"No doubt," murmured Betty, as she let the piece of
bark fall on the table and clasped her hands over her eyes,
"he rose and tried to reach the water. Praise God that
there is hope!"

She sat for a few seconds in profound silence, which
was broken by Paul and his friends re-entering the tent.

"It's all arranged, Betty," he said, taking down an old
rifle which hung above the door; "old Larkins has agreed

to look arter my claim and take care of you, lass, while
we 're away."

" I shall need no one to take care of me."

" Ah ! so you think, for you 're as brave as you 're good ;
but—I think otherwise. So he 'll look arter you."

" Indeed he won't, father !" returned Betty, smiling,
" because I intend that *you* shall look after me."

" Impossible, girl ! I 'm going to sarch for Tom Brixton,
you see, along with Mister Fred an' Flinders, so I can't
stop here with you."

" But I am going too, father !"

" But—but we can't wait for you, my good girl,"
returned Paul, with a perplexed look ; " we 're all ready
to start, an' there ain't a hoss for you except the poor
critters that Tolly Trevor brought wi' him, an', you know,
they need rest very badly."

" Well, well, go off, father ; I won't delay you," said
Betty ; "and don't disturb Tolly, let him sleep, he needs
it, poor boy. I will take care of him and his horses."

That Tolly required rest was very obvious, for he lay
sprawling on the deer-skin couch just as he had flung himself down, buried in the profoundest sleep he perhaps ever
experienced since his career in the wilderness began.

After the men had gone off, Betty Bevan—who was by
that time better known, at least among those young
diggers whose souls were poetical, as the Rose of Oregon,
and among the matter-of-fact ones as the Beautiful Nugget
—conducted herself in a manner that would have increased
the admiration of her admirers, if they had seen her, and
awakened their curiosity also. First of all she went out
to the half-ruined log-hut that served her father for a
stable, and watered, fed, and rubbed down the horse and
pony which Tolly had brought, in a manner that would
have done credit to a regular groom. Then, returning to

the tent, she arranged and packed a couple of saddle-bags with certain articles of clothing, as well as biscuits, dried meat, and other provisions. Next she cleaned and put in order a couple of revolvers, a bowie-knife, and a small hatchet; and ultimately, having made sundry other mysterious preparations, she lifted the curtain which divided the tent into two parts, and entered her own private apartment. There, after reading her nightly portion of God's Word and committing herself, and those who were out searching in the wilderness for the lost man, to His care, she lay down with her clothes on, and almost instantly fell into a slumber as profound as that which had already overwhelmed Tolly. As for that exhausted little fellow, he did not move during the whole night, save once, when an adventurous insect of the ear-wig type walked across his ruddy cheek and upper lip and looked up his nose. There are sensitive portions of the human frame which may not be touched with impunity. The sleeper sneezed, blew the earwig out of existence, rolled over on his back, flung his arms wide open, and, with his mouth in the same condition, spent the remainder of the night in motionless repose.

The sun was well up next morning, and the miners of Simpson's Gully were all busy, up to their knees in mud and gold, when Betty Bevan awoke, sprang up, ran into the outer apartment of her tent, and gazed admiringly at Tolly's face. A band of audacious and early flies were tickling it and causing the features to twitch, but they could not waken the sleeper. Betty gazed only for a moment with an amused expression, and then shook the boy somewhat vigorously.

"Come, Tolly, rise!"

"Oh! d-on'-t b-borrer."

"But I must bother. Wake up, I say. Fire!"

At the last word the boy sat up and gazed idiotically.

" Hallo !   Betty—my   dear   Nugget—is   that   you ?
Why, where am I ?"

" Your body is here," said Betty, laughing.   " When
your mind comes to the same place I 'll talk to you."

" I 'm *all* here now, Betty ; so go ahead," said the boy,
with a hearty yawn as he arose and stretched himself.
" Oh ! I remember now all about it.   Where is your
father ?"

" I will tell you presently, but first let me know what
you mean by calling me Nugget."

" Why, don't you know ?   It 's the name the men give
you everywhere—one of the names at least—the Beautiful Nugget."

" Indeed !" exclaimed the Nugget, with a laugh and
blush ; " very impudent of the men ; and, pray, if this is
one of the names, what may the others be ?"

" There 's only one other that I know of—the Rose of
Oregon.   But come, it 's not fair of you to screw my
secrets out o' me when I 'm only half awake ; and you
haven't yet told me where Paul Bevan is."

" I 'll tell you that when I see you busy with this pork
pie," returned the Rose.   " I made it myself, so you ought
to find it good.   Be quick, for I have work for you to do,
and there is no time to lose.   Content yourself with a
cold breakfast for once."

" Humph ! as if I hadn't contented myself with a cold
breakfast at any time.   Well, it *is* a good pie.   Now—
about Paul ?"

" He has gone away with Mr. Westly and Flinders to
search for Mr. Brixton."

" What ! without *me ?*" exclaimed Tolly, overturning
his chair as he started up and pushed his plate from
him.

"Yes, without you, Tolly ; I advised him not to awake you."

"It's the unkindest thing you've ever done to me," returned the boy, scarcely able to restrain his tears at the disappointment. "How can they know where to search for him without me to guide them ? Why didn't you let them waken me ?"

"You forget, Tolly, that my father knows every inch of these woods and plains for at least fifty miles round the old house they have blown up ; and, as to waking you, it would have been next to impossible to have done so, you were so tired, and you would have been quite unable to keep your eyes open. Besides, I had a little plan of my own which I want you to help me to carry out. Go on with your breakfast and I'll explain."

The boy sat down to his meal again without speaking, but with a look of much curiosity on his expressive face.

"You know, without my telling you," continued Betty, "that I, like my father, have a considerable knowledge of this part of the country, and of the ways of Indians and miners, and from what you have told me, coupled with what father has said, I think it likely that the Indians have carried poor T—Mr. Brixton, I mean—through the Long Gap rather than by the plains—"

"So I would have said, had they consulted me," interrupted the boy, with an offended air.

"Well, but," continued Betty, "they would neither have consulted you nor me, for father has a very decided will, you know, and a belief in his own judgment—which is quite right, of course, only I cannot help differing from him on this occasion—"

"No more can I," growled Tolly, thrusting his fork into the pie at a tempting piece of pork.

"So, you see, I'm going to take the big horse you

brought here and ride round by the Long Gap to see if I'm right, and I want you to go with me on the pony and take care of me."

Tolly Trevor felt his heart swell with gratification at the idea of his being the chosen protector of the Rose of Oregon—the Beautiful Nugget; selected by herself, too. Nevertheless his good sense partially subdued his vanity on the point.

"But, I say," he remarked, looking up with a half-serious expression, "d'you think that you and I are a sufficient party to make a good fight if we are attacked by Redskins? You know your father will hold me responsible, for carrying you off into the midst of danger in this fashion."

"I don't mean to fight at all," returned Betty, with a pleasant laugh, "and I will free you from all responsibility; so, have done, now, and come along."

"It's *so* good," said Tolly, looking as though he were loath to quit the pork pie; "but, come, I'm your man! Only don't you think it would be as well to get up a good fighting party among the young miners to go with us? They'd only be too happy to take service under the Beautiful Nugget, you know."

"Tolly," exclaimed the Nugget, with more than her wonted firmness, "if you are to take service under *me* you must learn to obey without question. Now, go and saddle the horses. The big one for me, the pony for yourself. Put the saddle-bags on the horse, and be quick."

There was a tone and manner about the usually quiet and gentle girl which surprised and quite overawed little Trevor, so that he was reduced at once to an obedient and willing slave. Indeed he was rather glad than otherwise that Betty had declined to listen to his suggestion about the army of young diggers—which an honest doubt as to his own capacity to fight and conquer all who might chance to come in his way had induced him to make— while he was by no means unwilling to undertake, single-handed, any duties his fair conductor should require of him.

In a few minutes, therefore, the steeds were brought round to the door of the tent, where Betty already stood equipped for the journey.

Our fair readers will not, we trust, be prejudiced against the Rose of Oregon when we inform them that she had adopted man's attitude in riding. Her costume was arranged very much after the pattern of the Indian women's dress—namely, a close-fitting body, a short woollen skirt reaching a little below the knees, and blue cloth leggings in continuation. These latter were elegantly wrought with coloured silk thread, and the pair of moccasins which covered her small feet were similarly ornamented. A little cloth cap, in shape resembling that of a cavalry foraging cap, but without ornaments, graced her head, from beneath which her wavy hair tumbled in luxuriant curls on her shoulders, and, as Tolly was wont to remark, looked after itself anyhow. Such a costume was well adapted to the masculine position on horseback, as well as to the conditions of a land in which no roads, but much underwood, existed.

Bevan's tent having been pitched near the outskirts of Simpson's Camp, the maiden and her gallant protector had no difficulty in quitting it unobserved. Riding slowly at first, to avoid attracting attention as well as to pick their steps more easily over the somewhat rugged ground near the camp, they soon reached the edge of an extensive plain, at the extremity of which a thin purple line indicated a range of hills. Here Tolly Trevor, unable to

restrain his joy at the prospect of adventure before him,
uttered a war-whoop, brought his switch down smartly
on the pony's flank, and shot away over the plain like a
wild creature. The air was bracing, the prospect was
fair, the sunshine was bright. No wonder that the
obedient pony, forgetting for the moment the fatigues
of the past, and strong in the enjoyment of the previous
night's rest and supper, went over the ground at a pace
that harmonised with its young rider's excitement; and
no wonder that the obstinate horse was inclined to
emulate the pony, and stretched its long legs into a wild
gallop, encouraged thereto by the Rose on its back.

The gallop was ere long pressed to racing speed, and
there is no saying when the young pair would have pulled
up had they not met with a sudden check by the pony
putting his foot into a badger-hole. The result was
frightful to witness, though trifling in result. The pony
went heels over head upon the plain like a rolling wheel,
and its rider shot into the air like a stone from a catapult.
Describing a magnificent curve, and coming down head
foremost, Tolly would then and there have ended his
career if he had not fortunately dropped into a thick bush,
which broke his fall instead of his neck, and saved him.
Indeed, excepting several ugly scratches, he was none the
worse for the misadventure.

Poor horrified Betty attempted to pull up, but the
obstinate horse had got the bit in his teeth and declined,
so that when Tolly had scrambled out of the bush she
was barely visible in the far distance, heading towards the
blue hills.

"Hallo!" was her protector's anxious remark as he
gazed at the flying fair one. Then, without another word,
he leaped on the pony and went after her at full speed,
quite regardless of recent experience.

The blue hills had become green hills, and the Long Gap was almost reached, before the obstinate horse suffered itself to be reined in—probably because it was getting tired. Soon afterwards the pony came panting up.

"You're not hurt, I hope?" said Betty, anxiously, as Tolly came alongside.

"Oh no. All right," replied the boy; "but, I say what a run you have given me! Why didn't you wait for me?"

"Ask that of the horse, Tolly."

"What! Did he bolt with you?"

"Truly he did. I never before rode such a stubborn brute. My efforts to check it were useless, as it had the bit in its teeth, and I did my best, for I was terribly anxious about you, and cannot imagine how you escaped a broken neck after such a flight."

"It was the bush that saved me, Betty. But, I say, we seem to be nearing a wildish sort of place."

"Yes; this is the Long Gap," returned the girl, flinging back her curls and looking round. "It cuts right through the range here, and becomes much wilder and more difficult to traverse on horseback farther on."

"And what d'ye mean to do, Betty?" inquired the boy as they rode at a foot-pace towards the opening, which seemed like a dark portal to the hills. "Suppose you discover that the Redskins *have* carried Tom Brixton off in this direction, what then? You and I won't be able to rescue him, you know."

"True, Tolly. If I find that they have taken him this way I will ride straight to father's encampment—he told me before starting where he intends to sleep to-night, so I shall easily find him—tell him what we have discovered and lead him back here."

"And suppose you don't find that the Redskins have come this way," rejoined Tolly, after a doubtful shake of his head, "what then?"

"Why, then, I shall return to our tent and leave father and Mr. Westly to hunt them down."

"And suppose," continued Tolly—but Tolly never finished the supposition, for at that moment two painted Indians sprang from the bushes on either side of the narrow track, and, almost before the riders could realise what had happened, the boy found himself on his back with a savage hand at his throat, and the girl found herself on the ground with the hand of a grinning savage on her shoulder.

Tolly Trevor struggled manfully, but, alas! also boyishly, for though his spirit was strong his bodily strength was small—at least, as compared with that of the savage who held him. Yes, Tolly struggled like a hero. He beheld the Rose of Oregon taken captive, and his blood boiled! He bit, he kicked, he scratched, and he hissed with indignation—but it would not do.

"Oh, if you'd only let me up and give me *one* chance!" he gasped.

But the red man did not consent—indeed, he did not understand. Nevertheless, it was obvious that the savage was not vindictive, for although Tolly's teeth and fists and toes and nails had wrought him some damage, he neither stabbed nor scalped the boy. He only choked him into a state of semi-unconsciousness, and then, turning him on his face, tied his hands behind his back with a deerskin thong.

Meanwhile the other savage busied himself in examining the saddle-bags of the obstinate horse. He did not appear to think it worth while to tie the hands of Betty! During the short scuffle between his comrade and the boy he had held her fast, because she manifested an intention to run to the rescue.   When that was ended he relieved her of the weapons she carried and let her go, satisfied, no doubt, that if she attempted to run away he could easily overtake her, and if she were to attempt anything else he could restrain her.

When, however, Betty saw that Tolly's antagonist meant no harm, she wisely attempted nothing, but sat down on a fallen tree to await the issue.

The savages did not keep her long in suspense.   Tolly's foe, having bound him, lifted him on the back of the pony, and then, taking the bridle, quietly led it away.   At the same time the other savage assisted Betty to remount the horse, and, grasping the bridle of that obstinate creature, followed his comrade.   The whole thing was so sudden, so violent, and the result so decisive, that the boy looked back at Betty and burst into a half-hysterical fit of laughter, but the girl did not respond.

" It 's a serious business, Tolly !" she said.

" So it is, Betty," he replied.

Then, pursing his little mouth, and gathering his eyebrows into a frown, he gave himself up to meditation, while the Indians conducted them into the dark recesses of the Long Gap.

CHAPTER XII.

NOW, the Indians into whose hands the Rose of Oregon and our little hero had fallen happened to be part of the tribe to which the three who had discovered Tom Brixton belonged, and although his friends little knew it, Tom himself was not more than a mile or so distant from them at the time, having been carried in the same direction, towards the main camp or headquarters of the tribe in the Sawback Hills.

They had not met on the journey, because the two bands of the tribe were acting independently of each other.

We will leave them at this point, and ask the reader to return to another part of the plain over which Tolly and Betty had galloped so furiously.

It is a small hollow, at the bottom of which a piece of marshy ground has encouraged the growth of a few willows. Paul Bevan had selected it as a suitable camping-ground for the night, and while Paddy Flinders busied himself with the kettle and frying-pan, he and Fred Westly went among the bushes to procure firewood.

Fred soon returned with small twigs sufficient to kindle the fire ; his companion went on further in search of larger boughs and logs.

While Fred was busily engaged on hands and knees, blowing the fire into a flame, a sharp " hallo !" from his companion caused him to look up.

"What is it?" he asked.

"Goliath of Gath—or his brother!" said Paddy, point-ing to a little eminence behind which the sun had but recently set.

The horseman, who had come to a halt on the eminence and was quietly regarding them, did indeed look as if he might have claimed kinship with the giant of the Philis-tines, for he and his steed looked stupendous. No doubt the peculiarity of their position, with the bright sky as a glowing background, had something to do with the gigan-tic appearance of horse and man, for, as they slowly descended the slope towards the fire, both of them assumed a more natural size.

The rider was a strange-looking as well as a large man, for he wore a loose shooting-coat, a tall wideawake with a broad brim, blue spectacles with side-pieces to them, and a pair of trousers which appeared to have been made for a smaller man, as, besides being too tight, they were much too short. Over his shoulder was slung a green tin botanical box. He carried no visible weapons save a small hatchet and a bowie-knife, though his capacious pockets might easily have concealed half a dozen revolvers.

"Goot night, my frunds," said the stranger, in broken English, as he approached.

"The same to yersilf, sor," returned Flinders.

Any one who had been closely watching the counten-ance of the stranger might have observed a sudden gleam of surprise on it when the Irishman spoke, but it passed instantly, and was replaced by a pleasant air of good fellowship as he dismounted and led his horse nearer the fire.

"Good night, and welcome to our camp. You are a foreigner, I perceive," said Fred Westly in French, but the stranger shook his head.

" I not un'erstan'."

" Ah ! a German, probably," returned Fred, trying him with the language of the Fatherland; but again the stranger shook his head.

" You mus' spok Eenglish. I is a Swedish man; knows noting but a leetil Eenglish."

" I 'm sorry that I cannot speak Swedish," replied Fred, in English; "so we must converse in my native tongue. You are welcome to share our camp. Have you travelled far ?"

Fred cast a keen glance of suspicion at the stranger as he spoke, and, in spite of himself, there was a decided diminution in the heartiness of his tones, but the stranger did not appear to observe either the change of tone or the glance, for he replied, with increased urbanity and openness of manner, " Yis; I has roden far—very far— an' moche wants meat an' sleep."

As he spoke Paul Bevan came staggering into camp under a heavy load of wood, and again it may be said that a close observer might have noticed on the stranger's face a gleam of surprise much more intense than the previous one when he saw Paul Bevan. But the gleam had utterly vanished when that worthy, having thrown down his load, looked up and bade him good evening.

The urbanity of manner and blandness of expression increased as he returned the salutation.

" T'anks, t'anks. I vill go for hubble—vat you call— hobble me horse," he said, taking the animal's bridle and leading it a short distance from the fire.

" I don't like the look of him," whispered Fred to Paul when he was out of earshot.

" Sure, an' I howld the same opinion," said Flinders.

" Pooh ! Never judge men by their looks," returned Bevan—"specially in the diggin's. They 're all black-

guards or fools, more or less.   This one seems to be one
o' the fools.   I 've seed sitch critters before.   They keep
fillin' their little boxes wi' grass an' stuff, an' never makes
any use of it that I could see.   But every man to his
taste.   I 'll be bound he 's a good enough feller when ye
come to know him an' git over yer contempt for his idle
ways.   Very likely he draws, too—an' plays the flute;
most o' these furriners do.   Come now, Flinders, look
alive wi' the grub."

When the stranger returned to the fire he spread his
huge hands over it and rubbed them with apparent satisfaction.

"Fat a goot t'ing is supper!" he remarked, with a
benignant look all round; "the very smell of him be
deliciowse!"

"An' no mistake!" added Flinders.   "Sure, the half
o' the good o' victuals would be lost av they had no smell."

"Where have you come from, stranger?" asked Bevan,
as they were about to begin supper.

"From de Sawbuk Hills," answered the botanist,
filling his mouth with an enormous mass of dried meat.

"Ay, indeed!   That 's just where *we* are goin' to,"
returned Bevan.

"An' vere may you be come from?" asked the stranger.

"From Simpson's Gully," said Fred.

"Ha! how cooriouse!   Dat be joost vere I be go to."

The conversation flagged a little at this point as they
warmed to the work of feeding; but after a little it was
resumed, and then their visitor gradually ingratiated
himself with his new friends to such an extent that the
suspicions of Fred and Flinders were somewhat, though
not altogether, allayed.   At last they became sufficiently
confidential to inform the stranger of their object in going
to the Sawback Hills.

K

"Ha! vat is dat you say?" he exclaimed, with well-feigned surprise; "von yoong man carried avay by Ridskins. I saw'd dem! Did pass dem not longe ago. T'ree mans carry von man. I t'ink him a sick comrade, but now I reklect hims face vas vhitish."

"Could ye guide us to the place where ye met them?" asked Bevan, quickly.

The botanist did not reply at once, but seemed to consider.

"Vell, I has not moche time to spare; but, come, I has pity for you, an' don't mind if I goes out of de vay to help you. I vill go back to the Sawbuk Hills so far as need be."

"Thank'ee kindly," returned Bevan, who possessed a grateful spirit; "I'll think better of yer grass-gatherin' after this, though it does puzzle me awful to make out what's the use ye put it to. If you kep' tame rabbits, now, I could understand it, but to carry it about in a green box an' go squeezin' it between the leaves o' books, as I've seed some of 'ee do, seems to me the most out-rageous—"

"Ha, ha!" interrupted the botanist, with a loud laugh; "you is not the first what t'ink hims nonsense. But you mus' know dere be moche sense in it"—(he looked very grave and wise here)—"very moche. First, ve finds him; den ve squeezes an' dries him; den ve sticks him in von book, an' names him; den ve talks about him; oh! dere is moche use in him, very moche!"

"Well, but arter you've found, an' squeezed, an' dried, an' stuck, an' named, an' talked about him," repeated Paul, with a slight look of contempt, "what the better are ye for it all?"

"Vy, ve is moche de better," returned the botanist, "for den ve tries to find out all about him. Ve magnifies

BETTY AND TOLLY TAKEN PRISONERS.

him, an' writes vat ve zee about him, an' compares him vid oders of de same family, an' boils, an' stews, an' fries, an' melts, an' dissolves, an' mixes him, till ve gits somet'ing out of him."

"It's little I'd expect to git out of him after tratin' him so badly," remarked Flinders, whose hunger was gradually giving way before the influence of venison steaks.

"True, me frund," returned the stranger, "it is ver' leetil ve gits ; but den dat leetil is ver' goot—valooable you calls it."

"Humph!" ejaculated Bevan, with an air that betokened doubt.   Flinders and Fred said nothing, but the latter felt more than ever inclined to believe that their guest was a deceiver, and resolved to watch him narrowly. On his part, the stranger seemed to perceive that Fred suspected him, but he was not rendered less hearty or free-and-easy on that account.

In the course of conversation Paul chanced to refer to Betty.

"Ah! me frund," said the stranger, "has you brought you's vife to dis vile contry ?"

"No, I haven't," replied Paul, bluntly.

"Oh, pardon.   I did t'ink you spoke of Bettie; an' surely dat is vooman's name ?"

"Ay, but Betty's my darter, not my wife," returned Paul, who resented this inquisition with regard to his private affairs.

"Is you not 'fraid," said the botanist, quietly helping himself to a marrow-bone, "to leave you's darter at Simpson's Gully ?"

"Who told you I left her there ?" asked Bevan, with increasing asperity.

"Oh! I only t'ink so, as you's come from dere."

"An' why should I be afraid ?"

"Because, me frund, de contry be full ob scoundrils."

"Yes, an' you are one of the biggest of them," thought Fred Westly, but he kept his thoughts to himself, while Paul muttered something about being well protected and having no occasion to be afraid.

Perceiving the subject to be distasteful, the stranger quickly changed it. Soon afterwards each man, rolling himself in his blanket, went to sleep—or appeared to do so. In regard to Paddy Flinders, at least, there could be no doubt, for the trombone-tones of his nose were eloquent. Paul, too, lay on his back with eyes tight shut and mouth wide open, while the regular heaving of his broad chest told that his slumbers were deep. But more than once Fred Westly raised his head gently and looked suspiciously round. At last, in his case also, tired Nature asserted herself, and his deep regular breathing proved that the "sweet restorer" was at work, though an occasional movement showed that his sleep was not so profound as that of his comrades.

The big botanist remained perfectly motionless from the time he lay down, as if the sleep of infancy had passed with him into the period of manhood. It was not till the fire had died completely down, and the moon had set, leaving only the stars to make darkness visible, that he moved. He did so, not as a sleeper awaking, but with the slow stealthy action of one who is already wide awake and has a purpose in view.

Gradually his huge shoulders rose till he rested on his left elbow.

A sense of danger, which had never left him even while he slept, aroused Fred, but he did not lose his self-possession. He carefully watched, from the other side of the extinct fire, the motions of the stranger, and lay perfectly still—only tightening his grasp on the knife-handle that he had been instinctively holding when he dropped asleep.

The night was too dark for Fred to distinguish the man's features. He could only perceive the outline of his black figure, and that for some time he rested on his elbow without moving, as if he were contemplating the stars. Despite his efforts to keep awake, Fred felt that drowsiness was again slowly but surely overcoming him. Maintaining the struggle, however, he kept his dreamy eyes riveted on their guest until he seemed to swell into gigantic proportions.

Presently Fred was again thoroughly aroused by observing that the right arm of the man moved slowly upwards, and something like a knife appeared in the hand; he even fancied he saw it gleam, though there was not light enough to render that possible.

Feeling restrained, as if under the horrible influence of nightmare, Fred lay there spell-bound and quite unable to move, until he perceived the stranger's form bend over in the direction of Paul Bevan, who lay on the other side of him.

Then, indeed, Fred's powers returned. Shouting, "Look out, Paul!" he sprang up, drew his bowie-knife, and leaped over the blackened logs, but, to his surprise and confusion, found that the stranger lay extended on the ground as if sound asleep. He roused himself, however, and sat up, as did the others, on hearing Fred's shout.

"Fat is wrong, yoong man?" he inquired, with a look of sleepy surprise.

"Ye may well ax that, sor," said Flinders, staggering to his feet and seizing his axe, which always lay handy at his side. Paul had glanced round sharply, like a man inured to danger, but seeing nothing to alarm him, had remained in a sitting position.

"Why, Westly, you've been dreaming," he said with a broad grin.

"So I must have been," returned the youth, looking very much ashamed, "but you've no notion what a horrible dream I had. It seemed so real, too, that I could not help jumping up and shouting. Pardon me, comrades, and, as bad boys say when caught in mischief, 'I won't do it again!'"

"Ve pardon you, by all means," said the botanist, stretching himself and yawning, "and ve do so vid de more pleasure for you has rouse us in time for start on de joorney."

"You're about right. It's time we was off," said Paul, rising slowly to his feet and looking round the horizon and up at the sky, while he proceeded to fill a beloved little black pipe, which invariably constituted his preliminary little breakfast.

Pat Flinders busied himself in blowing up the embers of the fire.

A slight and rapidly eaten meal sufficed to prepare these hardy backwoodsmen for their journey, and, long before daybreak illumined the plains, they were far on their way towards the Sawback mountain range.

During the journey of two days which this trip involved the botanist seemed to change his character to some extent. He became silent—almost morose; did not encourage the various efforts made by his companions to draw him into conversation, and frequently rode alone in advance of the party, or occasionally fell behind them.

The day after the stranger had joined them, as they were trotting slowly over the plains that lay between the Rangers Hill and the Sawbacks, Fred rode close up

to Bevan, and said in a low voice, glancing at the
botanist, who was in advance—

"I am convinced, Paul, that he is a scoundrel."

"That may be so, Mr. Fred, but what then?"

"Why, then I conclude that he is deceiving us for
some purpose of his own."

"Nonsense," replied Bevan, who was apt to express
himself bluntly, "what purpose can he serve in deceiving
strangers like us? We carry no gold-dust, and have
nothing worth robbing us of, even if he were fool enough
to think of attemptin' such a thing. Then, he can
scarcely be deceivin' us in sayin' that he met three Redskins carryin' off a white man—an' what good could it do
him if he is? Besides, he is goin' out of his way to sarve
us."

"It is impossible for me to answer your questions,
Paul, but I understand enough of both French and
German to know that his broken English is a mere sham
—a mixture, and a bad one too, of what no German or
Frenchman would use—so it's not likely to be the sort of
bad English that a Swede would speak. Moreover, I have
caught him once or twice using English words correctly at
one time and wrongly at another. No, you may depend on
it that, whatever his object may be, he is deceiving us."

"It's mesilf as agrees wid ye, sor," said Flinders, who
had been listening attentively to the conversation. "The
man's no more a Swede than an Irishman, but what can
we do wid oursilves? True or false, he's ladin' us in the
diriction we want to go, an' it would do no good to say
to him, 'Ye spalpeen, yer decavin' of us,' for he'd only
say he wasn't; or may be he'd cut up rough an' lave us
—but, after all, it might be the best way to push him up
to that."

"I think not," said Bevan. "Doesn't English law say

that a man should be held innocent till he's proved guilty?"

"It's little I know or care about English law," answered Flinders, "but I'm sure enough that Irish law howlds a bad man to be guilty till he's proved innocent—at laste av it dosn't it should."

"You'd better go an' pump him a bit, Mr. Fred," said Bevan; "we're close up to the Sawback range; another hour an' we'll be among the mountains.

They were turning round the spur of a little hillock as he spoke. Before Fred could reply a small deer sprang from its lair, cast on the intruders one startled gaze, and then bounded gracefully into the bush, too late, however, to escape from Bevan's deadly rifle. It had barely gone ten yards when a sharp crack was heard; the animal sprang high into the air, and fell dead upon the ground.

"Bad luck to ye, Bevan!" exclaimed Flinders, who had also taken aim at it, but not with sufficient speed, "isn't that always the way ye do?—plucks the baste out o' me very hand. Sure I had me sights lined on it as straight as could be; wan second more an' I'd have sent a bullet right into its brain, when *crack!* ye go before me. Och! it's onkind, to say the laste of it. Why cudn't ye gi' me a chance?"

"I'm sorry, Flinders, but I couldn't well help it. The critter rose right in front o' me."

"Vat a goot shote you is!" exclaimed the botanist, riding back to them and surveying the prostrate deer through his blue spectacles.

"Ay, and it's a lucky shot too," said Fred, "for our provisions are running low. But perchance we shan't want much more food before reaching the Indian camp. You said, I think, that you have a good guess where the camp lies, Mister—what shall we call you?"

"Call me vat you please," returned the stranger, with a peculiar smile; "I is not partickler. Some of me frunds calls me Mr. Botaniste."

"Well Mr. Botanist, the camp cannot be far off now, an' it seems to me that we should have overtaken men travelling on foot by this time."

"Ve vill surely come on de tracks dis naight or de morrow," replied the botanist, riding forward, after Bevan had secured the carcass of the deer to his saddlebow, "bot ve must have patience, yoong blood be alvays too hote. All in goot time."

With this reply Fred was fain to content himself, for no amount of pressure availed to draw anything more satisfactory out of their strange guide.

Before sunset they had penetrated some distance into the Sawback range, and then proceeded to make their encampment for the night under the spreading branches of a lordly pine.

CHAPTER XIII.

TABLES are frequently turned in this world in more senses than one. As was said in the last chapter, the romantic pair who were in search of the Indians did not find those for whom they sought, but, as fickle fortune willed it, those for whom they sought found *them*. It happened thus.

Soon after the Rose of Oregon and her young champion, with their captors, had passed through the Long Gap, crossed the plain, and entered the Sawback Hills, they fell in with a band of twenty Indians, who from their appearance and costume evidently belonged to the same tribe as their captors. From the manner in which they met, also, it seemed that they had been in search of each other, and had something interesting to communicate, for they gesticulated much, pointed frequently to the sky, and to various directions of the compass, chattered excitedly, showed their brilliant teeth in fitful gleams, and glittered quite awfully about the eyes.

They paid little attention at first to their prisoners, who remained sitting on their steeds looking on with interest and some anxiety.

" O Betty, what would I not give to have my arms free just now ! What a chance it would be for a bold dash and a glorious run !"

" You 'd make little of it on such rough ground, Tolly."

"Pooh! I'd try it on any ground. Just fancy, I'd begin with a clear leap over that chief's head—the one there wi' the feathers an' the long nose that's makin' such hideous faces—then away up the glen, over the stones, down the hollows, shoutin' like mad, an' clearin' the brooks and precipices with a band o' yellin' Redskins at my tail! Isn't it enough to drive a fellow wild to be on the brink of such a chance an' miss it? I say, haven't you got a penknife in your pocket—no? Not even a pair o' scissors? Why, I thought you women never travelled without scissors."

"Alas! Tolly, I have not even scissors; besides, if I had, it would take me at least two minutes with all the strength of my fingers to cut the thongs that bind you with scissors, and I don't think the Redskins would stand quietly by and look on while I did it. But what say you to *me* trying it by myself?"

"Quite useless," returned Tolly. "You'd be caught at once—or break your neck. And you'd never get on, you know, without me. No, no, we've got fairly into a fix, an' I don't see my way out of it. If my hands were free we might attempt anything, but what can a fellow do when tied up in this fashion?"

"He can submit, Tolly, and wait patiently."

Tolly did not feel inclined to submit, and was not possessed of much patience, but he was too fond of Betty to answer flippantly. He therefore let his feelings escape through the safety-valve of a great sigh, and relapsed into pensive silence.

Meanwhile the attention of the band of savages was attracted to another small band of natives which approached them from the eastward. That these were also friends was evident from the fact that the larger band made no hostile demonstration, but quietly awaited the coming up of the others. The new-comers were three in number, and two of them bore on their shoulders what appeared to be the body of a man wrapped up in a blanket.

"They've got a wounded comrade with them, I think," said little Trevor.

"So it would seem," replied Betty, with a dash of pity in her tone, for she was powerfully sympathetic.

The savages laid the form in the blanket on the ground, and began to talk earnestly with their comrades.

"It's not dead yet, anyhow," remarked Tolly, "for I see it move. I wonder whether it is a man or a woman. Mayhap it's their old grandmother they're giving a little exercise to. I've heard that some o' the Redskins are affectionate sort o' fellows, though most of 'em are hard enough on the old folk."

As he spoke he looked up in Betty's face. Just as he did so a startling change came over that face. It suddenly became ashy pale, the large eyes dilated to their utmost extent, and the mouth opened with a short gasp.

In great alarm the boy turned his eyes in the direction in which the girl gazed so fixedly, and then his own visage assumed a somewhat similar appearance as he beheld the pale, thin, cadaverous countenance of his friend Tom Brixton, from off which a corner of the blanket had just slipped. But for the slight motion above referred to Tom might have been mistaken for a dead man, for his eyes were closed and his lips bloodless.

Uttering a sudden shout, Tolly Trevor flung himself headlong off the pony and tried to get on his feet, but failed, owing to his hands being tied behind him. Betty also leaped to the ground, and, running to where Tom lay, went down on her knees and raised his head in her hands.

The poor youth, being roused, opened his eyes. They were terribly sunken and large, but when they met those of Betty they enlarged to an extent that seemed positively awful, and a ,faint tinge of colour came to his hollow cheeks.

"Betty!" he whispered; "can—can it be possible?"

"Yes, it is I! Surely God must have sent me to save your life!"

"I fear not, dear—"

He stopped abruptly and shut his eyes. For a few moments it seemed as if he were dead, but presently he opened them again, and said, faintly, "It is too late, I fear. You are very kind, but I—I feel so terribly weak that I think I am dying."

By this time Tolly, having managed to get on his feet, stood beside his friend, on whom he gazed with intense anxiety. Even the Indians were solemnised by what appeared to be a death-scene.

"Have you been wounded?" asked the girl, quickly.

"No; *only* starved!" returned Tom, a slight smile of humour flickering for a second on his pale face even in that hour of his extremity.

"Have the Indians given you anything to eat since they found you?"

"They have tried to, but what they offered me was dry and tough; I could not get it down."

The girl rose promptly. "Tolly, fetch me some water and make a fire. Quick!" she said, and going up to an Indian, coolly drew from its sheath his scalping-knife, with which she cut Tolly's bonds. The savage evidently believed that such a creature could not possibly do evil, for he made no motion whatever to check her. Then, without a word more, she went to the saddle-bags on the obstinate horse, and, opening one of them, took out some soft sugar. The savage who held the horse made no objection. Indeed, from that moment the whole band stood silently by observing the pretty maiden and the active boy as they moved about, regardless of everything but the work in hand.

The Rose of Oregon constituted herself a sick-nurse on that occasion with marvellous facility. True, she knew nothing whatever about the duties of a sick-nurse or a doctor, for her father was one of those fortunate men who are never ill, but her native tact and energy sufficed. It was not her nature to stand by inactive when anything urgent had to be done. If she knew not what to do, and no one else did, she was sure to attempt something. Whether sugar-and-water was the best food for a starving man she knew not, but she did know—at least she thought—that the starvation ought to be checked without delay.

"Here, Mr. Brixton, sip a little of this," she said, going down on her knees, and putting a tin mug to the patient's mouth.

Poor Tom would have sipped prussic acid cheerfully from *her* hand ! He obeyed, and seemed to like it.

"Now, a little more."

"God bless you, dear girl !" murmured Tom, as he sipped a little more.

"There, that will do you good till I can prepare something better."

She rose and ran to the fire which Tolly had already blown up almost to furnace heat.

"I filled the kettle, for I knew you 'd want it," said the boy, turning up his fiery-red visage for a moment, "It can't be long o' boiling with such a blaze below it."

He stooped again and continued to blow while Betty cut some dried meat into small pieces. Soon these were boiled, and the resulting soup was devoured by the starving man with a zest that he had never before experienced.

"Nectar!" he exclaimed faintly, smiling as he raised his eyes to Betty's face.

"But you must not take too much at a time," she said, gently drawing away the mug.

Tom submitted patiently. He would have submitted to anything patiently just then!

During these proceedings the Indians, who seemed to be amiably disposed, looked on with solemn interest, and then, coming apparently to the conclusion that they might as well accommodate themselves to circumstances, they quietly made use of Tolly's fire to cook a meal for themselves.

This done, one of them—a noble-looking savage, who, to judge from his bearing and behaviour, was evidently their chief—went up to Betty, and, with a stately bend of the head, said, in broken English, "White woman git on horse!"

"And what are you going to do with this man?" asked Betty, pointing to the prostrate form of Tom.

"Unaco will him take care," briefly replied the chief (meaning himself), while with a wave of his hand he turned away and went to Tolly, whom he ordered to mount the pony, which he styled the "littil horse."

The boy was not slow to obey, for he was by that time quite convinced that his only chance of being allowed to have his hands left free lay in prompt submission. Any lurking thought that might have remained of making a grand dash for liberty was effectually quelled by a big savage, who quietly took hold of the pony's rein and led it away. Another Indian led Betty's horse. Then the original three who had found Tom took him up quite gently and carried him off, while the remainder of the band followed in single file. Unaco led the way, striding over the ground at a rate which almost forced the pony to trot, and glancing from side to side with a keen look of inquiry that seemed to intimate an expectation of attack from an enemy in ambush.

But if any such enemy existed he was careful not to show himself, and the Indian band passed through the defiles and fastnesses of the Sawback Hills unmolested until the shades of evening began to descend.

Then, on turning round a jutting rock that obstructed the view up a mountain gorge, Unaco stopped abruptly and held up his hand. This brought the band to a sudden halt, and the chief, apparently sinking on his knees, seemed to melt into the bushes. In a few minutes he returned with a look of stern resolve on his well-formed countenance.

" He has discovered something o' some sort, I—"

Tolly's remark to his fair companion was cut short by the point of a keen knife touching his side, which caused him to end with " hallo !"

The savage who held his bridle gave him a significant look that said, " Silence !"

After holding a brief whispered conversation with several of his braves, the chief advanced to Betty and said—

" White man's in the bush. Does white woman know why ?"

Betty at once thought of her father and his companions, and said—

" I have not seen the white men. How can I tell why they are here ? Let me ride forward and look at them—then I shall be able to speak."

A very slight smile of contempt curled the chief's lip for an instant as he replied—

THROUGH THE DEFILES OF THE SAWBACK HILLS.—Page 160.

"No. The white woman see them when they be trapped. Unaco knows one. He is black—a devil with two face—many face, but Unaco's eyes be sharp. They see far."

So saying, he turned and gave some directions to his warriors, who at once scattered themselves among the underwood and disappeared. Ordering the Indians who carried Tom Brixton to follow him, and the riders to bring up the rear, he continued to advance up the gorge.

"A devil with two faces!" muttered Tolly; "that must be a queer sort o' beast. I *have* heard of a critter called a Tasmanian devil, but never before heard of an Oregon one with two faces."

An expressive glance from the Indian who guarded him induced the lad to continue his speculations in silence.

On passing round the jutting rock, where Unaco had been checked in his advance, the party at once beheld the cause of anxiety. Close to the track they were following were seen four men busily engaged in making arrangements to encamp for the night.

It need scarcely be said that these were our friends Paul Bevan, Fred Westly, Flinders, and the botanist.

The moment that these caught sight of the approaching party they sprang to their arms, which of course lay handy, for in those regions, at the time we write of, the law of might was in the ascendant. The appearance and conduct of Unaco, however, deceived them, for that wily savage advanced towards them with an air of confidence and candour which went far to remove suspicion, and when, on drawing nearer, he threw down his knife and tomahawk, and held up his empty hands, their suspicions were entirely dispelled.

"They're not likely to be onfriendly," observed Flinders,

" for there's only five o' them altogither, an' wan o' them's only a bit of a boy an' another looks uncommon like a wo—"

He had got thus far when he was checked by Paul Bevan's exclaiming, with a look of intense surprise, " Why, that's Betty !—or her ghost !"

Flinders's astonishment was too profound to escape in many words. He only gave vent to " Musha ! there's Tolly !" and let his lower jaw drop.

" Yes, it's me an' the Beautiful Nugget," cried Tolly, jumping off the pony and running to assist the Nugget to dismount, while the bearers of Tom Brixton laid him on the ground, removed the blanket, and revealed his face.

The exclamations of surprise would no doubt have been redoubled at this sight if the power of exclamation had not been for the time destroyed. The sham botanist in particular was considerably puzzled, for he at once recognised Tom and also Betty, whom he had previously known. Of course he did not know Tolly Trevor ; still less did he know that Tolly knew *him !*

Unaco himself was somewhat surprised at the mutual recognitions, though his habitual self-restraint enabled him to conceal every trace of emotion. Moreover, he was well aware that he could not afford to lose time in the development of his little plot. Taking advantage, therefore, of the surprise which had rendered every one for the moment more or less confused, he gave a sharp signal which was well understood by his friends in the bush.

Instantly, and before Tolly or Betty could warn their friends of what was coming, the surrounding foliage parted, as if by magic, and a circle of yelling and painted Redskins sprang upon the white men. Resistance was utterly out of the question. They were overwhelmed as if by a cataract, and, almost before they could realise what had happened, the arms of all the men were pinioned behind them.

At that trying hour little Tolly Trevor proved himself to be more of a man than most of his friends had hitherto given him credit for.

The savages, regarding him as a weak little boy, had paid no attention to him, but confined their efforts to the overcoming of the powerful and by no means submissive men with whom they had to deal.

Tolly's first impulse was to rush to the rescue of Paul Bevan; but he was remarkably quick-witted, and, when on the point of springing, observed that no tomahawk was wielded or knife drawn. Suddenly grasping the wrist of Betty, who had also naturally felt the impulse to succour her father, he exclaimed—

"Stop! Betty. They don't mean murder. You an' I can do nothing against so many. Keep quiet; p'r'aps they'll leave us alone.

As he spoke a still deeper idea flashed into his little brain. To the surprise of Betty, he suddenly threw his arms round her waist and clung to her as if for protection with a look of fear in his face, and when the work of binding the captives was completed the Indians found him still labouring to all appearance under great alarm. Unaco cast on him one look of supreme scorn, and then, leaving him, like Betty, unbound, turned towards Paul Bevan.

"The white man is one of wicked band?" he said, in his broken English.

"I don't know what ye mean, Redskin," replied Paul; "but speak your own tongue, I understand it well enough to talk with ye."

The Indian repeated the question in his native language, and Paul, replying in the same, said—

"No, Redskin, I belong to no band, either wicked or good."

"How come you, then, to be in company with this man?" demanded the Indian.

In reply Paul gave a correct account of the cause and object of his being there, explained that the starving man before them was the friend for whom he sought, that Betty was his daughter, though how she came to be there beat his comprehension entirely, and that the botanist was a stranger, whose name even he did not yet know.

"It is false," returned the chief. "The white man speaks with a forked tongue. He is one of the murderers who have slain my wife and my child."

A dark fierce frown passed over the chief's countenance as he spoke, but it was quickly replaced by the habitual look of calm gravity.

"What can stop me," he said, reverting again to English as he turned and addressed Betty, "from killing you as my wife was killed by white man?"

"My God can stop you," answered the girl, in a steady voice, though her heart beat fast and her face was very pale.

"Your God!" exclaimed the savage. "Will your God defend the wicked?"

"No, but He will pardon the wicked who come to Him in the name of Jesus, and He will defend the innocent."

"Innocent!" repeated Unaco, vehemently, as he turned and pointed to the botanist. "Does you call *this* man innocent?"

"I know nothing about that man," returned the girl, earnestly; "but I do know that my father and I, and all the rest of us, are innocent of any crime against you."

For a few seconds the savage chief gazed steadily at Betty, then turning towards the botanist, he took a step towards the spot where he sat and looked keenly into his face.

The botanist returned the gaze with equal steadiness through his blue spectacles.

CHAPTER XIV.

" THE big man with the blue glass eyes is a villain,"
said the Indian chief, after a long scrutiny of
the botanist's countenance.

"So some of my mistaken friends have thought,"
returned the man, speaking for the first time in his
natural voice, which caused a thrill to pass through Paul
Bevan's frame.

"He is a thief," continued the chief, still gazing
steadily at the blue glasses, "and a murderer !"

"He's all that, and liar and deceiver into the bargain,"
thought Tolly Trevor, but Tolly did not speak ; he only
vented his feelings in a low chuckle, for he saw, or thought
he saw, that the robber's career was about to receive a
check.   As the thought passed through his brain, however, he observed from the position in which he stood
that Stalker—for, as the reader has doubtless perceived,
it was he—was working his hands about in a very soft,
slow, mysterious, and scarcely observable manner.

"Oho !" thought Tolly, "is that your little game ?
Ha ! I 'll spoil it for you !"

He quietly took up a piece of firewood and began, as
it were, to amuse himself therewith.

"You has many faces, many colours," continued Unaco,
"and too many eyes."

At the last word he plucked the blue glasses off the
botanist's nose and flung them into the fire.

A TALE OF THE OREGON GOLDFIELDS.

"My enemy!" gasped Paul Bevan, turning first very pale and then very red, as he glared like a chained tiger at his foe.

"You knows him *now?*" said Unaco, turning abruptly to Paul.

"Yes; *I* knows him!"

"The white man with the forked tongue say jus' now he *not* knows him."

"Ay, Redskin, an' I said the truth, for he's a rare deceiver—always has been—an' can pass himself off for a'most anything. I knows him as my mortal foe. Cast my hands loose an' give me a knife an' you shall see."

"O father! your promise—remember!" exclaimed Betty.

"True, dear lass, true; I forgot," returned Paul, with a humbled look; "yet it *is* hard for a man to see him there, grinning like a big baboon, an' keep his hands off him."

During this dialogue the Indians looked from one speaker to another with keen interest, although none but their chief understood a word of what was said; and Stalker took advantage of their attention being turned for the moment from himself to carry out what Tolly had styled his "little game," all unaware that the boy was watching him like a lynx.

Among other shifts and devices with which the robber chief had become familiar, he had learned the conjuror's method of so arranging his limbs while being bound, that he could untie his bonds in a marvellous manner. On the present occasion, however, he had been tied by men who were expert in the use of deerskin thongs, and he found some difficulty in loosening them without attracting attention, but he succeeded at last. He had been secured only by the wrists and forearms, and remained sitting still a few seconds after he was absolutely free ; then, seizing what he believed to be his opportunity, he leapt up, dashed the Indian nearest him to the earth, and sprang like a deer towards the bushes.

But Tolly Trevor was ready for him. That daring youth plunged right in front of the big botanist and stooped. Stalker tripped over him and came violently to the ground on his forehead and nose. Before he could rise Tolly had jumped up, and swinging his billet of wood once in the air, brought it down with all his little might on the robber's crown. It sufficed to stupefy him, and when he recovered he found himself in the close embrace of three muscular Redskins.

"Well done, Tolly Trevor!" shouted Paul Bevan, enthusiastically.

Even Tom Brixton, who had been looking on in a state of inexpressible surprise, managed to utter a feeble cheer.

But the resources of the robber were not yet exhausted. Finding himself in the grasp of overwhelming numbers, he put forth all his strength, as if to make a final effort, and then, suddenly collapsing, dropped limp and helpless to the ground, as a man does when he is stabbed to the heart.

The savages knew the symptoms well—too well! They rose, breathless, and each looked inquiringly at the other, as though to say, "Who did the deed?" Before they discovered that the deed had not been done at all, Stalker sprang up, knocked down two of them, overturned the third, and, bounding into the bushes, was out of sight in a few seconds.

The whole band, of course, went yelling after him, except their chief, who stood with an angry scowl upon his visage, and awaited the return of his braves.

One by one they came back panting and discomfited, for the white robber had outrun them all and got clear away.

"Well, now, it was cliverly done," remarked Paddy Flinders, finding his tongue at last; "an' I raly can't but feel that he desarves to git off this time. All the same I hope he 'll be nabbed at last an' recaive his due—bad luck to him !"

"Now, Redskin—" began Bevan.

"My name is Unaco," interrupted the chief, with a look of dignity.

"Well, then, Unaco," continued Bevan, "since ye must see that we have nothing whatever to do wi' the blackguard that's just given ye the slip, I hope you 'll see your way to untie our hands an' let us go."

"You may not belong to that man's band," answered the chief, in his own tongue, "but you are a white man, and by white men I have been robbed of my wife and child. Your lives are forfeited. You shall be slaves to those whom you call Redskins, and this girl with the sunny hair shall replace the lost one in my wigwam."

Without deigning to listen to a reply, Unaco turned and gave orders to his men, who at once brought up the horse and pony, set Betty and Tolly thereon, lifted Tom Brixton on their shoulders as before, and resumed their march deeper into the fastnesses of the Sawback Hills.

It was growing rapidly dark as they advanced, but the chief who led the party was intimately acquainted with every foot of the way, and as the moon rose before daylight had quite disappeared, they were enabled to continue their journey by night.

"No doubt," remarked Fred Westly to Paul, who was permitted to walk beside him, though Flinders was obliged to walk behind—"no doubt the chief fears that

Stalker will pursue him when he is rejoined by his robber band, and wants to get well out of his way."

"Very likely," returned Bevan ; "an' it's my opinion that he'll find some more of his tribe hereabouts, in which case Master Stalker and his blackguards will have pretty stiff work cut out for them."

"What think you of the threat of the chief to take Betty to be one of his wives ?" asked Fred.

"Well, I don't think he'll do it."

"Why not?"

"Because I've got a hold over him that he's not aware of just yet."

"What is that, and why did you not make use of it just now to prevent our being needlessly led farther into these mountains ?" asked Fred, in surprise.

"What the hold is," returned Bevan, "you shall know at supper-time. The reason why I didn't make use of it sooner is that, on the whole, I think it better to stick by the Redskins yet awhile—first, because if Stalker should look for us, as he's sartin sure to do, we would not be strong enough to fight him in the open ; and, secondly, because poor Tom Brixton needs rest, and he has more chance o' that, in the circumstances, wi' the Redskins than he could have with us while being hunted by robbers ; and, lastly, because Betty would come to grief if she fell into that villain Stalker's hands just now."

While Paul and Fred were thus conversing, the Rose of Oregon and her little protector rode silently beside each other, buried, apparently, in profound thought.

At last Tolly raised his head and voice.

"Betty," said he, "what a lucky thing it was that we fell in wi' Tom Brixton, and that you were able to give him somethin' to eat."

"Yes, thank God," replied the girl, fervently.

"He'd have died but for you," said the boy.

"And you, Tolly," added Betty.

"Well, yes, I did have a finger in the pie," returned the boy, with a self-satisfied air; "but I say, Betty," he added, becoming suddenly serious, "what d'ye think o' what that rascally chief said about takin' you to his wigwam? You know that means he intends to make you his wife."

"Yes, I know; but God will deliver me," answered the girl.

"How d'ye know that?"

"Because I put my trust in Him."

"Oh! but," returned the boy, with a slight look of surprise, "unless God works a miracle I don't see how He can deliver us from the Redskins, and you know He doesn't work miracles nowadays."

"I'm not so sure of that," replied the girl. "More than once I have seen a man who had been nearly all his life given to drinking, fighting, thieving, and swearing, and every sort of wickedness, surrender himself body and soul to Jesus Christ, so that he afterwards gave up all his evil ways, and led a pure and peaceable life, trying not only to serve God himself, but doing his best to bring his old companions to the same state of mind. What would you call that, Tolly?"

"Well, I'm bound to say it's as near a miracle as can be, if not one altogether. But in what way do you think God will deliver you just now?"

"That I cannot tell; but I know this, it is written in His Word that those who put their trust in Him shall never be confounded, and I have put my trust in Him. He will never forsake me."

"I wish I had as strong faith as you, Betty," said the boy, with a grave look.

"You may have it—and stronger than I have, for faith is the gift of God, and we shall get it, not in proportion to our trying to get it, or to our trying to rouse it, or to our working for it, but according as we *ask* for it. The Holy Spirit can work anything in us and by us, and *He* is promised to those who merely ask in the name of Jesus. Ah! Tolly, have I not often told you this, that in God's Word it is written, 'Ye have not because ye ask not'?"

While these two were yet speaking, the chief called a halt, and, after a brief consultation with some of his braves, ordered the band to encamp for the night.

Soon the camp fires were lighted under the spreading trees, and their bright blaze and myriad sparks converted the gloomy forest into a brilliant banqueting hall, in which, unlike civilised halls, the decorations were fresh and natural, and the atmosphere was pure.

There were at least six camp-fires, each with its circle of grave red warriors, its roasting steaks and its bubbling kettle, in which latter was boiled a rich mixture of dried meat and flour. Some of the Indians stood conversing in low tones, their faces ruddy with the brilliant blaze and their backs as black as the surrounding background. Others lay at length on the ground or squatted thereon, placidly smoking their calumets, or the little iron pipes which formed part of the heads of their tomahawks, or tending the steaks and kettles. To an observer outside the circle of light the whole scene was intensely vivid and picturesque, for the groups, being at different distances, were varied in size, and the intense light that shone on those nearest the fires shed a softer glow on those who were more distant, while on the few Indians who moved about in search of firewood it cast a pale light which barely sufficed to distinguish them from surrounding darkness.

Paul Bevan and his friends occupied a fire by themselves, the only native who stood beside them being Unaco. It is probable that the savage chief constituted himself their guard in order to make quite sure of them, for the escape of Stalker weighed heavily on his mind. To secure this end more effectively, and at the same time enable the captives to feed themselves, the right arm of each was freed, while the left was tied firmly to his body. Of course, Betty and Tom Brixton were left altogether unbound.

"I feel uncommon lopsided goin' about in this one-armed fashion," remarked Paul, as he turned the stick on which his supper was roasting. "Couldn't ye make up yer mind to trust us, Unaco? I'd promise for myself an' friends that we wouldn't attempt to cut away like that big thief Stalker."

The chief, who sat a little apart near the farther end of the blazing pile of logs, smoking his pipe in motionless gravity, took not the slightest notice.

"Arrah! howld yer tongue, Paul," said Flinders, who made so much use of his one arm, in stirring the kettle, turning a roasting venison rib, and arranging the fire, that it seemed as if he were in full possession of two; "why d'ye disturb his majesty? Don't ye see that he's meditatin', or suthin' o' that sort—maybe about his forefathers?"

"Well, well, I hope his aftermothers won't have many sulky ones like him," returned Paul, rather crossly. "It's quite impossible to cut up a steak wi' one hand, so here goes i' the next best fashion."

He took up the steak in his fingers, and was about to tear off a mouthful with his teeth, when Betty came to the rescue.

"Stay, father; I'll cut it into little bits for you if Unaco will kindly lend me his scalping-knife."

Without a word or look the chief quietly drew the glittering weapon from its sheath and handed it to Betty, who at once, using a piece of sharpened stick as a fork, cut her father's ·portion into manageable lumps.

"That's not a bad notion," said Fred. "Perhaps you'll do the same for me, Betty."

"With pleasure, Mr. Westly."

"Ah, now, av it wouldn't be axin' too much, might I make so bowld—"

Flinders did not finish the sentence, but laid his pewter plate before the Rose of Oregon with a significant smile.

"I'm glad to be so unexpectedly useful," said Betty, with a laugh.

When she had thus aided her half-helpless companions, Betty returned the knife to its owner, who received it with a dignified inclination of the head. She then filled a mug with soup, and went to Tom, who lay on a deer-skin robe, gazing at her in rapt admiration, and wondering when he was going to awake out of this most singular dream, for, in his weak condition, he had taken to disbelieving all that he saw.

"And yet it can't well be a dream," he murmured, with a faint smile, as the girl knelt by his side, "for I never dreamed anything half so real. What is this—soup?"

"Yes; try to take a little. It will do you good, with God's blessing."

"Ah, yes, with God's blessing," repeated the poor youth, earnestly. "You know what that means, Betty, and—and—I *think* I am beginning to understand it."

Betty made no reply, but a feeling of profound gladness crept into her heart.

When she returned to the side of her father she found

that he had finished supper, and was just beginning to use his pipe.

"When are you going to tell me, Paul, about the—the —subject we were talking of on our way here?" asked Fred, who was still devoting much of his attention to a deer's rib.

"I'll tell ye now," answered Paul, with a short glance at the Indian chief, who still sat, profoundly grave, in the dreamland of smoke. "There's no time like after supper for a good pipe an' a good story—not that what I'm goin' to tell ye is much of a story either, but it's true, if that adds vally to it, an' it'll be short. It's about a brave young Indian I once had the luck to meet with. His name was Oswego."

At the sound of the name Unaco cast a sharp glance at Bevan. It was so swift that no one present observed it save Bevan himself, who had expected it. But Paul pretended not to notice it, and turning himself rather more towards Fred, addressed himself pointedly to him.

"This young Indian," said Paul, "was a fine specimen of his race, tall and well made, with a handsome coun- tenance, in which truth was as plain as the sun in the summer sky. I was out after grizzly b'ars at the time, but hadn't had much luck, an' was comin' back to camp one evenin' in somethin' of a sulky humour, when I fell upon a trail which I knowed was the trail of a Redskin. The Redskins was friendly at that time wi' the whites, and as I was out alone, an' am somethin' of a sociable critter, I thought I'd follow him up an' take him to my camp wi' me, if he was willin', an' give him some grub an' baccy. Well, I hadn't gone far when I came to a precipiece. The trail followed the edge of it for some distance, an' I went along all right till I come to a bit where the trail seemed to go right over it. My heart

gave a jump, for I seed at a glance that a bit o' the cliff
had given way there, an' as there was no sign o' the trail
farther on, of course I knowed that the Injin, whoever he
was, must have gone down with it.

"I tried to look over, but it was too steep an' dangerous, so I sought for a place where I could clamber
down. Sure enough, when I reached the bottom, there
lay the poor Redskin. I thought he was dead, for he'd
tumbled from a most awful height, but a tree had broke
his fall to some extent, and when I went up to him I
saw by his eyes that he was alive, though he could
neither speak nor move.

"I soon found that the poor lad was damaged past
recovery; so, after tryin' in vain to get him to speak to
me, I took him in my arms as tenderly as I could and
carried him to my camp. It was five miles off, and the
road was rough, and although neither groan nor com-
plaint escaped him, I knew that poor Oswego suffered
much by the great drops o' perspiration that rolled from
his brow; so, you see, I had to carry him carefully.
When I'd gone about four miles I met a small Injin boy
who said he was Oswego's brother, had seen him fall,
an', not bein' able to lift him, had gone to seek for help,
but had failed to find it.

"That night I nursed the lad as I best could, gave him
some warm tea, and did my best to arrange him comfort-
ably. The poor fellow tried to speak his gratitude but
couldn't; yet I could see it in his looks. He died next
day, and I buried him under a pine-tree. The poor
heart-broken little brother said he knew the way back to
the wigwams of his tribe, so I gave him the most of the
provisions I had, told him my name, and sent him away."

At this point in the story Unaco rose abruptly, and
said to Bevan—

"The white man will follow me."

Paul rose, and the chief led him into the forest a short way, when he turned abruptly, and, with signs of emotion unusual in an Indian, said—

"Your name is Paul Bevan?"

"It is."

"I am the father of Oswego," said the chief, grasping Paul by the hand and shaking it vigorously in the white man's fashion.

"I know it, Unaco, and I know you by report, though we've never met before, and I told that story in your ear to convince ye that my tongue is *not* ' forked.' "

When Paul Bevan returned to the camp fire, soon afterwards, he came alone, and both his arms were free. In a few seconds he had the satisfaction of undoing the bonds of his companions and relating to them the brief but interesting conversation which had just passed between him and the Indian chief.

CHAPTER XV.

A T the edge of a small plain, or bit of prairie land,
that shone like a jewel in a setting of bush-clad
hills, dwelt the tribe of natives who owned Unaco as
their chief.

It was a lovely spot, in one of the most secluded portions
of the Sawback range, far removed at that time from the
evil presence of the gold-diggers, though now and then an
adventurous "prospector" would make his way to these
remote solitudes in quest of the precious metal.   Up to
that time those prospectors had met with nothing to reward them for their pains, save the gratification to be
derived from fresh mountain air and beautiful scenery.

It required three days of steady travelling to enable
the chief and his party to reach the wigwams of the tribe.
The sun was just setting, on the evening of the third day,
when they passed out of a narrow defile and came in
sight of the Indian village.

" It seems to me, Paul," remarked Fred Westly, as they
halted to take a brief survey of the scene, "that these
Indians have found an admirable spot on which to lead
a peaceful life, for the region is too high and difficult of
access to tempt many gold-hunters, and the approaches
to it could be easily defended by a handful of resolute
men."

" That is true," replied Bevan, as they continued

on their way. "Nevertheless, it would not be very difficult for a few resolute men to surprise and capture the place."

"Perchance Stalker and his villains may attempt to prove the truth of what you say," suggested Fred.

"They will certainly attempt it," returned Paul, "but they are not what I call resolute men. Scoundrels are seldom blessed wi' much resolution, an' they're never heartily united."

"What makes you feel so sure that they will follow us up, Paul?"

"The fact that my enemy has followed me like a bloodhound for six years," answered Bevan, with a frown.

"Is it touching too much on private matters to ask why he is your enemy, and why so vindictive?"

"The reason is simple enough. Buxley hates me, and would kill me if he could. Indeed I'm half afraid that he will manage it at last, for I've promised my little gal that I won't kill *him* 'cept in self-defence, an' of course if I don't kill him he's pretty sure to kill me."

"Does Betty know why this man persecutes you so?"

"No—she don't."

As it was evident, both from his replies and manner, that Bevan did not mean to be communicative on the subject, Fred forbore to ask more questions about it.

"So you think Unaco may be depended on?" he asked, by way of changing the subject.

"Ay, surely. You may depend on it that the Almighty made all men pretty much alike as regards their feelin's. The civilised people an' the Redskins ain't so different as some folk seem to think. They can both of 'em love an' hate pretty stiffly, an' they are both able to feel an' show gratitude as well as the reverse—also, they're pretty equal in the matter of revenge."

"But don't we find," said Fred, "that among Christians revenge is pretty much held in check?"

"Among Christians—ay," replied Bevan; "but white men ain't always Christians, any more than red men are always devils. Seems to me it's six o' one an' half a dozen o' the other. Moreover, when the missionaries git among the Redskins, some of 'em turns Christians an' some hypocrites—just the same as white men. What Unaco is, in the matter o' Christianity, is not for me to say, for I don't know; but from what I do know, from hearsay, of his character, I'm sartin sure that he's a good man and true, an' for that little bit of sarvice I did to his poor boy he'd give me his life if need be."

"Nevertheless, I can't help thinking that we might have returned to Simpson's Gully, and taken the risk of meeting with Stalker," said Fred.

"Ha! that's because you don't know him," returned Bevan. "If he had met with his blackguards soon after leaving us, he'd have overtook us by this time. Any way, he's sure to send scouts all round, and follow up the trail as soon as he can."

"But think what a trial this rough journey has been to poor Tom Brixton," said Fred.

"No doubt," returned Paul; "but haven't we got him on Tolly's pony to-day? and isn't that a sign he's better? An' would you have me risk Betty fallin' into the hands o' Buxley?"

Paul looked at his companion as if this were an unanswerable argument, and Fred admitted that it was.

"Besides," he went on, "it will be a pleasant little visit this, to a friendly tribe o' Injins, an' we may chance to fall in wi' gold, who knows? An' when the ugly thieves do succeed in findin' us, we shall have the help o' the Redskins, who are not bad fighters when their cause is a good 'un an' their wigwams are in danger."

"It may be so, Paul. However, right or wrong, here we are, and a most charming spot it is, the nearer we draw towards it."

As Fred spoke, Betty Bevan, who rode in advance, reined in her horse,—which, by the way, had become much more docile in her hands,—and waited till her father overtook her.

"Is it not like paradise, father?"

"Not havin' been to paradise, dear, I can't exactly say," returned her matter-of-fact sire.

"Oh, I say, ain't it splendatious!" said Tolly Trevor, coming up at the moment, and expressing Betty's idea in somewhat different phraseology; just look at the lake —like a lookin'-glass, with every wigwam pictur'd upside down, so clear that a feller can't well say which is which. An' the canoes in the same way, bottom to bottom, Red-skins above and Redskins below. Hallo! I say, what's that?"

The excited lad pointed, as he spoke, to the bushes, where a violent motion and crashing sound told of some animal disturbed in its lair. Next moment a beautiful little antelope bounded into an open space, and stopped to cast a bewildered gaze for one moment on the in-truders. That pause proved fatal. A concealed hunter seized his opportunity; a sharp crack was heard, and the animal fell dead where it stood, shot through the head.

"Poor, poor creature!" exclaimed the tender-hearted Betty.

"Not a bad supper for somebody," remarked her practical father.

As he spoke the bushes parted at the other side of the

open space, and the man who had fired the shot appeared.

He was a tall and spare, but evidently powerful fellow. As he advanced towards our travellers they could see that he was not a son of the soil, but a white man—at least as regards blood, though his face, hands, neck, and bared bosom had been tanned by exposure to as red a brown as that of any Indian.

"He's a trapper," exclaimed Tolly, as the man drew nearer, enabling them to perceive that he was middle-aged and of rather slow and deliberate temperament, with a sedate expression on his rugged countenance.

"Ay, he looks like one o' these wanderin' chaps," said Bevan, "that seem to be fond of a life o' solitude in the wilderness. I've knowed a few of 'em. Queer customers some, that stick at nothin' when their blood's up; though I have met wi' one or two that desarved an easier life, an' more o' this world's goods. But most of 'em prefer to hunt for their daily victuals, an' on'y come down to the settlements when they run out o' powder an' lead, or want to sell their furs. Hallo! Why, Tolly, boy, it is—yes! I do believe it's Mahogany Drake himself!"

Tolly did not reply, for he had run eagerly forward to meet the trapper, having already recognised him.

"His name is a strange one," remarked Fred Westly, gazing steadily at the man as he approached.

"Drake is his right name," explained Bevan, "an' Mahogany is a handle some fellers gave him 'cause he's so much tanned wi' the sun. He's one o the right sort, let me tell ye. None o' your boastin', bustin' critters, like Gashford, but a quiet, thinkin' man, as is ready to tackle any subject a'most in the univarse, but can let his tongue lie till it's time to speak. He can hold his own, too

A BEAUTIFUL ANTELOPE BOUNDED FORTH. – Page 181.

wi' man or beast. Ain't he friendly wi' little Tolly
Trevor? He'll shake his arm out o' the socket if he don't
take care. I'll have to go to the rescue."

In a few seconds Paul Bevan was having his own arm
almost dislocated by the friendly shake of the trapper's
hand, for, although fond of solitude, Mahogany Drake
was also fond of human beings, and especially of old
friends.

"Glad to see you, gentlemen," he said, in a low, soft
voice, when introduced by Paul to the travellers. At the
same time he gave a friendly little nod to Unaco, thus
indicating that with the Indian chief he was already
acquainted.

"Well, Drake," said Bevan, after the first greetings
were over, "all right at the camp down there?"

"All well," he replied, "and the Leaping Buck quite
recovered."

He cast a quiet glance at the Indian chief as he spoke,
for the Leaping Buck was Unaco's little son, who had
been ailing when his father left his village a few weeks
before.

"No sign o' gold-seekers yet?" asked Paul.

"None—'cept one lot that ranged about the hills for a
few days, but they seemed to know nothin'. Sartinly
they found nothin', an' went away disgusted."

The trapper indulged in a quiet chuckle as he said
this.

"What are ye larfin' at?" asked Paul.

"At the gold-seekers," replied Drake.

"What was the matter wi' 'em," asked Tolly.

"Not much, lad, only they was blind, and also ill of a
strong appetite."

"Ye was always fond o' speakin' in riddles," said Paul.
"What d'ye mean, Mahogany?"

"I mean that though there ain't much gold in these
hills, maybe, what little there is the seekers couldn't
see, though they was walkin' over it, an' they was so
blind they couldn't hit what they fired at, so their appetites
was stronger than was comfortable. I do believe they'd
have starved if I hadn't killed a buck for them."

During this conversation Paddy Flinders had been
listening attentively and in silence. He now sidled up
to Tom Brixton, who, although bestriding Tolly's pony,
seemed ill able to travel.

"D'ye hear what the trapper says, Muster Brixton?"

"Yes, Paddy, what then?"

"Och! I only thought to cheer you up a bit by p'intin'
out that he says there's goold hereabouts."

"I'm glad for your sake and Fred's," returned Tom,
with a faint smile, "but it matters little to me; I feel
that my days are numbered."

"Ah! then, sor, don't spake like that," returned
Flinders, with a woebegone expression on his countenance.
"Sure, it's in the dumps ye are, an' no occasion for that
same. Isn't Miss—"

The Irishman paused. He had it in his heart to say,
"Isn't Miss Betty smilin' on ye like one o'clock?" but,
never yet having ventured even a hint on that subject to
Tom, an innate feeling of delicacy restrained him. As
the chief who led the party gave the signal to move on
at that moment, it was unnecessary for him to finish the
sentence.

The Indian village, which was merely a cluster of
tents made of deerskins stretched on poles, was now
plainly visible from the commanding ridge along which
the party travelled. It occupied a piece of green level
land on the margin of the lake before referred to, and,
with its background of crag and woodland and its distance

of jagged purple hills, formed as lovely a prospect as the
eye of man could dwell upon.

The distance of the party from it rendered every sound
that floated towards them soft and musical. Even the
barking of the dogs and the shouting of the little Redskins at play came up to them in a mellow, almost peaceful,
tone. To the right of the village lay a swamp, from out
of which arose the sweet and plaintive cries of innumerable gulls, plovers, and other wild-fowl, mingled with the
trumpeting of geese and the quacking of ducks, many of
which were flying to and fro over the glassy lake, while
others were indulging in aquatic gambols among the
reeds and sedges.

After they had descended the hill-side by a zigzag
path, and reached the plain below, they obtained a nearer
view of the eminently joyful scene, the sound of the
wild-fowl became more shrill, and the laughter of the
children more boisterous. A number of the latter who
had observed the approaching party were seen hurrying
towards them with eager haste, led by a little lad, who
bounded and leaped as if wild with excitement. This
was Unaco's little son, Leaping Buck, who had recognised
the well-known figure of his sire a long way off, and ran
to meet him.

On reaching him the boy sprang like an antelope into
his father's arms and seized him round the neck, while
others crowded round the gaunt trapper and grasped his
hands and legs affectionately. A few of the older boys
and girls stood still somewhat shyly, and gazed in silence
at the strangers, especially at Betty, whom they evidently
regarded as a superior order of being—perhaps an angel
—in which opinion they were undoubtedly backed by
Tom Brixton.

After embracing his father, Leaping Buck recognised

Paul Bevan as the man who had been so kind to him and his brother Oswego at the time when the latter got his death-fall over the precipice. With a shout of joyful surprise he ran to him, and, we need scarcely add, was warmly received by the kindly backwoodsman.

"I cannot help thinking," remarked Betty to Tom, as they gazed on the pleasant meeting, "that God must have some way of revealing the Spirit of Jesus to these Indians that we Christians know not of."

"It is strange," replied Tom, "that the same thought has occurred to me more than once of late, when observing the character and listening to the sentiments of Unaco. And I have also been puzzled with this thought—if God has some method of revealing Christ to the heathen that we know not of, why are Christians so anxious to send the Gospel to the heathen ?"

"That thought has never occurred to me," replied Betty, "because our reason for going forth to preach the Gospel to the heathen is the simple one that God commands us to do so. Yet it seems to me quite consistent with that command that God may have other ways and methods of making His truth known to men, but this being a mere speculation does not free us from our simple duty."

"You are right. Perhaps I am too fond of reasoning and speculating," answered Tom.

"Nay, that you are not," rejoined the girl, quickly; "it seems to me that to reason and speculate is an important part of the duty of man, and cannot but be right, so long as it does not lead to disobedience. 'Let every man be fully persuaded in his own mind,' is our title from God to *think* fully and freely; but ' Go ye into all the world and preach the Gospel to every creature,' is a command so plain and peremptory that it does not admit of speculative objection."

"Why, Betty, I had no idea you were such a reasoner!"
said Tom, with a look of surprise. "Surely it is not your
father who has taught you to think thus?"

"I have had no teacher, at least of late years, but the
Bible," replied the girl, blushing deeply at having been
led to speak so freely on a subject about which she was
usually reticent. "But see," she added hastily, giving a
shake to the reins of her horse, "we have been left
behind. The chief has already reached his village. Let
us push on."

The obstinate horse went off at an accommodating amble
under the sweet sway of gentleness, while the obedient
pony followed at a brisk trot which nearly shook all the
little strength that Tom Brixton possessed out of his
wasted frame.

The manner in which Unaco was received by the
people of his tribe, young and old, showed clearly that
he was well beloved by them; and the hospitality with
which the visitors were welcomed was intensified when it
was made known that Paul Bevan was the man who had
shown kindness to their chief's son Oswego in his last
hours. Indeed, the influence which an Indian chief can
have on the manners and habits of his people was well
exemplified by this small and isolated tribe, for there
was among them a pervading tone of contentment and
goodwill which was one of Unaco's most obvious characteristics. Truthfulness, also, and justice were more or
less manifested by them. Even the children seemed to
be free from disputation; for, although there were of
course differences of opinion during games, these differences were usually settled without quarrelling, and the
noise, of which there was abundance, was the result of
gleeful shouts or merry laughter. They seemed, in short,
to be a happy community, the various members of which

had learned—to a large extent from their chief—" how good a thing it is for brethren to dwell together in unity."

A tent was provided for Bevan, Flinders, and Tolly Trevor near to the wigwam of Unaco, with a separate little one for the special use of the Rose of Oregon. Not far from these another tent was erected for Fred and his invalid friend Tom Brixton. As for Mahogany Drake, that lanky, lantern-jawed individual encamped under a neighbouring pine-tree in quiet contempt of any more luxurious covering.

But, although the solitary wanderer of the western wilderness thus elected to encamp by himself, he was by no means permitted to enjoy privacy, for during the whole evening and greater part of that night his camp-fire was surrounded by an admiring crowd of boys, and not a few girls, who listened in open-eyed-and-mouthed attention to his thrilling tales of adventure, giving vent now and then to a " waugh !" or a " ho !" of surprise at some telling point in the narrative, or letting fly sudden volleys of laughter at some humorous incident, to the amazement, no doubt, of the neighbouring bucks and bears and wild-fowl.

" Tom," said Fred that night, as he sat by the couch of his friend, " we shall have to stay here some weeks, I suspect, until you get strong enough to travel, and, to say truth, the prospect is a pleasant as well as an unexpected one, for we have fallen amongst amiable natives."

" True, Fred. Nevertheless I shall leave the moment my strength permits—that is, if health be restored to me —and I shall go off by myself."

" Why, Tom, what do you mean ?"

" I mean exactly what I say. Dear Fred," answered the sick man, feebly grasping his friend's hand, " I feel that it is my duty to get away from all who have ever known me, and begin a new career of honesty, God permitting. I will not remain with the character of a thief stamped upon me to be a drag round your neck, and I have made up my mind no longer to persecute dear Betty Bevan with the offer of a dishonest and dishonoured hand. In my insolent folly I had once thought her somewhat below me in station. I now know that she is far, far above me in every way, and also beyond me."

"Tom, my dear boy," returned Fred, earnestly, "you are getting weak. It is evident that they have delayed supper too long. Try to sleep now, and I'll go and see why Tolly has not brought it."

So saying, Fred Westly left the tent and went off in quest of his little friend.

CHAPTER XVI.

LITTLE Tolly Trevor and Leaping Buck—being about the same age, and having similar tastes and propensities, though very unlike each other in temperament —soon became fast friends, and they both regarded Mahogany Drake, the trapper, with almost idolatrous affection.

"Would you care to come wi' me to-day, Tolly? I'm goin' to look for some meat on the heights."

It was thus that Drake announced his intention to go a-hunting one fine morning after he had disposed of a breakfast that might have sustained an ordinary man for several days.

"Care to go with ye!" echoed Tolly, "I just think I should. But, look here, Mahogany," continued the boy, with a troubled expression, "I've promised to go out on the lake to-day wi' Leaping Buck, an' I *must* keep my promise. You know you told us only last night in that story about the Chinaman and the grizzly that no true man ever breaks his promise."

"Right, lad, right," returned the trapper, "but you can go an' ask the little Buck to jine us, an' if he's inclined you can both come—only you must agree to leave yer tongues behind ye if ye do, for it behoves hunters to be silent, and from my experience of you I rather think yer too fond o' chatterin'."

Before Drake had quite concluded his remark Tolly was off in search of his red-skinned bosom friend.

The manner in which the friendship between the red boy and the white was instituted and kept up was somewhat peculiar and almost incomprehensible, for neither spoke the language of the other except to a very slight extent. Leaping Buck's father had, indeed, picked up a pretty fair smattering of English during his frequent expeditions into the gold-fields, which, at the period we write of, were being rapidly developed. Paul Bevan, too, during occasional hunting expeditions among the red men, had acquired a considerable knowledge of the dialect spoken in that part of the country, but Leaping Buck had not visited the diggings with his father, so that his knowledge of English was confined to the smattering which he had picked up from Paul and his father. In like manner Tolly Trevor's acquaintance with the native tongue consisted of the little that had been imparted to him by his friend Paul Bevan. Mahogany Drake, on the contrary, spoke Indian fluently, and it must be understood that in the discourses which he delivered to the two boys he mixed up English and Indian in an amazing compound which served to render him intelligible to both, but which, for the reader's sake, we feel constrained to give in the trapper's ordinary English.

" It was in a place just like this," said Drake, stopping with his two little friends on reaching a height, and turning round to survey the scene behind him, " that a queer splinter of a man who was fond o' callin' himself an ornithologist, shot a grizzly b'ar wi' a mere popgun that was only fit for a squawkin' babby's plaything."

" Oh ! do sit down, Mahogany," cried little Trevor, in a voice of entreaty; " I'm so fond of hearin' about grizzlies, an' I'd give all the world to meet one myself, so would Buckie here, wouldn't you ?"

The Indian boy, whose name Tolly had thus modified, tried to assent to this proposal by bending his little head in a stately manner, in imitation of his dignified father.

" Well, I don't mind if I do," replied the trapper, with a twinkle of his eyes.

Mahogany Drake was blessed with that rare gift the power to invest with interest almost any subject, no matter how trivial or commonplace, on which he chose to speak. Whether it was the charm of a musical voice, or the serious tone and manner of an earnest man, we cannot tell, but certain it is that whenever or wherever he began to talk, men stopped to listen, and were held enchained until he had finished.

On the present occasion the trapper seated himself on a green bank that lay close to the edge of a steep precipice, and laid his rifle across his knees, while the boys sat down one on each side of him.

The view from the elevated spot on which they sat was most exquisite, embracing the entire length of the valley at the other end of which the Indian village lay, its inhabitants reduced to mere specks and its wigwams to little cones by distance. Owing also to the height of the spot the view of surrounding mountains was extended, so that range upon range was seen in softened perspective, while a variety of lakelets, with their connecting watercourses, which were hidden by foliage in the lower grounds, were now opened up to view. Glowing sunshine glittered on the waters and bathed the hills and valleys, deepening the near shadows and intensifying the purple and blue of those more distant.

" It often makes me wonder," said the trapper, in a reflective tone, as if speaking rather to himself than to his companions, "why the Almighty has made the world so beautiful an' parfect, an' allowed mankind to grow so awful bad."

The boys did not venture to reply, but as Drake sat gazing in dreamy silence at the far-off hills, little Trevor, who recalled some of his conversations with the Rose of Oregon, ventured to say, " P'r'aps we 'll find out some day, though we don't understand it just now."

" True, lad, true," returned Drake. " It would be well for us if we always looked at it in that light, instead o' findin' fault wi' things as they are, for it stands to reason that the Maker of all can fall into no mistakes."

" But what about the ornithologist?" said Tolly, who had no desire that the conversation should drift into abstruse subjects.

" Ay, ay, lad, I 'm comin' to him," replied the trapper, with the humorous twinkle that seemed to hover always about the corners of his eyes, ready for instant development. " Well, you must know, this was the way of it— and it do make me larf yet when I think o' the face o' that spider-legged critter goin' at the rate of twenty miles an hour or thereabouts wi' that most awful-lookin' grizzly b'ar peltin' after him—Hist! Look there, Tolly. A chance for your popgun."

The trapper pointed as he spoke to a flock of wild duck that was coming straight towards the spot on which they sat. The " popgun " to which he referred was one of the smooth-bore flint-lock single-barrelled fowling-pieces which traders were in the habit of supplying to the natives at that time, and which Unaco had lent to the boy for the day, with his powder-horn and ornamented shot-pouch.

For the three hunters to drop behind the bank on which they had been sitting was the work of a moment.

Young though he was, Tolly had already become a fair and ready shot. He selected the largest bird in the flock, covered it with a deadly aim, and pulled the trigger. But the click of the lock was not followed by an explosion as the birds whirred swiftly on.

"Ah! my boy," observed the trapper, taking the gun quietly from the boy's hand and proceeding to chip the edge of the flint, "you should never go a-huntin' without seein' that your flint is properly fixed."

"But I did see to it," replied Tolly, in a disappointed tone, "and it struck fire splendidly when I tried it before startin'."

"True, boy, but the thing is worn too short, an' though its edge is pretty well you didn't screw it firm enough, so it got drove back a bit, and the hammer-head as well as the flint strikes the steel, d'ye see? There now, prime it again, an' be sure ye wipe the pan before puttin' in the powder. It's not worth while to be disap'inted about so small a matter. You'll git plenty more chances. See, there's another flock comin'. Don't hurry, lad. If ye want to be a good hunter always keep cool, an' take time. Better lose a chance than hurry. A chance lost, you see, is only a chance lost, but blazin' in a hurry is a bad lesson that ye've got to unlarn."

The trapper's advice was cut short by the report of Tolly's gun, and next moment a fat duck, striking the ground in front of them, rolled fluttering to their feet.

"Not badly done, Tolly," said the trapper, with a nod, as he reseated himself on the bank, while Leaping Buck picked up the bird, which was by that time dead, and the young sportsman recharged his gun; "just a leetle too hurried. If you had taken only half a second more time to put the gun to your shoulder, you'd have brought the bird to the ground dead; and you boys can't larn too soon that you should never give needless pain to critters that you've got to kill. You must shoot, of course, or you'd starve ; but always make sure of killin' at once, an' the only way to do that is to keep cool an' take time. You see, it ain't the aim you take that matters so much as the coolness an' steadiness with which ye put the gun to your shoulder. If you only do that steadily an' without hurry, the gun is sure to p'int straight for'ard an' the aim'll look arter itself. Nevertheless, it was smartly done, lad, for it's a difficult shot when a wild duck comes straight for your head like a cannon-ball."

"But what about the ornithologist ;" said Tolly, who, albeit well pleased at the trapper's complimentary remarks, did not quite relish his criticism.

"Yes, yes ; I'm comin' to that. Well, as I was sayin', it makes me larf yet when I thinks on it. How he did run, to be sure ! Greased lightnin' could scarce have kep' up wi' him."

"But where was he a-runnin' to, an' why ?" asked little Trevor, impatiently.

"Now, you leetle boy," said Drake, with a look of grave remonstrance, "don't you go an' git impatient. Patience is one o' the backwoods vartues, without which you'll never git on at all. If you don't cultivate patience you may as well go an' live in the settlements or the big cities —where it don't much matter what a man is—but it'll be o' no use to stop in the wilderness. There's Leapin' Buck, now, a-sittin' as quiet as a Redskin warrior on guard ! Take a lesson from him, lad, an' restrain yourself. Well, as I was goin' to say, I was out settin' my traps somewheres about the head-waters o' the Yellowstone river at the time when I fell in wi' the critter. I couldn't rightly make out what he was, for, though I've seed mostly all sorts o' men in my day, I'd never met in wi' one o' this

sort before.   It wasn't his bodily shape that puzzled me,
though that was queer enough, but his occupation that
staggered me.   He was a long, thin, spider-shaped article
that seemed to have run to seed—all stalk with a frowsy
top, for his hair was long an' dry an' fly-about.   I 'm six-
futt one myself, but my step was a mere joke to his stride !
He seemed split up to the neck, like a pair o' human
compasses, an' his clo's fitted so tight that he might have
passed for a livin' skeleton !

"Well, it was close upon sundown, an' I was joggin'
along to my tent in the bush when I came to an' openin'
where I saw the critter down on one knee an' his gun up
takin' aim at somethin'.   I stopped to let him have his
shot, for I count it a mortal sin to spoil a man's sport, an'
I looked hard to see what it was he was goin' to let drive
at, but never a thing could I see, far or near, except a
small bit of a bird about the size of a big bee, sittin' on
a branch not far from his nose an' cockin' its eye at him
as much as to say, ' Well, you air a queer 'un !' ' Surely,'
thought I, ' he ain't a-goin' to blaze at *that!*' But I 'd
scarce thought it when he did blaze at it, an' down it
came flop on its back, as dead as mutton !

" ' Well, stranger,' says I, goin' for'ard, ' you do seem to
be hard up for victuals when you 'd shoot a small thing
like that !'   ' Not at all, my good man,' says he—an' the
critter had a kindly smile an' a sensible face enough—
' you must know that I am shootin' birds for scientific
purposes.   I am an ornithologist.'

" ' Oh !' say I, for I didn't rightly know what else to
say to that.

" ' Yes,' says he ; ' an' see here.'

" Wi' that he opens a bag he had on his back an'
showed me a lot o' birds, big an' small, that he 'd been
shootin' ; an' then he pulls out a small book, in which

he'd been makin' picturs of 'em—an' r'ally I was raither took wi' that, for the critter had got 'em down there almost as good as natur'. They actooally looked as if they was alive!

"'Shut the book, sir,' says I, ' or they'll all escape!'

"It was only a small joke I meant, but the critter took it for a big 'un an' larfed at it till he made me half ashamed.

"'D'ye know any of these birds?' he axed, arter we'd looked at a lot of 'em.

"'Know 'em?' says I; 'I should think I does! Why, I've lived among 'em ever since I was a babby!'

"'Indeed!' says he, an' he got quite excited, 'how interestin'! An' do you know anythin' about their habits?'

"'If you mean by that their ways o' goin' on,' says I, 'there's hardly a thing about 'em that I don't know, except what they *think,* an' sometimes I've a sort o' notion I could make a pretty fair guess at that too.'

"'Will you come to my camp and spend the night with me?' he asked, gettin' more an' more excited.

"'No, stranger, I won't,' says I; 'but if you'll come to mine I'll feed you an' make you heartily welcome,' for somehow I'd took quite a fancy to the critter.

"'I'll go,' says he, an' he went, an' we had such a night of it! He didn't let me have a wink o' sleep till pretty nigh daylight the next mornin', an' axed me more questions about birds an' beasts an' fishes than I was iver axed before in the whole course o' my life—an' it warn't yesterday I was born. I began to feel quite like a settlement boy at school. An' he set it all down, too, as fast as I could speak, in the queerest hand-writin' you ever did see. At last I couldn't stand it no longer.

"'Mister Ornithologist,' says I.

"'Well,' says he.

"'There's a pecooliar beast in them parts,' says I, 'as has got some pretty stiff an' settled habits.'

"'Is there?' says he, wakin' up again quite fresh, though he had been growin' sleepy.

"'Yes,' says I, 'an' it's a obstinate sort o' brute that won't change its habits for nobody. One o' these habits is that it turns in of a night quite reg'lar an' has a good snooze before goin' to work next day. Its name is Mahogany Drake, an' that's me, so I'll bid you good-night, stranger.'

"Wi' that I knocked the ashes out o' my pipe, stretched myself out wi' my feet to the fire, an' rolled my blanket round me. The critter larfed again at this as if it was a great joke, but he shut up his book, put it and the bag o' leetle birds under his head for a pillow, spread himself out over the camp like a great spider that was awk'ard in the use o' its limbs, an' went off to sleep even before I did—an' that was sharp practice, let me tell you.

"Well," continued the trapper, clasping his great bony hands over one of his knees, and allowing the lines of humour to play on his visage, while the boys drew nearer in open-eyed expectancy, "we slep' about three hours, an' then had a bit o' breakfast, after which we parted, for he said he knew his way back to the camp, where he left his friends; but the poor critter didn't know nothin'—'cept ornithology. He lost himself an' took to wanderin' in a circle arter I left him. I came to know it 'cause I struck his trail the same arternoon, an' there could be no mistakin' it, the length o' stride bein' somethin' awful! So I followed it up.

"I hadn't gone far when I came to a place pretty much like this, as I said before, and when I was lookin' at the view—for I'm fond of a fine view, it takes a man's mind off trappin' an' victuals somehow—I heerd a most awful screech, an' then another. A moment later an' the ornithologist busted out o' the bushes with his long legs goin' like the legs of a big water-wagtail. He was too fur off to see the look of his face, but his hair was tremendous to behold. When he saw the precipice before him he gave a most horrible yell, for he knew that he couldn't escape that way from whatever was chasin' him. I couldn't well help him, for there was a wide gully between him an' me, an' it was too fur off for a fair shot. Howsever, I stood ready. Suddenly I seed the critter face right about, an' down on one knee like a pair o' broken compasses; up went the shot-gun, an' at the same moment out busted a great old grizzly b'ar from the bushes. Crack! went my rifle at once, but I could see that the ball didn't hurt him much, although it hit him fair on the head. Loadin' in hot haste, I observed that the ornithologist sat like a post till that b'ar was within six foot of him, when he let drive both barrels of his popgun straight into its face. Then he jumped a one side with a spurt like a grasshopper, an' the b'ar tumbled heels over head and got up with an angry growl to rub its face, then it made a savage rush for'ard and fell over a low bank, jumped up again, an' went slap agin a face of rock. I seed at once that it was blind. The small shot used by the critter for his leetle birds had put out both its eyes, an' it went blunderin' about, while the ornithologist kep' well out of its way. I knew he was safe, so waited to see what he'd do, an' what d'ye think he did?"

"Shoved his knife into him," suggested Tolly Trevor, in eager anxiety.

"What! shove his knife into a healthy old b'ar with nothin' gone but his sight? No, lad, he did do nothing

so mad as that, but he ran coolly up to it an' screeched
in its face. Of course the b'ar went straight at the
sound, helter-skelter, and the ornithologist turned an' ran
to the edge o' the precipice, screechin' as he went.
When he got there he pulled up an' darted a one side,
but the b'ar went slap over, an' I believe I 'm well within
the mark when I say that that b'ar turned five complete
somersaults before it got to the bottom, where it came to
the ground with a whack that would have busted an
elephant. I don't think we found a whole bone in its
carcass when the ornithologist helped me to cut it up
that night in camp."

"Well done!" exclaimed little Trevor, with enthusiasm, "an' what came o' the orny-what-d'ye-callum?"

"That's more than I can tell, lad. He went off wi'
the b'ar's claws to show to his friends, an' I never saw
him again. But look there, boys," continued the trapper
in a suddenly lowered tone of voice, while he threw
forward and cocked his rifle, "d'ye see our supper?"

"What? Where?" exclaimed Tolly, in a soft whisper,
straining his eyes in the direction indicated.

The sharp crack of the trapper's rifle immediately
followed, and a fine buck lay prone upon the ground.

"'Twas an easy shot," said Drake, recharging his
weapon, "only a man needs a leetle experience before
he can fire down a precipice correctly. Come along,
boys."

CHAPTER XVII.

NOTHING further worth mentioning occurred to the hunters that day, save that little Tolly Trevor was amazed—we might almost say petrified—by the splendour and precision of the trapper's shooting, besides which he was deeply impressed with the undercurrent of what we may style grave fun, coupled with calm enthusiasm, which characterised the man, and the utter absence of self-assertion or boastfulness.

But if the remainder of the day was uneventful, the stories round the camp-fire more than compensated him and his friend Leaping Buck. The latter was intimately acquainted with the trapper, and seemed to derive more pleasure from watching the effect of his anecdotes on his new friend than in listening to them himself. Probably this was in part owing to the fact that he had heard them all before more than once.

The spot they had selected for their encampment was the summit of a projecting crag, which was crowned with a little thicket, and surrounded on three sides by sheer precipices. The neck of rock by which it was reached was free from shrubs, besides being split across by a deep chasm of several feet in width, so that it formed a natural fortress, and the marks of old encampments seemed to indicate that it had been used as a camping-place by the red man long before his white brother—too often his white foe—had appeared in that western wilderness to disturb him. The Indians had no special name for the spot, but the roving trappers who first came to it had named it the Outlook, because from its summit a magnificent view of nearly the whole region could be obtained. The great chasm or fissure already mentioned descended sheer down, like the neighbouring precipices, to an immense depth, so that the Outlook, being a species of aërial island, was usually reached by a narrow plank which bridged the chasm. It had stood many a siege in times past, and when used as a fortress, whether by white hunters or savages, the plank bridge was withdrawn, and the place rendered—at least esteemed—impregnable.

When Mahogany Drake and his young friends came up to the chasm a little before sunset, Leaping Buck took a short run and bounded clear over it.

"Ha! I knowed he couldn't resist the temptation," said Mahogany, with a quiet chuckle, "an' it's not many boys—no, nor yet men—who could jump that. I wouldn't try it myself for a noo rifle—no, though ye was to throw in a silver-mounted powder-horn to the bargain."

"But you *have* jumped it?" cried the Indian boy, turning round with a gleeful face.

"Ay, lad, long ago, and then I was forced to, when runnin' for my life. A man 'll do many a deed when so sitooate that he couldn't do in cold blood. Come, come, young feller," he added, suddenly laying his heavy hand on little Trevor's collar and arresting him, "you wasn't thinkin' o' tryin' it, was ye?"

"Indeed I was, and I *think* I could manage it," said the foolishly ambitious Tolly.

"Thinkin' is not enough, boy," returned the trapper, with a grave shake of the head. "You should always make *sure*. Suppose you was wrong in your thinkin', now, who d'ee think would go down there to pick up the bits of 'ee an' carry them home to your mother."

"But I haven't got a mother," said Tolly.

"Well, your father, then."

"But I haven't got a father."

"So much the more reason," returned the trapper, in a softened tone, "that you should take care o' yourself, lest you should turn out to be the last o' your race. Come, help me to carry this plank. After we 're over I 'll see you jump on safe ground, and if you can clear enough, mayhap I 'll let 'ee try the gap. Have you a steady head?"

"Ay, like a rock," returned Tolly, with a grin.

"See that you 're *sure*, lad, for if you ain't I 'll carry you over."

In reply to this Tolly ran nimbly over the plank bridge like a tight-rope dancer. Drake followed, and they were all soon busily engaged clearing a space on which to en-camp, and collecting firewood.

"Tell me about your adventure at the time you jumped the gap, Mahogany," begged little Trevor, when the first volume of smoke arose from their fire and went straight up like a pillar into the calm air.

"Not now, lad. Work first, talk afterwards. That 's my motto."

"But work is over now—the fire lighted and the kettle on," objected Tolly.

"Nay, lad, when you come to be an old hunter you 'll look on supper as about the most serious work o' the day. When that 's over, an' the pipe a-goin', an' maybe a little stick-whittlin' for variety, a man may let his tongue wag to some extent."

Our small hero was fain to content himself with this reply, and for the next half-hour or more the trio gave

their undivided attention to steaks from the loin of the
fat buck and slices from the breast of the wild duck
which had fallen to Tolly's gun. When the pipe-and-
stick-whittling period arrived, however, the trapper dis·
posed his bulky length in front of the fire, while his young
admirers lay down beside him.

The stick-whittling, it may be remarked, devolved
upon the boys, while the smoking was confined to the
man.

" I can't see why it is," observed Tolly, when the first
whiffs curled from Mahogany Drake's lips, " that you men
are so strong in discouragin' us boys from smokin'. You
keep it all selfishly to yourselves, though Buckie an' I
would give anythin' to be allowed to try a whiff now an'
then.   Paul Bevan's just like you—won't hear o' *me*
touchin' a pipe, though he smokes himself like a wigwam
wi' a greenwood fire !' "

Drake pondered a little before replying.

" It would never do, you know," he said, at length,
" for you boys to do 'zackly as we men does."

" Why not ?" demanded Tolly, developing an early bud
of independent thought.

" Why, 'cause it wouldn't," replied Drake.   Then,
feeling that his answer was not a very convincing argument, he added, " You see, boys ain't men, no more than
men are boys, an' what's good for the one ain't good for
the tother."

" I don't see that," returned the radical-hearted Tolly.
" Isn't eatin', an' drinkin', an' sleepin', an' walkin', an'
runnin', an' talkin', an' thinkin', an' huntin', equally good
for boys and men ?   If all these things is good for us
both, why not smokin' ?"

" That's more than I can tell 'ee, lad," answered the
honest trapper, with a somewhat puzzled look.

If Mahogany Drake had thought the matter out a little more closely he might perhaps have seen that smoking *is* as good for boys as for men—or, what comes to much the same thing, is equally bad for both of them ! But the sturdy trapper liked smoking; hence, like many wiser men, he did not care to think the matter out. On the contrary, he changed the subject, and, as the change was very much for the better in the estimation of his companions, Tolly did not object.

"Well now, about that jump," he began, emitting a prolonged and delicate whiff.

"Ah, yes ! How did you manage to do it ?" asked little Trevor, eagerly.

"Oh, for the matter o' that, it 's easy to explain ; but it wasn't *my* jump I was goin' to tell about, it was the jump o' a poor critter—a sort o' ne'er-do-well who jined a band o' us trappers the day before we arrived at this place on our way through the mountains on a huntin' expedition. He was a miserable specimen o' human natur' —all the worse that he had a pretty stout body o' his own, an' might have made a fairish man if he 'd had the spirit even of a cross-grained rabbit. His name was Miffy, an' it sounded nat'ral to him, for there was no go in him whatever. I often wonder what sitch men was made for. They 're o' no use to anybody, an' a nuisance to themselves."

"P'r'aps they wasn't made for any use at all," suggested Tolly, who, having whittled a small piece of stick down to nothing, commenced another piece with renewed interest.

"No, lad," returned the trapper, with a look of deeper gravity. "Even poor, foolish man does not construct anything without some sort o' purpose in view. It 's an outrage on common sense to think the Almighty could

do so.　Mayhap sitch critters was meant to act as warnin's
to other men.　He told us that he'd runned away from
home when he was a boy 'cause he didn't like school.
Then he engaged as a cabin-boy aboard a ship tradin' to
some place in South America, an' runned away from his
ship the first port they touched at 'cause he didn't like
the sea.　Then he came well-nigh to the starvin' p'int,
an' took work on a farm as a labourer, but left that 'cause
it was too hard, after which he got a berth as watchman
at a warehouse, or some place o' the sort, but left that,
for it was too easy.　Then he tried gold-diggin', but
could make nothin' of it; engaged in a fur company, but
soon left it; an' then tried his hand at trappin' on his
own account, but gave it up 'cause he could catch nothin'.
When he fell in with our band he was redooced to two
rabbits an' a prairie hen, wi' only three charges o' powder
in his horn, an' not a drop o' lead.

"Well, we tuck pity on the miserable critter, an' let
him come along wi' us.　There was ten of us altogether,
an' he made eleven.　At first we thought he'd be of some
use to us, but we soon found he was fit for nothin'.
However, we couldn't cast him adrift in the wilderness,
for he'd have bin sure to come to damage somehow, so we
let him go on with us.　When we came to this neighbourhood we made up our minds to trap in the valley, and
as the Injins were wild at that time, owin' to some rascally white men who had treated them badly and killed
a few, we thought it advisable to pitch our camp on the
Outlook here.　It was a well-known spot to most o' my
comrades, tho' I hadn't seen it myself at that time.

"When we came to the gap, one of the young fellows
named Bounce gave a shout, took a run, and went clear
over it, just as Leapin' Buck did.　He was fond o' showin'
off, you know !　He turned about with a laugh, and asked

us to follow. We declined, and felled a small tree to bridge it. Next day we cut the tree down to a plank, as bein' more handy to shove across in a hurry if need be.

"Well, we had good sport—plenty of b'ar and moose steaks, no end of fresh eggs of all sorts, and enough o' pelts to make it pay. You see we didn't know there was gold here in those days, so we didn't look for it, an' wouldn't ha' knowed it if we'd seen it. But I never myself cared to look for gold. It's dirty work, grubbin' among mud and water like a beaver. It's hard work, too, an' I've observed that the men who get most gold at the diggin's are not the diggers but the storekeepers, an' a bad lot they are, many of 'em, though I'm bound to say that I've knowed a few as was real honest men, who kep' no false weights or measures, an' had some sort of respec' for their Maker.

"However," continued the trapper, filling a fresh pipe, while Tolly and his little red friend, whittling their sticks less vigorously as the story went on and at length dropping them altogether, kept their bright eyes riveted on Drake's face. "However, that's not what I've got to tell 'ee about. You must know that one evening, close upon sundown, we was all returnin' from our traps more or less loaded wi' skins an' meat, all except Miffy, who had gone, as he said, a huntin'. Bin truer if he'd said he meant to go around scarin' the animals. Well, just as we got within a mile o' this place we was set upon by a band o' Redskins. There must have bin a hundred of 'em at least. I've lived a longish time now in the wilderness, but I never, before or since, heard sitch a yellin' as the painted critters set up in the woods all around when they came at us, sendin' a shower o' arrows in advance to tickle us up ; but they was bad shots, for only one took effect, an' that shaft just grazed the point o' young Bounce's nose as neat as if it was only meant to make him sneeze. It made him jump, I tell 'ee, higher than I ever seed him jump before. Of course fightin' was out o' the question. Ten trappers under cover might hold their own easy enough agin a hundred Redskins, but not in the open. We all knew that, an' had no need to call a council o' war. Every man let his pack fall, an' away we went for the Outlook, followed by the yellin' critters closer to our heels than we quite liked. But they couldn't shoot runnin', so we got to the gap. The plank was there all right. Over we went, faced about, and while one o' us hauled it over, the rest gave the savages a volley that sent them back faster than they came.

"'Miffy's lost!' obsarved one o' my comrades as we got in among the bushes here an' prepared to fight it out.

"'No great loss,' remarked another.

"'No fear o' Miffy,' said Bounce, feelin' his nose tenderly, 'he's a bad shillin', and bad shillin's always turn up, they say.'

"Bounce had barely finished when we heard another most awesome burst o' yellin in the woods, followed by a deep roar.

"'That's Miffy,' says I, feelin' quite excited, for I'd got to have a sneakin' sort o' pity for the miserable critter. 'It's a twin roar to the one he gave that day when he mistook Hairy Sam for a grizzly b'ar, an' went up a spruce-fir like a squirrel.' Sure enough, in another moment Miffy burst out o' the woods an' came tearin' across the open space straight for the gap, followed by a dozen or more savages.

"'Run, Bounce—the plank!' says I, jumpin' up. 'We'll drive the reptiles back!'

"While I was speakin' we were all runnin' full split to meet the poor critter, Bounce far in advance. Whether it

was over-haste, or the pain of his nose, I never could
make out, but somehow, in tryin' to shove the plank over,
Bounce let it slip. Down it went an' split to splinters on
the rocks a hundred feet below! Miffy was close up at
the time. His cheeks was yaller an' his eyes starin' as he
came on, but his face turned green and his eyes took to
glarin' when he saw what had happened. I saw a kind o'
hesitation in his look as he came to the unbridged gulf.
The savages, thinkin' no doubt it was all up with him,
gave a fiendish yell o' delight. That yell saved the poor
ne'er-do-well. It was as good as a Spanish spur to a wild
horse. Over he came with legs an' arms out like a
flyin' squirrel, and down he fell flat on his stummick at our
feet wi' the nearest thing to a fair bu'st that I ever saw,
or raither heard, for I was busy sightin' a Redskin at the
time an' didn't actually see it. When the savages saw
what he'd done they turned tail an' scattered back into
the woods, so we only gave them a loose volley, for we
didn't want to kill the critters. I just took the bark off
the thigh of one to prevent his forgettin' me. We held
the place here for three days, an' then findin' they could
make nothin' of us, or havin' other work on hand, they
went away an' left us in peace."

"An' what became o' poor Miffy?" asked little Trevor,
earnestly.

"We took him down with us to a new settlement that
had been started in the prairie-land west o' the Blue
Mountains, an' there he got a sitooation in a store, but I
s'pose he didn't stick to it long. Anyhow that was the
last I ever saw of him. Now, boys, it's time to turn
in."

That night, when the moon had gone down and the
stars shed a feeble light on the camp of those who
slumbered on the Outlook rock, two figures, like darker

shades among the surrounding shadows, glided from the
woods, and, approaching the edge of the gap, gazed down
into the black abyss.

"I told you, redskin, that the plank would be sure to
be drawn over," said one of the figures, in a low but gruff
whisper.

"When the tomahawk is red men do not usually
sleep unguarded," replied the other, in the Indian
tongue.

"Speak English, Maqua, I don't know enough o' your
gibberish to make out what you mean. Do you think,
now, that the villain Paul Bevan is in the camp?"

"Maqua is not a god, that he should be able to tell
what he does not know."

"No, but he could guess," retorted Stalker—for it was
the robber-chief. "My scouts said they thought it was
his figure they saw. However, it matters not. If you are
to earn the reward I have offered, you must creep into the
camp, put your knife in Bevan's heart, and bring me his
scalp. I would do it myself, redskin, and be indebted to
nobody, but I can't creep as you and your kindred can.
I'd be sure to make row enough to start them in time for
self-defence. As to the scalp, I don't want it—only want
to make certain that you've done the deed. You may
keep it to ornament your dress or to boast about to your
squaw. If you should take a fancy to do a little murder
on your own account, do so. It matters nothin' to me.
I'll be ready to back you up if they give chase."

While the robber-chief was speaking he searched
about for a suitable piece of wood to span the chasm.
He soon found what he wanted, for there was much
felled timber lying about, the work of previous visitors to
the Outlook.

In a few minutes Maqua had crossed, and glided in

a stealthy, stooping position towards the camp, seeming more like a moving shadow than a real man. When pretty close he went down on hands and knees and crept forward, with his scalping-knife between his teeth.

It would have been an interesting study to watch the savage had his object been a good one—the patience ; the slow, gliding movements ; the careful avoidance of growing branches, and the gentle removal of dead ones from his path, for well did Maqua know that a snapping twig would betray him if the camp contained any of the Indian warriors of the Far West.

At last he drew so near that by stretching his neck he could see over the intervening shrubs and observe the sleepers. Just then Drake chanced to waken. Perhaps it was a presentiment of danger that roused him, for the Indian had up to that moment made not the slightest sound. Sitting up and rubbing his eyes, the trapper looked cautiously round ; then he lay down and turned over on his other side to continue his slumbers.

Like the tree-stems around him, Maqua remained absolutely motionless until he thought the trapper was again sleeping. Then he retired, as he had come, to his anxiously-awaiting comrade.

"Bevan not there," he said briefly, when they had retired to a safe distance ; "only Mahogany Drake an' two boy."

"Well, why didn't ye scalp them ?" asked Stalker, savagely, for he was greatly disappointed to find that his enemy was not in the camp. "You said that all white men were your enemies."

"No, not all," replied the savage. "Drake have the blood of white mans, but the heart of red mans. He have be good to Injins."

"Well, well ; it makes no odds to me," returned Stalker.

"Come along, an' walk before me, for I won't trust ye behind.   As for slippery Paul, I 'll find him yet; you shall see.   When a man fails in one attempt, all he 's got to do is to make another.   Now then, redskin, move on l"

CHAPTER XVIII.

A S widely different as night is from day, summer
from winter, heat from cold, are some members of
the human family; yet God made them all, and has a
purpose of love and mercy towards each! Common
sense says this; the general opinion of mankind holds
this; highest of all, the Word clearly states this: "God
willeth not the death of a sinner, but rather that he
should turn from his wickedness and live;" and "He
maketh His sun to shine upon the just and on the
unjust." Nevertheless, it seemed difficult to believe that
the same God formed and spared and guarded and fed
the fierce, lawless man Stalker, and the loving, gentle,
delicate Rose of Oregon.

About the same hour that the former was endeavouring to compass the destruction of Paul Bevan, Betty was
on her knees in her little tented room, recalling the
deeds, the omissions, and the shortcomings of the past
day, interceding alike for friends and foes—if we may
venture to assume that a rose without a thorn could have
foes! Even the robber-chief was remembered among
the rest, and you may be very sure that Tom Brixton was
not forgotten.

Having slept the sleep of innocence and purity, Betty
rose refreshed on the following day, and, before the Indian
village was astir, went out to ramble along a favourite

walk in a thicket on the mountain-side. It so fell out
that Tom had selected the same thicket for his morning
ramble. But poor Tom did not look like one who hoped
to meet with his lady-love that morning. He had, under
good nursing, recovered some of his former strength and
vigour of body with wonderful rapidity, but his face was
still haggard and careworn in an unusual degree for one
so young. When the two met Tom did not pretend
to be surprised. On the contrary, he said :—

"I expected to meet you here, Betty, because I have
perceived that you are fond of the place, and, believe me,
I would not have presumed to intrude were it not that I
wish to ask one or two questions, the answers to which
may affect my future movements."

He paused, and Betty's heart fluttered, for she could
not help remembering former meetings when Tom had
tried to win her affections, and when she had felt it her
duty to discourage him. She made no reply to this
rather serious beginning to the interview, but dropped
her eyes on the turf, for she saw that the youth was gazing
at her with a very mingled and peculiar expression.

"Tell me," he resumed, after a few moments' thought,
"do you feel quite safe with these Indians?"

"Quite," replied the girl, with a slight elevation of the
eyebrows; "they are unusually gentle and good-natured
people. Besides, their chief would lay down his life for
my father—he is so grateful. Oh yes, I feel perfectly
safe here."

"But what does your father think. He is always so
fearless—I might say reckless—that I don't feel certain
as to his real opinion. Have you heard him speaking
about the chance of that rascal Stalker following him
up?"

"Yes; he has spoken freely about that. He fully

expects that Stalker will search for us, but considers that he will not dare to attack us while we live with so strong a band of Indians, and, as Stalker's followers won't hang about here very long for the mere purpose of pleasing their chief, especially when nothing is to be gained by it, father thinks that his enemy will be forced to go away. Besides, he has made up his mind to remain here for a long time—many months, it may be."

"That will do," returned Tom, with a sigh of relief; "then there will be no need for me to—"

"To what?" asked Betty, seeing that the youth paused.

"Forgive me if I do not say what I meant to. I have reasons for—" (he paused again)—"Then you are pleased with the way the people treat you?"

"Of course I am. They could not be kinder if I were one of themselves. And some of the women are so intelligent, too! You know I have picked up a good deal of the Indian language, and understand them pretty well, though I can't speak much, and you've no idea what deep thinkers some of them are! There is Unaco's mother, who looks so old and dried up and stupid—she is one of the dearest old things I ever knew. Why," continued the girl, with increasing animation, as she warmed with her subject, "that old creature led me, the other night, into quite an earnest conversation about religion, and asked me ever so many questions about the ways of God with man—speculative, difficult questions too, that almost puzzled me to answer. You may be sure I took the opportunity to explain to her God's great love to man in and through Jesus, and—"

She stopped abruptly, for Tom Brixton was at that moment regarding her with a steady and earnest gaze.

"Yes," he said, slowly, almost dreamily, "I can well

believe you took your opportunity to commend Jesus to her. You did so once to me, and—"

Tom checked himself, as if with a great effort. The girl longed to hear more, but he did not finish the sentence. "Well," he said, with a forced air of gaiety, " I have sought you here to tell you that I am going off on—on—a long hunting expedition. Going at once— but I would not leave without bidding you good-bye."

" Going away, Mr. Brixton !" exclaimed Betty, in genuine surprise.

" Yes. As you see, I am ready for the field, with rifle and wallet, firebag and blanket."

" But you are not yet strong enough," said Betty.

" Oh ! yes, I am—stronger than I look. Besides, that will mend every day. I don't intend to say good- bye to Westly or any one, because I hate to have people try to dissuade me from a thing when my mind is made up. I only came to say good-bye to you, because I wish you to tell Fred and your father that I am grateful for all their kindness to me, and that it will be useless to follow me. Perhaps we may meet again, Betty," he added, still in the forced tone of lightness, while he gently took the girl's hand in his and shook it; " but the dangers of the wilderness are numerous, and, as you have once or twice told me, we ' know not what a day or an hour may bring forth.'" (His tone had deepened suddenly to that of intense earnestness)—" God bless you, Betty ; farewell."

He dropped her hand, turned sharply on his heel, and walked swiftly away, never once casting a look behind.

Poor Tom ! It was a severe wrench, but he had fought the battle manfully and gained the victory. In his new-born sense of personal unworthiness and strict justice, he had come to the conclusion that he had for-

HE WALKED SWIFTLY AWAY.—Page 218.

feited the right to offer heart or hand to the Rose of
Oregon.   Whether he was right or wrong in his opinion
we do not pretend to judge, but this does not alter the
fact that a hard battle with self had been fought by him,
and a great victory won.

But Tom neither felt nor looked very much like a
conqueror.   His heart seemed to be made of lead, and
the strength of which he had so recently boasted seemed
to have deserted him altogether after he had walked a
few miles, insomuch that he was obliged to sit down on
a bank to rest.   Fear lest Fred or Paul should follow up
his trail, however, infused new strength into his limbs,
and he rose and pushed steadily on, for he was deeply
impressed with the duty that lay upon him—namely, to
get quickly, and as far as possible, away from the girl
whom he could no longer hope to wed.

Thus, advancing at times with great animation, sitting
down occasionally for short rests, and then resuming the
march with renewed vigour, he travelled over the mountains without any definite end in view beyond that to
which we have already referred.

For some time after he was gone Betty stood gazing at
the place in the thicket where he had disappeared, as if
she half expected to see him return ; then, heaving a
deep sigh, and with a mingled expression of surprise,
disappointment, and anxiety on her fair face, she hurried
away to search for her father.

She found him returning to their tent with a load of
firewood, and at once told him what had occurred.

" He'll soon come back, Betty," said Paul, with a
significant smile.   " When a young feller is fond of a
lass, he's as sure to return to her as water is sure to find
its way as fast as it can to the bottom of a hill."

Fred Westly thought the same, when Paul afterwards

told him about the meeting, though he did not feel quite
so sure about the return being immediate; but Mahogany
Drake differed from them entirely.

"Depend on 't," he said to his friend Paul, when, in
the privacy of a retired spot on the mountain-side, they
discussed the matter—"depend on 't, that young feller
ain't made o' butter. What he says he will do he 'll
stick to, if I 'm any judge o' human natur. Of course
it ain't for me to guess why he should fling off in this
fashion. Are ye sure he 's fond o' your lass ?"

"Sure ? Ay, as sure as I am that yon is the sun an'
not the moon a-shinin' in the sky."

"H'm ! that 's strange. An' they 've had no quarrel ?"

"None that I knows on. Moreover, they ain't bin
used to quarrel. Betty 's not one o' that sort—dear lass.
She 's always fair an' above board; honest an' straight-
for'ard. Says 'zactly what she means, an' means what
she says. Mister Tom ain't given to shilly-shallyin',
neither. No, I 'm sure they 've had no quarrel."

"Well, it 's the old story," said Drake, while a puzzled
look flitted across his weather-beaten countenance, and
the smoke issued more slowly from his unflagging pipe,
"the conduct o' lovers is not to be accounted for. Howsever, there 's one thing I 'm quite sure of—that he must
be looked after."

"D'ye think so ?" said Paul. "I 'd have thought he
was quite able to look arter himself."

"Not just now," returned the trapper, "he 's not yet
got the better of his touch o' starvation, an' there 's a
chance o' your friend Stalker, or Buxley, which d'ye call
him ?"

"Whichever you like; he answers to either, or neither,
as the case may be. He 's best known as Stalker in
these parts, though Buxley is his real name."

"Well, then," resumed Drake, "there's strong likelihood o' him prowlin' about here, and comin' across the tracks o' young Brixton ; so, as I said before, he must be looked after, and I'll take upon myself to do it."

"Well, I'll jine ye," said Paul, "for of course ye'll have to make up a party."

"Not at all," returned the trapper, with decision. "I'll do it best alone ; leastwise I'll take only little Tolly Trevor an' Leapin' Buck with me, for they're both smart an' safe lads, and are burnin' keen to learn somethin' o' woodcraft."

In accordance with this determination, Mahogany Drake, Leaping Buck, and little Trevor set off next day and followed Tom Brixton's trail into the mountains. It was a broad trail and very perceptible, at least to an Indian or a trapper, for Tom had a natural swagger, which he could not shake off even in the hour of his humiliation, and, besides, he had never been an adept at treading the western wilderness with the care which the red man finds needful in order to escape from or baffle his foes.

"'Tis as well marked, a'most," said Drake, pausing to survey the trail, "as if he'd bin draggin' a toboggan behind him."

"Yet a settlement man wouldn't see much of. it," remarked little Trevor ; "eh ! Buckie ?"

The Indian boy nodded gravely. He emulated his father in this respect, and would have been ashamed to have given way to childish levity on what he was pleased to consider the war-path, but he had enough of the humorous in his nature to render the struggle to keep grave in Tolly's presence a pretty severe one. Not that Tolly aimed at being either witty or funny, but he had a peculiarly droll expression of face, which added much point to whatever he said.

"Ho !" exclaimed the trapper, after they had gone a little farther ; "here's a trail that even a settlement man could hardly fail to see. There's bin fifty men or more. D'ye see it, Tolly'?"

"See it ? I should think so. D'you suppose I carry my eyes in my pocket ?"

"Come now, lad," said Drake, turning to Leaping Buck, "you want to walk in your father's tracks, no doubt. Read me this trail if ye can."

The boy stepped forward with an air of dignity that Drake regarded as sublime and Tolly thought ludicrous, but the latter was too fond of his red friend to allow his feelings to betray themselves.

"As the white trapper has truly said," he began, "fifty men or more have passed this way. They are most of them white men, but three or four are Indians."

"Good !" said Drake, with an approving nod; "I thought ye'd notice that. Well, go on."

"They were making straight for my father's camp," continued the lad, bending a stern look on the trail, "but they turned sharp round, like the swallow, on coming to the trail of the white man Brixton, and followed it."

"How d'ye know that, lad ?" asked the trapper.

"Because I see it," returned the boy, promptly, pointing at the same time to a spot on the hill-side considerably above them, where the conformation of the land at a certain spot revealed enough of the trail of the "fifty men or more" to show the change of direction.

"Good again, lad. A worthy son of your father. I didn't give 'e credit for sharpness enough to perceive that. Can you read anything more ?"

"One man was a horseman, but he left his horse behind on getting to the rough places of the hills and walked with the rest. He is Paul Bevan's enemy."

"And how d'ye know all *that*?" said Drake, regarding the little fellow with a look of pride.

"By the footprints," returned Leaping Buck. "He wears boots and spurs."

"Just so," returned the trapper, "and we've bin told by Paul that Stalker was the only man of his band who wouldn't fall in wi' the ways o' the country, but sticks to the clumsy Jack-boots and spurs of old England. Yes, the scoundrel has followed you up, Tolly, as Paul Bevan said he would, and, havin' come across Brixton's track, has gone after him, from all which I now come to the conclusion that your friend Mister Tom is a prisoner, an' stands in need of our sarvices. What say you, Tolly?"

"Go at 'em at once," replied the warlike Trevor, "an' set him free."

"What! us three attack fifty men?"

"Why not?" responded Tolly, "We're more than a match for 'em. Paul Bevan has told me oftentimes that honest men are, as a rule, ten times more plucky than dishonest ones. Well, you are one honest man, that's equal to ten; an' Buckie and I are two honest boys, equal, say, to five each, that's ten more, making twenty among three of us. Three times twenty's sixty, isn't it? so, surely that's more than enough to fight fifty."

"Ah, boy," answered the trapper, with a slightly puzzled expression, "I never could make nothin' o' 'rithmetic, though my mother put me to school one winter with a sort o' half-mad parson that came to the head waters o' the Yellowstone river, an' took to teachin'—dear me, how long ago was it now? Well, I forget, but somehow you seem to add up the figgurs raither faster than I was made to do. Howsever, we'll go an' see what's to be done for Tom Brixton."

The trapper, who had been leaning on his gun, looking

down at his bold little comrades during the foregoing conversation, once more took the lead, and, closely following the trail of the robber-band, continued the ascent of the mountains.

The Indian village was by that time far out of sight behind them, and the scenery in the midst of which they were travelling was marked by more than the average grandeur and ruggedness of the surrounding region.

On their right arose frowning precipices which were fringed and crowned with forests of pine, intermingled with poplar, birch, maple, and other trees. On their left a series of smaller precipices, or terraces, descended to successive levels, like giant steps, till they reached the bottom of the valley up which our adventurers were moving, where a brawling river appeared in the distance like a silver thread. The view both behind and in advance was extremely wild, embracing almost every variety of hill scenery, and in each case was shut in by snow-capped mountains. These, however, were so distant and so soft in texture as to give the impression of clouds rather than solid earth.

Standing on one of the many jutting crags from which could be had a wide view of the vale lying a thousand feet below, Tolly Trevor threw up his arms and waved them to and fro as if in an ecstasy, exclaiming—

"Oh, if I had only wings, *what* a swoop I'd make down there!"

"Ah, boy, you ain't the first that's wished for wings in the like circumstances. But we've bin denied these advantages. P'r'aps we'd have made a bad use of 'em. Sartinly we've made a bad use o' sich powers as we do possess. Just think, now, if men could go about through the air as easy as the crows, what a row they'd kick up all over the 'arth! As it is, when we want to fight,

we 've got to crawl slowly from place to place, an' make
roads for our wagins, an' big guns, an' supplies, to go
along with us ; but if we 'd got wings—why, the first fire-
eatin' great man that could lead his fellows by the nose
would only have to give the word, when up would start a
whole army o' men, like some thousand Jack-in-the-boxes,
an' away they 'd go to some place they 'd took a fancy to,
an' down they 'd come, all of a heap, quite onexpected—
take their enemy by surprise, sweep him off the face o'
the 'arth, and enter into possession."

"Well, it would be a blue lookout," remarked Tolly,
"if that was to be the way of it. There wouldn't be
many men left in the world before long."

"That 's true, lad, an' sitch as was left would be the
worst o' the race. No, on the whole I think we 're better
without wings."

While he was talking to little Trevor, the trapper had
been watching the countenance of the Indian boy with
unusual interest. At last he turned to him and asked—

"Has Leaping Buck nothin' to say ?"

"When the white trapper speaks the Indian's tongue
should be silent," replied the youth.

"A good sentiment, and does you credit, lad. But I
am silent now. Has Leaping Buck no remark to make
on what he sees ?"

"He sees the smoke of the robber's camp far up the
heights," replied the boy, pointing as he spoke.

"Clever lad !" exclaimed the trapper, "I know'd he
was his father's son."

"Where ? I can see nothing," cried Tolly, who understood the Indian tongue sufficiently to make out the
drift of the conversation.

"Of course ye can't ; the smoke is too far off an' too
thin for eyes not well practised in the signs o' the wilder-

ness.   But come; we shall go and pay the robbers a visit; mayhap disturb their rest a little—who knows !"

With a quiet laugh, Mahogany Drake withdrew from the rocky ledge, and, followed by his eager satellites, continued to wend his way up the rugged mountain-sides, taking care, however, that he did not again expose himself to view, for well did he know that sharp eyes and ears would be on the *qui vive* that night.

CHAPTER XIX.

WHEN Tom Brixton sternly set his face like a flint to
what he believed to be his duty, he wandered, as
we have said, into the mountains, with a heavy heart and
without any definite intentions as to what he intended to
do.

If his thoughts had taken the form of words they
would probably have run somewhat as follows :—

"Farewell for ever, sweet Rose of Oregon! Dear
Betty! You have been the means, in God's hand, of
saving at least one soul from death, and it would be
requiting you ill indeed were I to persuade you to unite
yourself to a man whose name is disgraced even among
rough men whose estimate of character is not very high.
No! henceforth our lives diverge wider and wider apart.
May God bless you and give you a good hus—give you
happiness in His own way! And now I have the world
before me where to choose. It is a wide world, and there
is much work to be done. Surely I shall be led in the
right way to fill the niche which has been set apart for
me. I wonder what it is to be! Am I to hunt for gold,
or to become a fur-trader, or go down to the plains and
turn cattle-dealer, or to the coast and become a sailor, or
try farming? One thing is certain, I must not be an
idler; must not join the ranks of those who merely hunt
that they may eat and sleep, and who eat and sleep that

they may hunt. I have a work to do for Him who bought me with His precious blood, and my first step must be to commit my way to Him."

Tom Brixton took that step at once. He knelt down on a mossy bank, and there, with the glorious prospect of the beautiful wilderness before him, and the setting sun irradiating his still haggard countenance, held communion with God.

That night he made his lonely bivouac under a spreading pine, and that night, while he was enjoying a profound and health-giving slumber, the robber-chief stepped into his encampment and laid his hand roughly on his shoulder.

In his days of high health Tom would certainly have leaped up and given Stalker a considerable amount of trouble, but starvation and weakness, coupled with self-condemnation and sorrow, had subdued his nerves and abated his energies, so that when he opened his eyes and found himself surrounded by as disagreeable a set of cut-throats as could well be brought together, he at once resigned himself to his fate, and said, without rising, and with one of his half-humorous smiles—

"Well, Mister Botanist, sorry I can't say it gives me pleasure to see you. I wonder you 're not ashamed to return to the country of the great chief Unaco after running away from him as you did."

"I 'm in no humour for joking," answered Stalker, gruffly. "What has become of your friend Paul Bevan ?"

"I 'm not aware that anything particular has become of him," replied Tom, sitting up with a look of affected surprise.

"Come, you know what I mean. Where is he ?"

"When I last saw him he was in Oregon. Whether

he has now gone to Europe or the moon or the sun I
cannot tell, but I should think it unlikely."

"If you don't give me a direct and civil answer I'll
roast you alive, you young puppy!" growled Stalker.

"If you roast me dead instead of alive you'll get no
answer from me but such as I choose to give, you
middle-aged villain!" retorted Tom, with a glare of his
eyes which quite equalled that of the robber-chief in
ferocity, for Tom's nature was what we may style volcanic,
and he found it hard to restrain himself when roused to
a certain point, so that he was prone to speak unadvisedly
with his lips.

A half-smothered laugh from some of the band who
did not care much for their chief rendered Stalker furious.

He sprang forward with a savage oath, drew the small
hatchet which he carried in his belt, and would certainly
then and there have brained the rash youth with it, if
his hand had not been unexpectedly arrested. The
gleaming weapon was yet in the air when the loud report
of a rifle close at hand burst from the bushes with a
sheet of flame and smoke, and the robber's right arm
fell powerless at his side, hit between the elbow and
shoulder.

It was the rifle of Mahogany Drake that had spoken
so opportunely.

That stalwart backwoodsman had, as we have seen,
followed up the trail of the robbers, and with Tolly
Trevor and his friend Leaping Buck had lain for a considerable time safely ensconced in a moss-covered crevice
of the cliff that overlooked the camping-place. There,
quietly observing the robbers, and almost enjoying the
little scene between Tom and the chief, they remained
inactive until Stalker's hatchet gleamed in the air. The
boys were almost petrified by the suddenness of the act.

Not so the trapper, who with rapid aim saved Tom's life, as we have seen.

Dropping his rifle, he seized the boys by the neck and thrust their faces down on the moss : not a moment too soon, for a withering volley was instantly sent by the bandits in the direction whence the shots had come.   It passed harmlessly over their heads.

"Now, home like two arrows, and rouse your father, Leaping Buck," whispered the trapper, "and keep well out o' sight."

Next moment, picking up his empty rifle, he stalked from the fringe of bushes that partially screened the cliff, and gave himself up.

"Ha ! I know you—Mahogany Drake !   Is it not so ?" cried Stalker, savagely.   "Seize him, men.   You shall swing for this, you rascal."

Two or three of the robbers advanced, but Drake quietly held up his hand, and they stopped.

"I'm in your power, you see," he said, laying his rifle on the ground.   "Yes," he continued, drawing his tall figure up to its full height, and crossing his arms on his breast, "my name is Drake.   As to Mahogany, I've no objection to it, though it ain't complimentary.   If, as you say, Mister Stalker, I'm to swing for this, of course I must swing.   Yet it do seem raither hard that a man should swing for savin' his friend's life an' his enemy's at the same time."

"How—what do you mean ?"

"I mean that Mister Brixton is my friend," answered the trapper, "and I've saved his life just now, for which I thank the Lord.   At the same time, Stalker is my enemy—leastwise I fear he's no friend—an' didn't I save *his* life too when I put a ball in his arm that I could have as easily put into his head or his heart ?"

"Well," responded Stalker, with a fiendish grin, that the increasing pain of his wound did not improve, "at all events you have not saved your own life, Drake. As I said, you shall swing for it. But I'll give you one chance. If you choose to help me I will spare your life. Can you tell me where Paul Bevan and his daughter are?"

"They are with Unaco and his tribe."

"I could have guessed as much as that. I ask you *where* they are."

"On the other side of yonder mountain range, where the chief's village lies."

Somewhat surprised at the trapper's readiness to give the information required, and rendered a little suspicious, Stalker asked if he was ready and willing to guide him to the Indian village.

"Surely. If that's the price I'm to pay for my life, it can be easily paid," replied the trapper.

"Ay, but you shall march with your arms bound until we are there, and the fight wi' the redskins is over," said the robber-chief, "and if I find treachery in your acts or looks I'll blow your brains out on the spot. My left hand, you shall find, can work as well as the right wi' the revolver."

"A beggar, they say, must not be a chooser," returned the trapper. "I accept your terms."

"Good. Here, Goff," said Stalker, turning to his lieutenant, "bind his hands behind him after he's had some supper, and then come an' fix up this arm o' mine. I think the bone has escaped."

"Hadn't we better start off at once," suggested Drake, "an' catch the redskins when they're asleep?"

"Is it far off?" asked Stalker.

"A goodish bit. But the night is young. We might

git pretty near by midnight, and then encamp so as to
git an hour's sleep before makin' the attack.   You see,
redskins sleep soundest just before daybreak."

While he was speaking the trapper coughed a good
deal, and sneezed once or twice, as if he had a bad cold.

" Can't you keep your throat and nose quieter ?" said
the chief, sternly.

" Well, p'r'aps I might," replied Drake, emitting a
highly suppressed cough at the moment, " but I 've got a
queer throat just now.   The least thing affects it."

After consultation with the principal men of his band,
Stalker determined to act on Drake's advice, and in a few
minutes the trapper was guiding them over the hills in a
state of supreme satisfaction, despite his bonds, for had
he not obtained the power to make the robbers encamp
on a spot which the Indians could not avoid passing on
their way to the rescue, and had he not established a
sort of right to emit sounds which would make his
friends aware of his exact position, and thus bring both
parties into collision before daybreak, which could not
have been the case if the robbers had remained in the
encampment where he found them ?

Turn we now to Leaping Buck and Tolly Trevor.
Need it be said that these intelligent lads did not, as the
saying is, allow grass to grow under their feet ?   The
former went over the hills at a pace and in a manner
that fully justified his title ; and the latter followed with
as much vigour and resolution, if not as much agility, as
his friend.

In a wonderfully short space of time, considering the
distance, they burst upon the Indian village, and aroused
it with the startling news.

Warfare in those regions was not the cumbrous and
slow affair that it is in civilised places.   There was no

commissariat, no ammunition wagons, no baggage, no camp-followers to hamper the line of march. In five or ten minutes after the alarm was given about two hundred Indian braves marched out from the camp in a column which may be described as one-deep—*i.e.* one following the other—and took their rapid way up the mountain-sides, led by Unaco in person. Next to him marched Paul Bevan, who was followed in succession by Fred Westly, Paddy Flinders, Leaping Buck, and Tolly.

For some time the long line could be seen by the Rose of Oregon passing swiftly up the mountain-side. Then, as distance united the individuals, as it were, to each other, it assumed the form of a mighty snake crawling *slowly* along. By degrees it crawled over the nearest ridge and disappeared, after which Betty went to discuss the situation with Unaco's old mother.

It was near midnight when the robber-band encamped in a wooded hollow which was backed on two sides by precipices and on the third by a deep ravine.

"A good spot to set a host at defiance," remarked Stalker, glancing round with a look that would have expressed satisfaction if the wounded arm had allowed.

"Yes," added the trapper, "and—" A violent fit of coughing prevented the completion of the sentence, which, however, when thought out in Drake's mind ran—"a good spot for hemming you and your scoundrels in and starving you into submission!"

A short time sufficed for a bite of cold supper and a little whiff, soon after which the robber camp, with the exception of the sentinels, was buried in repose.

Tom Brixton was not allowed to have any intercourse whatever with his friend Drake. Both were bound and made to sleep in different parts of the camp. Nevertheless, during one brief moment, when they chanced to be near each other, Drake whispered, "Be ready!" and Tom heard him.

Ere long no sound was heard in the camp save an occasional snore or sigh, and Drake's constant and hacking, but highly suppressed, cough. Poor fellow! He was obviously consumptive, and it was quite touching to note the careful way in which he tried to restrain himself, giving vent to as little sound as was consistent with his purpose.

Turning a corner of jutting rock in the valley which led to the spot, Unaco's sharp and practised ear caught the sound. He stopped and stood like a bronze statue by Michael Angelo in the attitude of suddenly arrested motion. Upwards of two hundred bronze arrested statues instantly tailed away from him.

Presently a smile, such as Michael Angelo probably never thought of reproducing, rippled on the usually grave visage of the chief.

"M'ogany Drake!" he whispered, softly, in Paul Bevan's ear.

"I didn't know Drake had sitch a horrid cold," whispered Bevan, in reply.

Tolly Trevor clenched his teeth and screwed himself up internally to keep down the laughter that all but burst him, for he saw through the device at once. As for Leaping Buck, he did more than credit to his sire, because he kept as grave as Michael Angelo himself could have desired while chiselling his features.

"Musha! but that is a quare sound," whispered Flinders to Westly.

"Hush!" returned Westly.

At a signal from their chief the whole band of Indians sank, as it seemed, into the ground, melted off the face of the earth, and only the white men and the chief remained.

" I must go forward alone," whispered Unaco, turning
to Paul. " White man knows not how to go on his belly
like the serpent."

" Mahogany Drake would be inclined to dispute that
p'int with 'ee," returned Bevan. " However, you know
best, so we 'll wait till you give us the signal to
advance."

Having directed his white friends to lie down, Unaco
divested himself of all superfluous clothing, and glided
swiftly but noiselessly towards the robber camp, with
nothing but a tomahawk in his hand and a scalping-knife
in his girdle. He soon reached the open side of the
wooded hollow, guided thereto by Drake's persistent
and evidently distressing cough. Here it became
necessary to advance with the utmost caution. Fortunately for the success of his enterprise, all the sentinels
that night had been chosen from among the white men.
The consequence was that, although they were wide
awake and on the *qui vive,* their unpractised senses failed
to detect the very slight sounds that Unaco made while
gliding slowly—inch by inch, and with many an anxious
pause—into the very midst of his foes. It was a trying
situation, for instant death would have been the result of
discovery.

As if to make matters more difficult for him just then,
Drake's hacking cough ceased, and the Indian could not
make out where he lay. Either his malady was depart-
ing or he had fallen into a temporary slumber ! That the
latter was the case became apparent from his suddenly
recommencing the cough. This, however, had the effect
of exasperating one of the sentinels.

" Can't you stop that noise ?" he muttered, sternly.

" I 'm doin' my best to smother it," said Drake in a
conciliatory tone.

Apparently he had succeeded, for he coughed no more after that. But the fact was that a hand had been gently laid upon his arm.

" So soon !" he thought. " Well done, boys !" But he said never a word, while a pair of lips touched his ear and said, in the Indian tongue—

" Where lies your friend ?"

Drake sighed sleepily, and gave a short and intensely subdued cough, as he turned his lips to a brown ear which seemed to rise out of the grass for the purpose, and spoke something that was inaudible to all save that ear. Instantly hand, lips, and ear withdrew, leaving the trapper in apparently deep repose. A sharp knife, however, had touched his bonds, and he knew that he was free.

A few minutes later, and the same hand touched Tom Brixton's arm. He would probably have betrayed himself by an exclamation, but, remembering Drake's " Be ready," he lay perfectly still while the hands, knife, and lips did their work. The latter merely said, in broken English, " Rise when me rise, an' run !"

Next instant Unaco leaped to his feet, and, with a terrific yell of defiance, bounded into the bushes. Tom Brixton followed him like an arrow, and so prompt was Mahogany Drake to act that he and Tom came into violent collision as they cleared the circle of light thrown by the few sinking embers of the camp-fires. No damage, however, was done. At the same moment the band of Indians in ambush sprang up with their terrible war-whoop and rushed towards the camp. This effectually checked the pursuit which had been instantly begun by the surprised bandits, who at once retired to the shelter of the mingled rocks and shrubs in the centre of the hollow, from out of which position they fired several tremendous volleys.

UNACO ON THE TRAIL.

"That's right—waste yer ammunition," said Paul
Bevan, with a short laugh, as he and the rest lay quickly
down to let the leaden shower pass over.

"It's always the way wi' men taken by surprise," said
Drake, who, with Brixton and the chief, had stopped in
their flight and turned with their friends. "They blaze
away wildly for a bit, just to relieve their feelin's, I s'pose.
But they'll soon stop."

"An' what'll we do now?" inquired Flinders, "for it
seems to me we've got all we want out o' them, an' it's
no use fightin' them for mere fun—though it's mesilf
that used to like fightin' for that same; but I think the
air of Oregon has made me more peaceful inclined."

"But the country has been kept for a long time in
constant alarm and turmoil by these men," said Fred
Westly, "and, although I like fighting as little as
any man, I cannot help thinking that we owe it as a
duty to society to capture as many of them as we can,
especially now that we seem to have caught them in a
sort of trap."

"What says Mahogany Drake on the subject?" asked
Unaco.

"I vote for fightin', 'cause there'll be no peace in the
country till the band is broken up."

"Might it not be better to hold them prisoners here?"
suggested Paul Bevan. "They can't escape, you tell me,
except by this side, and there's nothin' so good for tamin'
men as hunger."

"Ah!" said Tom Brixton, "you speak the truth, Bevan;
I have tried it."

"But what does Unaco himself think?" asked
Westly.

"We must fight 'em at once, an' root them out neck
and crop!"

These words were spoken, not by the Indian, but by a deep bass voice which sent a thrill of surprise, not unmingled with alarm, to more hearts than one; and no wonder, for it was the voice of Gashford, the big bully of Pine Tree Diggings!

CHAPTER XX.

TO account for the sudden appearance of Gashford, as told in our last chapter, it is necessary to explain that two marauding Indians chanced to pay Pine Tree Diggings a visit one night almost immediately after the unsuccessful attack made by Stalker and his men. The savages were more successful than the white robbers had been. They managed to carry off a considerable quantity of gold without being discovered, and Gashford, erroneously attributing their depredations to a second visit from Stalker, was so enraged that he resolved to pursue and utterly root out the robber-band. Volunteers were not wanting. Fifty stout young fellows offered their services and at the head of these Gashford set out for the Saw-back Mountains, which were known to be the retreat of the bandits. An Indian, who knew the region well, and had once been ill-treated by Stalker, became a willing guide.

He led the gold-diggers to the robbers' retreat, and there, learning from a brother savage that the robber-chief and his men had gone off to hunt up Paul Bevan in the region that belonged to Unaco, he led his party by a short cut over the mountains, and chanced to come on the scene of action at the critical moment when Unaco and his party were about to attack the robbers. Ignorant of who the parties were that contended, yet feeling pretty sure that the men he sought for probably formed one of

Q

them, he formed the somewhat hazardous determination, personally and alone, to join the rush of the assailants, under cover of the darkness; telling his lieutenant, Crossby, to await his return, or to bring on his men at the run if they should hear his well-known signal.

On joining the attacking party without having been observed—or, rather, having been taken for one of the band in the uncertain light—he recognised Westly's and Flinders's voices at once, and thus it was that he suddenly gave his unasked advice on the subject then under discussion.

But Stalker's bold spirit settled the question for them in an unexpected manner. Perceiving at once that he had been led into a trap, he felt that his only chance lay in decisive and rapid action.

" Men," he said to those who crowded round him in the entre of the thicket which formed their encampment, " we've bin caught. Our only chance lies in a bold rush and then scatter. Are you ready ?"

" Ready !" responded nearly every man. Those who might have been unwilling were silent, for they knew that objection would be useless. " Come on, then, an' give them a screech when ye burst out !"

Like an avalanche of demons the robber band rushed down the slope and crashed into their foes, and a yell that might well have been born of the regions below rang from cliff to cliff, but the Indians were not daunted. Taken by surprise, however, many of them were overturned in the rush, when high above the din arose the bass roar of Gashford.

Crossby heard the signal and led his men down to the scene of battle at a rapid run. But the robbers were too quick for them ; most of them were already scattering far and wide through the wilderness. Only one group had been checked, and, strange to say, that was the party that happened to cluster round and rush with their chief.

But the reason was clear enough, for that section of the foe had been met by Mahogany Drake, Bevan, Westly, Brixton, Flinders, and the rest, while Gashford at last met his match in the person of the gigantic Stalker. But they did not meet on equal terms, for the robber's wounded arm was almost useless. Still, with the other arm he fired a shot at the huge digger, missed, and, flinging the weapon at his head, grappled with him. There was a low precipice or rocky ledge, about fifteen feet high, close to them. Over this the two giants went after a brief but furious struggle, and here, after the short fight was over, they were found, grasping each other by their throats, and in a state of insensibility.

Only two other prisoners were taken besides Stalker— one by Bevan, the other by Flinders. But these were known by Drake to be poor wretches who had only joined the band a few weeks before, and as they protested that they had been captured and forced to join, they were set free.

"You see, it's of no manner o' use hangin' the wretched critters," observed Drake to Bevan, confidentially, when they were returning to the Indian village the following morning. "It would do them no good. All that we wanted was to break up the band and captur' the chief, which bein' done, it would be a shame to shed blood uselessly."

"But we must hang Stalker," said little Tolly, who had taken part in the attack, and whose sense of justice, it seems, would have been violated if the leader of the band had been spared.

"I'm inclined to think he won't want hangin', Tolly," replied Drake, gravely. "That tumble didn't improve his wounded arm, for Gashford fell atop of him."

The trapper's fear was justified.   When Stalker was
carried into the Indian village and examined by Fred
Westly, it was found that, besides other injuries, two of
his ribs had been broken, and he was already in high
fever.

Betty Bevan, whose sympathy with all sufferers was
strong, volunteered to nurse him, and, as she was
unquestionably the best nurse in the place, her services
were accepted.   Thus it came about that the robber-chief
and the Rose of Oregon were for a time brought into
close companionship.

On the morning after their return to the Indian village,
Paul Bevan and Betty sauntered away towards the lake.
The Rose had been with Stalker the latter part of the
night, and after breakfast had said she would take a stroll
to let the fresh air blow sleepiness away.   Paul had
offered to go with her.

"Well, Betty, lass, what think ye of this robber-chief,
now you've seen somethin' of him at close quarters?"
asked Paul, as they reached the margin of the lake.

"I have scarcely seen him in his right mind, father,
for he has been wandering a little at times during the
night; and, oh! you cannot think what terrible things he
has been talking about."

"Has he?" said Paul, glancing at Betty with sudden
earnestness.   "What did he speak about?"

"I can scarcely tell you, for at times he mixed up his
ideas so that I could not understand him, but I fear he
has led a very bad life and done many wicked things.
He brought in your name, too, pretty often, and seemed
to confuse you with himself, putting on you the blame of
deeds which just a minute before he had confessed he had
himself done."

"Ay, did he?" said Paul, with a peculiar expression

and tone. " Well, he warn't far wrong, for I *have* helped him sometimes."

" Father !" exclaimed Betty, with a shocked look— " but you misunderstand. He spoke of such things as burglary and highway robbery, and you could never have helped him in deeds of that kind."

" Oh ! he spoke of such things as these, did he ?" returned Paul. " Well, yes, he's bin up to a deal of mischief in his day. And what did you say to him, lass ? Did you try to quiet him ?"

" What could I say, father, except tell him the old, old story of Jesus and His love ; that He came to seek and to save the lost, even the chief of sinners ?"

" An' how did he take it ?" inquired Paul, with a grave, almost an anxious look.

" At first he would not listen, but when I began to read the Word to him, and then tried to explain what seemed suitable to him, he got up on his unhurt elbow and looked at me with such a peculiar and intense look that I felt almost alarmed, and was forced to stop. Then he seemed to wander again in his mind, for he said such a strange thing "

" What was that, Betty ?"

" He said I was like his mother."

" Well, lass, he wasn't far wrong, for you *are* uncommon like her."

" Did you know his mother, then ?"

" Ay, Betty, I knowed her well, an' a fine, good-lookin' woman she was, wi' a kindly, religious soul, just like yours. She was a'most heartbroken about her son, who was always wild, but she had a strong power over him, for he was very fond of her, and I 've no doubt that your readin' the Bible an' telling him about Christ brought back old times to his mind."

"But if his mother was so good and taught him so carefully, and, as I doubt not, prayed often and earnestly for him, how was it that he fell into such awful ways?" asked Betty.

"It was the old, old story, lass, on the other side o' the question—drink and bad companions—and—and *I* was one of them."

"You, father, the companion of a burglar and highway robber?"

"Well, he wasn't just that at the time, though both him and me was bad enough. It was my refusin' to jine him in some of his jobs that made a coolness between us, an' when his mother died I gave him some trouble about money matters, which turned him into my bitterest foe. He vowed he would take my life, and as he was one o' those chaps that when they say they'll do a thing are sure to do it, I thought it best to bid adieu to old England, especially as I was wanted at the time by the police."

Poor Rose of Oregon! The shock to her feelings was terrible, for, although she had always suspected from some traits in his character that her father had led a wild life, it had never entered her imagination that he was an outlaw. For some time she remained silent with her face in her hands, quite unable to collect her thoughts or decide what to say, for whatever her father might have been in the past he had been invariably kind to her, and, moreover, had given very earnest heed to the loving words which she often spoke when urging him to come to the Saviour. At last she looked up quickly.

"Father," she said, "I will nurse this man with more anxious care and interest, for his mother's sake."

"You may do it, dear lass, for his own sake," returned Paul, impressively, "for he is your own brother."

"My brother?" gasped Betty. "Why, what do you mean, father? Surely you are jesting!"

"Very far from jesting, lass. Stalker is your brother Edwin, whom you haven't seen since you was a small girl and you thought was dead. But, come, as the cat's out o' the bag at last, I may as well make a clean breast of it. Sit down here on the bank, Betty, and listen."

The poor girl obeyed almost mechanically, for she was well-nigh stunned by the unexpected news which Paul had given her, and of which, from her knowledge of her father's character, she could not doubt the truth.

"Then Stalker—Edwin—must be your own son!" she said, looking at Paul earnestly.

"Nay, he's not my son, no more than you are my daughter. Forgive me, Betty. I've deceived you throughout, but I did it with a good intention. You see, if I hadn't passed myself off as your father, I'd never have bin able to git ye out o' the boardin'-school where ye was putt. But I did it for the best, Betty, I did it for the best; an' all to benefit your poor mother an' you. That is how it was."

He paused, as if endeavouring to recall the past, and Betty sat with her hands clasped, gazing in Paul's face like a fascinated creature, unable to speak or move.

"You see, Betty," he resumed, "your real father was a doctor in the army, an' I'm sorry to have to add, he was a bad man—so bad that he went and deserted your mother soon after you was born. I raither think that your brother Edwin must have got his wickedness from him, just as you got your goodness from your mother; but I've bin told that your father became a better man before he died, an' I can well believe it, wi' such a woman as your mother prayin' for him every day as long as he lived. Well, when you was about six, your

brother Edwin, who was then about twenty, had got so
bad in his ways, an' used to kick up sitch shindies in the
house, an' swore so terrible, that your mother made up
her mind to send you to a boardin'-school, to keep you
out o' harm's way, though it nigh broke her heart; for
you seemed to be the only comfort she had in life.

"About that time I was goin' a good deal about the
house, bein', as I've said, a chum o' your brother. But
he was goin' too fast for me, and that made me split with
him. I tried at first to make him hold in a bit; but
what was the use of a black sheep like me tryin' to make
a white sheep o' *him ?* The thing was so absurd that he
laughed at it; indeed, we both laughed at it. Your mother
was at that time very poorly off—made a miserable livin'
by dressmakin'. Indeed, she'd have bin half starved if
I hadn't given her a helpin' hand in a small way now an'
then. She was very grateful, and very friendly wi' me,
for I was very fond of her, and she know'd that, bad as I
was, I tried to restrain her son to some extent. So she
told me about her wish to git you well out o' the house,
an' axed me if I'd go an' put you in a school down at
Brighton, which she know'd was a good an' a cheap one.

"Of course I said I would, for, you see, the poor thing
was that hard worked that she couldn't git away from
her stitch-stitchin' not even for an hour, much less a day.
When I got down to the school, before goin' up to the
door it came into my head that it would be better that
the people should know you was well looked after, so
says I to you, quite sudden, 'Betty, remember you're to
call me father when you speak about me.' You turned
your great blue eyes to my face, dear lass, when I said
that, with a puzzled look.

"'Me sought mamma say father was far far away in
other country,' says you.

"'That's true,' says I, 'but I've come home from the other country, you see, so don't you forget to call me father.'

"'Vewy well, fadder,' says you, in your own sweet way, for you was always a biddable child, an' did what you was told without axin' questions.

"Well, when I'd putt you in the school an' paid the first quarter in advance, an' told 'em that the correspondence would be done chiefly through your mother, I went back to London, puzzlin' my mind all the way what I'd say to your mother for what I'd done. Once it came into my head I would ax her to marry me—for she was a widow by that time—an' so make the deception true. But I quickly putt that notion a one side, for I know'd I might as well ax an angel to come down from heaven an' dwell wi' me in a backwoods shanty—but, after all," said Paul, with a quiet laugh, "I did get an angel to dwell wi' me in a backwoods shanty when I got you, Betty! Howsever, as things turned out I was saved the trouble of explainin'.

"When I got back I found your mother in a great state of excitement. She'd just got a letter from the West Indies, tellin' her that a distant relation had died an' left her a small fortin! People's notions about the size o' fortins differs. Enough an' to spare is oceans o' wealth to some. Thousands o' pounds is poverty to others. She'd only just got the letter, an' was so taken up about it that she couldn't help showin' it to me.

"'Now,' says I, 'Mrs. Buxley'—that was her name, an' your real name too, Betty—says I, 'make your will right off, an putt it away safe, leavin' every rap o' that fortin to Betty, for you may depend on 't, if Edwin gits wind o' this, he'll worm it out o' you, by hook or by crook—you know he will—and go straight to the dogs at full gallop.'

"'What!' says she, 'an' leave nothin' to my boy?—
my poor boy, for whom I have never ceased to pray!
He may repent, you know—he *will* repent, I feel sure of
it—and then he will find that his mother left him
nothing, though God had sent her a fortune.'

"'Oh! as to that,' says I, 'make your mind easy. If
Edwin does repent an' turn to honest ways he's got
talents and go enough in him to make his way in the world
without help; but you can leave him what you like, you
know, only make sure that you leave the bulk of it to
Betty.'

"This seemed to strike her as a plan that would do, for
she was silent for some time, and then, suddenly makin'
up her mind, she said, 'I'll go and ask God's help in this
matter, an' then see about gettin' a lawyer—for I suppose
a thing o' this sort can't be done without one.'

"'No, mum,' says I, 'it can't. You may, if you
choose, 'make a muddle of it without a lawyer, but you
can't do it right without one.'

"'Can you recommend one to me?' says she.

"I was greatly tickled at the notion o' the likes o' me
bein' axed to recommend a lawyer. It was so like your
mother's innocence and trustfulness. Howsever, she'd
come to the right shop, as it happened, for I did know a
honest lawyer! Yes, Betty, from the way the world
speaks, an' what's often putt in books, you'd fancy there
warn't such'n a thing to be found on 'arth. But that's
all bam, Betty. Leastwise I know'd one honest firm.
'Yes, Mrs. Buxley,' says I, 'there's a firm o' the name o'
Truefoot, Tickle, and Badger in the City, who can do
a'most anything that's possible to man. But you'll have
to look sharp, for if Edwin comes home an' diskivers
what's doin', it's all up with the fortin an' Betty.'

"Well, to make a long story short, your mother went

to the lawyer's an' had her will made, leavin' a good lump
of a sum to your brother, but the most of the fortin to
you. By the advice o' Truefoot, Tickle, and Badger, she
made it so that you shouldn't touch the money till you
come to be twenty-one, 'for,' says she, 'there's no sayin'
what bad men will be runnin' after the poor thing an'
deceivin' her for the sake of her money before she is of
an age to look after herself.' 'Yes,' thought I, 'an'
there's no sayin' what bad men 'll be runnin' after the
poor thing an' deceivin' of her for the sake of her money
after she's of an age to look after herself,' but I didn't
say that out, for your mother was excited enough and
over-anxious about things, I could see that.

"Well, when the will was made out all right she took
it out of her chest one night an' read it all over to me.
I could see it was shipshape, though I couldn't read a
word of its crabbed letters myself.

"'Now Mrs. Buxley,' says I. 'where are you goin' to
keep that dockiment?'

"'In my chest,' says she.

"'Won't be safe there,' says I, for I knowed her for-
givin' and confidin' natur' too well, an' that she'd never
be able to keep it from your brother; but, before I could
say more, there was a tremendous knockin' wi' a stick at
the front door. Your poor mother turned pale—she know'd
the sound too well. 'That's Edwin,' she says, jumpin' up
an' runnin' to open the door, forgetting all about the will,
so I quietly folded it up an' shoved it in my pocket.

"When Edwin was comin' up stairs I know'd he was
very drunk and savage by the way he was goin' on, an'
when he came into the room an' saw me he gave a yell of
rage. 'Didn't I tell you never to show your face here
again?' says he. 'Just so,' says I, 'but not bein' subjec'
to your orders, d'ye see, I *am* here again.'

"Wi' that he swore a terrible oath an' rushed at me, but he tripped over a footstool and fell flat on the floor. Before he could recover himself I made myself scarce an' went home.

"Next mornin', when I'd just finished breakfast, a thunderin' rap came to the door. I know'd it well enough. 'Now look out for squalls,' said I to myself, as I went an' opened it. Edwin jumped in, banged the door to, an' locked it.

"'You've no occasion to do that,' says I, 'for I don't expect no friends—not even bobbies.'

"'You double-faced villain!' says he; 'you've bin robbin' my mother!'

"'Come, come,' says I, 'civility, you know, between pals. What have I done to your mother?'

"'You needn't try to deceive me, Paul,' says he, tryin' to keep his temper down. 'Mother's bin took bad, wi' over-excitement the doctor says, an' she's told me all about the fortin an' the will, an' where Betty is down at Brighton.'

"'My Betty at Brighton!' says I—pretendin' great surprise, for I had a darter at that time whom I had called after your mother, for that was her name too—but she's dead, poor thing!—she was dyin' in hospital at the very time we was speakin', though I didn't know at the time that her end was so near—'my Betty at Brighton!' says I. 'Why, she's in hospital. Bin there for some weeks.'

"'I don't mean *your* brat, but my sister,' says Edwin, quite fierce. 'Where have you put her? What's the name of the school? What have you done wi' the will?'

"'You'd better ax your mother,' says I. 'It's likely that she knows the partiklers better nor me.'

"He lost patience altogether at this, an' sprang at me

like a tiger. But I was ready for him. We had a regular set-to then an' there. By good luck there was no weapons of any kind in the room, not even a table knife, for I'd had to pawn a'most everything to pay my rent, and the clasp-knife I'd eat my breakfast with was in my pocket. But we was both handy with our fists. We kep' at it for about half an hour. Smashed all the furniture, an' would have smashed the winders too, but there was only one, an' it was a skylight. In the middle of it the door was burst open, an' in rushed half a dozen bobbies, who put a stop to it at once.

"'We're only havin' a friendly bout wi' the gloves,' says I, smilin' quite sweet.

"'I don't see no gloves,' says the man as held me.

"'That's true,' says I, lookin' at my hands. 'They must have dropped off an' rolled up the chimbly.'

"'Hallo! Edwin Buxley!' said the sargeant, lookin' earnestly at your brother; 'why you've bin wanted for some time. Here, Joe! the bracelets.'

"In half a minute he was marched off. 'I'll have your blood, Paul, for this,' he said bitterly, looking back as he went out.

"As *I* wasn't 'wanted' just then, I went straight off to see your mother, to find out how much she had told to Edwin, for from what he had said I feared she must have told all. I was anxious, also, to see if she'd bin really ill. When I got to the house I met a nurse who said she was dyin' an' would hardly let me in, till I got her persuaded I was an intimate friend. On reachin' the bedroom I saw by the looks o' two women who were standin' there that it was serious. And so it was, for there lay your poor mother, as pale as death; her eyes closed and her lips white; but there was a sweet, contented smile on her face, and her thin hands clasped her well-worn Bible to her breast."

Paul Bevan stopped, for the poor girl had burst into tears.   For a time he was silent and laid his heavy hand gently on her shoulder.

" I did not ventur' to speak to her," he continued, " an' indeed it would have been of no use, for she was past hearin'.   A few minutes later and her gentle spirit went up to God.

" I had no time now to waste, for I knew that your brother would give information that might be bad for me, so I asked the nurse to write down, while I repeated it, the lawyer's address.

" ' Now,' says I, ' go there an' tell 'em what 's took place. It 'll be the better for yourself if you do.'   An' then I went straight off to Brighton."

CHAPTER XXI.

"WELL, you must know," said Paul Bevan, continuing his discourse to the Rose of Oregon, "when I got to Brighton I went to the school, told 'em that your mother was just dead, and brought you straight away. I wasn't an hour too soon, for, as I expected, your brother had given information, an' the p'lice were on my heels in a jiffy, but I was too sharp for 'em. I went into hidin' in London; an' you 've no notion, Betty, what a rare place London is to hide in! A needle what takes to wanderin' in a haystack ain't safer than a feller is in London, if he only knows how to go about the business.

"I lay there nigh three months, durin' which time my own poor child Betty continued hoverin' 'tween life an' death. At last, one night when I was at the hospital sittin' beside her, she suddenly raised her sweet face, an' fixin' her big eyes on me, said—

"'Father, I 'm goin' home. Shall I tell mother that you 're comin'?'

"'What d'ye mean, my darlin'?' says I, while an awful thump came to my heart, for I saw a great change come over her.

"'I 'll be there soon, father,' she said, as her dear voice began to fail; 'have you no message for mother?'

"I was so crushed that I couldn't speak, so she went on—

"'You 'll come—won't you, father? an' we 'll be so glad to welcome you to heaven. An' so will Jesus.

Remember, He is the only door, father, no name but that of Jesus—' She stopped all of a sudden, and I saw that she had gone home.

"After that," continued Paul, hurrying on as if the memory of the event was too much for him, "havin' nothin' to keep me in England, I came off here to the gold-fields with you, an' brought the will with me, intendin', when you came of age, to tell you all about it, an' see justice done both to you an' to your brother, but—"

"Fath—Paul," said Betty, checking herself, "that brown parcel you gave me long ago with such earnest directions to keep it safe, and only to open it if you were killed, is—"

"That's the will, my dear."

"And Edwin—does he think that I am your real daughter Betty ?"

"No doubt he does, for he never heard of her bein' dead, and he never saw you since you was quite a little thing, an' there's a great change on you since then—a wonderful change."

"Yes fath— Oh ! it is so hard to lose my father," said Betty, almost breaking down, and letting her hands fall listlessly into her lap.

"But why lose him, Betty ? I did it all for the best," said Paul, gently taking hold of one of the poor girl's hands.

She made a slight motion to withdraw it, but checked herself and let it rest in the man's rough but kindly grasp, while tears silently coursed down her rounded cheeks. Presently she looked up and said—

"How did Edwin find out where you had gone to ?"

"That's more than I can tell, Betty, unless it was through Truefoot, Tickle, and Badger. I wrote to them after gettin' here, tellin' them to look well after the property, and it would be claimed in good time, an' I raither fear that the postmark on the letter must have let the cat out o' the bag. Anyhow, not long after that Edwin found me out, an' you know how he has persecuted me, though you little thought he was your own brother when you were beggin' of me not to kill him—no more did you guess that I was as little anxious to kill him as you were, though I did pretend I'd have to do it now an' then in self-defence. Sometimes, indeed, he riled me up to sitch an extent that there wasn't much pretence about it; but, thank God! my hand has been held back."

"Yes, thank God for that; and now I must go to him," said Betty, rising hastily and hurrying back to the Indian village.

In a darkened tent, on a soft couch of deerskins, the dying form of Buxley, alias Stalker, lay extended. In the fierceness of his self-will he had neglected his wounds until too late to save his life. A look of stern resolution sat on his countenance—probably he had resolved to "die game," as hardened criminals express it. His determination, on whatever ground based, was evidently not shaken by the arguments of a man who sat by his couch. It was Tom Brixton.

"What's the use o' preachin' to me, young fellow?" said the robber-chief, testily. "I dare say you are pretty nigh as great a scoundrel as I am."

"Perhaps a greater," returned Tom. "I have no wish to enter into comparisons, but I'm quite prepared to admit that I am as bad."

"Well, then, you've as much need as I have to seek salvation for yourself."

"Indeed I have, and it is because I have sought it and obtained it," said Tom, earnestly, "that I am anxious to point out the way to you. I've come through much the same experiences, no doubt, as you have. I have been a scouter of my mother's teachings, a thief, and, in heart if not in act, a murderer.   No one could be more urgently in need of salvation *from sin* than I, and I used to think that I was so bad that my case was hopeless, until God opened my eyes to see that Jesus came to save His people *from their sins.*   That is what you need, is it not?"

"Ay, but it is too late," said Stalker, bitterly.

"The crucified thief did not find it too late," returned Tom, "and it was the eleventh hour with him."

Stalker made no reply, but the stern, hard expression of his face did not change one iota until he heard a female voice outside asking if he were asleep.   Then the features relaxed ; the frown passed like a summer cloud before the sun, and, with half-open lips and a look of glad, almost childish expectancy, he gazed at the curtain-door of the tent.

"Mother's voice !" he murmured, apparently in utter forgetfulness of Tom Brixton's presence.

Next moment the curtain was raised, and Betty, entering quickly, advanced to the side of the couch.   Tom rose, as if about to leave.

"Don't go, Mr. Brixton," said the girl, "I wish you to hear us."

"My brother !" she continued, turning to the invalid, and grasping his hand, for the first time, as she sat down beside him.

"If you were not so young I'd swear you were my mother," exclaimed Stalker, with a slight look of surprise at the changed manner of his nurse.   "Ha ! I wish that I were indeed your brother."

"But you *are* my brother, Edwin Buxley," cried the girl with intense earnestness, "my dear and only brother, whom God will save through Jesus Christ."

"What do you mean, Betty ?" asked Stalker, with an anxious and puzzled look.

"IT IS TOO LATE."—Page 258.

"I mean that I am *not* Betty Bevan. Paul Bevan has told me so—told me that I am Betty Buxley, and your sister!"

The dying man's chest heaved with labouring breath, for his wasted strength was scarcely sufficient to bear this shock of surprise.

"I would not believe it," he said, with some difficulty, "even though Paul Bevan were to swear to it, were it not for the wonderful likeness both in look and tone." He pressed her hand fervently, and added, "Yes, dear Betty, I *do* believe that you are my very sister."

Tom Brixton, from an instinctive feeling of delicacy, left the tent, while the Rose of Oregon related to her brother the story of her life with Paul Bevan, and then followed it up with the story of God's love to man in Jesus Christ.

Tom hurried to Bevan's tent to have the unexpected and surprising news confirmed, and Paul told him a good deal, but was very careful to make no allusion to Betty's "fortin."

"Now, Mister Brixton," said Paul, somewhat sternly, when he had finished, "there must be no more shilly-shallyin' wi' Betty's feelin's. You 're fond o' *her*, an' she's fond o' *you*. In them circumstances a man is bound to wed—all the more that the poor thing has lost her nat'ral protector, so to speak, for I 'm afraid she 'll no longer look upon me as a father."

There was a touch of pathos in Paul's tone as he concluded, which checked the rising indignation in Brixton's breast.

"But you forget, Paul, that Gashford and his men are here, and will probably endeavour to lay hold of me. I can scarce look on myself as other than an outlaw."

"Pooh! lay hold of you!" exclaimed Paul, with

contempt; "d'ye think Gashford or any one else will dare
to touch you with Mahogany Drake an' Mister Fred an'
Flinders an' me; and Unaco with all his Injins at your
back?   Besides, let me tell you that Gashford seems
a changed man.   I've had a talk wi' him about you,
an' he said he was done persecutin' of you—that you
had made restitootion when you left all the goold on
the river's bank for him to pick up, and that as nobody
else in partikler wanted to hang you, you'd nothin' to
fear."

"Well, that does change the aspect of affairs," said Tom,
"and it may be that you are right in your advice about
Betty.   I have twice tried to get away from her and have
failed.   Perhaps it may be right now to do as you suggest,
though after all the time seems not very suitable; but, as
you truly observe, she has lost her natural protector, for
of course you cannot be a father to her any longer.   Yes,
I'll go and see Fred about it."

Tom had considerable qualms of conscience as to the
propriety of the step he meditated, and tried to argue with
himself as he went in search of his friend.

"You see," he soliloquised aloud, "her brother is dying;
and then, though I am not a whit more worthy of her than
I was, the case is nevertheless altered, for she has no
father now.   Then by marrying her I shall have a right
to protect her—and she stands greatly in need of a protector in this wild country at this time, poor thing! and
some one to work for her, seeing that she has no means
whatever!"

"Troth, an' that's just what she does need, sor!" said
Paddy Flinders, stepping out of the bush at the moment.
"Excuse me, sor, but I cudn't help hearin' ye, for ye was
spakin' out loud.   But I agree with ye intirely; an', if I
may make so bowld, I'm glad to find ye in that state o'

mind. Did ye hear the news, sor? They 've found goold at the hid o' the valley here."

"Indeed," said Tom, with a lack of interest that quite disgusted his volatile friend.

"Yes, indade," said he. "Why, sor, they 've found it in big nuggets in some places, an' Muster Gashford is off wid a party not half an hour past. I 'm goin' mesilf, only I thought I 'd see first if ye wouldn't jine me; but ye don't seem to care for goold no more nor if it was copper; an' that 's quare, too, whin it was the very objec' that brought ye here."

"Ah! Flinders, I have gained more than my object in coming. I *have* found gold—most fine gold, too, that I won't have to leave behind me when it pleases God to call me home. But, never fear, I 'll join you. I owe you and other friends a debt, and I must dig to pay that. Then, if I succeed in the little scheme which you overheard me planning, I shall need some gold to keep the pot boiling!"

"Good luck to ye, sor! so ye will. But plaze don't mintion the little debt you say you owe me an' the other boys. Ye don't owe us nothin' o' the sort. But who comes here? Muster Fred it is—the very man I want to see."

"Yes, and I want to see him too, Paddy, so let me speak first, for a brief space, in private, and you can have him as long as you like afterwards."

Fred Westly's opinion on the point which his friend put before him entirely coincided with that of Paul Bevan.

"I 'm not surprised to learn that Paul is not her father," he said. "It was always a puzzle to me how she came to be so lady-like and refined in her feelings, with such a rough though kindly father. But I can easily understand it now that I hear who and what her mother was."

But the principal person concerned in Tom Brixton's

little scheme held an adverse opinion to his friends Paul
and Fred and Flinders.   Betty would by no means listen
to Tom's proposals until, one day, her brother said that
he would like to see her married to Tom Brixton before
he died.   Then the obdurate Rose of Oregon gave in!

"But how is it to be managed without a clergyman?"
asked Fred Westly one evening over the camp fire when
supper was being prepared.

"Ay, how indeed?" said Tom, with a perplexed look.

"Oh, bother the clergy!" cried the irreverent Flinders.

"That's just what I'd do if there was one here,"
responded Tom; "I'd bother him till he married us."

"I say, what did Adam and Eve an' those sort o'
people do?" asked Tolly Trevor, with the sudden animation resulting from the budding of a new idea; "there
was no clergy in their day, I suppose?"

"True for ye, boy," remarked Flinders, as he lifted a
large pot of soup off the fire.

"I know and care not, Tolly, what those sort o' people
did," said Tom; "and as Betty and I are not Adam and
Eve, and the nineteenth century is not the first, we need
not inquire."

"I'll tell 'ee what," said Mahogany Drake, "it's just
comed into my mind that there's a missionary goes up
once a year to an outlyin' post o' the fur-traders, an' this
is about the very time.   What say ye to make an excursion there to get spliced, it's only about two hundred
miles off?   We could soon ride there an' back, for the
country's all pretty flattish after passin' the Sawback
range."

"The very thing!" cried Tom; "only— perhaps Betty
might object to go, her brother being so ill."

"Not she," said Fred; "since the poor man found in
her a sister as well as a nurse he seems to have got a

new lease of life.   I don't, indeed, think it possible that he can recover, but he may yet live a good while; and the mere fact that she has gone to get married will do him good."

So it was finally arranged that they should all go, and, before three days had passed, they went, with a strong band of their Indian allies.   They found the missionary as had been expected.   The knot was tied, and Tom Brixton brought back the Rose of Oregon as a blooming bride to the Sawback range.

From that date onward Tom toiled at the goldfields as if he had been a galley-slave, and scraped together every speck and nugget of gold he could find, and hoarded it up as if he had been a very miser, and, strange to say, Betty did not discourage him.

One day he entered his tent with a large canvas bag in his hand quite full.

"It's all here at last," he said, holding it up.   "I've had it weighed, and I'm going to square up."

"Go, dear Tom, and God speed you," said the Rose, giving him a kiss that could not have been purchased by all the gold in Oregon.

Tom went off, and soon returned with the empty bag.

"It was hard work, Betty, to get them to take it, but they agreed when I threatened to heave it all into the lake if they didn't!   Then—I ventured," said Tom, looking down with something like a blush—"it does seem presumptuous in me, but I couldn't help it—I preached to them!   I told them of my having been twice bought; of the gold that never perishes; and of the debt I owe, which I could never repay, like theirs, with interest, because it is incalculable.   And now, dear Betty, we begin the world afresh from to-day."

"Yes, and with clear consciences," returned Betty. "I like to re-commence life thus."

"But with empty pockets," added Tom, with a peculiar twist of his mouth.

"No, not quite empty," rejoined the young wife, drawing a very business-looking envelope from her pocket and handing it to her husband. "Read that, Tom."

Need we say that Tom read it with mingled amusement and amazement; that he laughed at it, and did not believe it; that he became grave, and inquired into it; and that, finally, when Paul Bevan detailed the whole affair, he was forced to believe it?

"An estate in the West Indies," he murmured to himself in a condition of semi-bewilderment, "yielding over fifteen hundred a year !"

"A tidy little fortin," remarked Paddy Flinders, who overheard him. "I hope, sor, ye won't forgit yer owld frinds in Oregon when ye go over to take possession."

"I won't, my boy—you may depend on that."

And he did not !

But Edwin Buxley did not live to enjoy his share of the fortune. Soon after the wedding he began to sink rapidly, and finally died while gazing earnestly in his sister's face, with the word "mother" trembling faintly on his lips. He was laid under a lordly tree not far from the Indian village in the Sawback range.

It was six months afterwards that Betty became of age and was entitled to go home and claim her own. She and Tom went first to a small village in Kent, where dwelt an old lady who for some time past had had her heart full to the very brim with gratitude because of a long-lost prodigal son having been brought back to her —saved by the blood of the Lamb. When at last she set her longing eyes on Tom, and heard his well-remem-

bered voice say "Mother!" the full heart overflowed and
rushed down the wrinkled cheeks in floods of inexpressible
joy.   And the floods were increased, and the joy intensified, when she turned at last to gaze on a little modest,
tearful, sympathetic flower, whom Tom introduced to her
as the Rose of Oregon!

Thereafter Tom and the Rose paid a visit to London
City and called upon Truefoot, Tickle, and Badger.

Truefoot was the only partner in the office at the time,
but he ably represented the firm, for he tickled them
with information and badgered them with questions to
such an extent that they left the place of business in a
state of mental confusion, but, on the whole, very well
satisfied.

The result of all these things was that Tom Brixton
settled down near the village where his mother dwelt,
and Fred Westly, after staying long enough among the
Sawback Mountains to dig out of them a sufficiency,
returned home and bought a small farm beside his old
chum.

And did Tom forget his old friends in Oregon? No!
He became noted for the length and strength of his
correspondence. He wrote to Flinders begging him to
come home and help him with his property, and
Flinders accepted. He wrote to Mahogany Drake and
sent him a splendid rifle, besides good advice and many
other things; at different times, too numerous to mention.
He wrote to little Tolly Trevor endeavouring to persuade
him to come to England and be "made a man of," but
Tolly politely declined, preferring to follow the fortunes
of Mahogany and be made a man of in the backwoods
sense of the expression, in company with his fast friend
the Leaping Buck. Tolly sent his special love to the
Rose of Oregon, and said that she would be glad to hear

that the old place in the Sawback range had become a little colony, and that a missionary had settled in it, and Gashford had held by his promise to her—not only giving up drink and gambling entirely, but had set up a temperance coffee-house and a store, both of which were in the full blast of prosperity.

Tolly also said, in quite a poetical burst, that the fragrance of the Rose not only remained in the Colony, but was still felt as a blessed memory and a potent influence for good throughout all the land.

Finally, Tom Brixton settled down to a life of usefulness beside his mother—who lived to a fabulous old age—and was never tired of telling, especially to his young friends, of his wonderful adventures in the Far West, and how he had been twice bought—once with gold and once with blood.

If you are interested in more books from
The Old West Series
Contact:
Mantle Ministries Press:
228 Still Ridge, Bulverde, Texas 78163
Office Phone: 830-438-3777
E-mail: mantleministries@cs.com
Web Page: www.mantlemin.com